WHEN AT LAST I FIND YOU

AARON GUDMUNSON

Dedicated to the BT
In return for their prolonged and continued dedication

If you ever looked at me once with what I know is in you, I would be your slave.

- Emily Brontë, Wuthering Heights

Chapter One

On Sunday mornings, wagonloads of elders descend on Dot's Place to drink coffee out of cloudy decanters and overwhelm the place with tales of days gone by. Paul felt like an outcast anytime he happened into the restaurant during their slow, watchful guard. All eyes swung his way, instantly disdaining him for his youth. They saw a man decades their junior, fair of face—handsome, even—tall, confident, unbitten yet by life. He wore no eyeglasses to correct poor vision, walked without a broke-back hunch, had no earlobes dangling to his jawline. The elders saw a man who'd only just begun his journey, and they hated him for it.

Paul felt their crisp contempt and tried to ignore it. He considered himself a likeable fellow who'd been voted Nicest Boy in Lake Winona High's senior yearbook, and if the elder population didn't choose to see that aspect of him, it was their loss. He found a back booth, far from the malicious squints, and dumped a drift of yesterday's mail onto the table.

"Coffee, hon?" a server asked, thrusting one of those decanters of questionable cleanliness at him. He held a hand over the mug before him.

"No, thank you. I'll take the farm-fresh skillet and a Diet Sprite, please."

The server gave him an inscrutable look. It didn't hold the same naked scorn the elders displayed, but it certainly bore no outward pleasure. *Someone who doesn't take morning coffee cannot be trusted*, that stare said. She must have sensed his understanding, for she put on a harried smile. "You seem like a man who knows what he wants."

"That would be a fair appraisal," Paul replied, offering a taut grin of his own. The server scribbled his order and sashayed it away.

The mail he'd brought in had been on the passenger seat since yesterday. Paul Jeske considered himself fastidious about reviewing correspondence promptly but yesterday had been his eighth wedding anniversary and the mail had understandably gone forgotten until this morning.

He flipped through the usual suspects and noticed nothing of interest among the bills and circulars until he reached the last item. He held it up to the light streaming through the frosty glass. The address read:

Lucine Korth
200 Pace Ln.
Lake Winona, IL

The neighborhood in which the Jeskes lived had gotten a new postal carrier around Halloween, and he had an excruciating habit of leaving mail addressed to neighbors in their box. Paul had twice called the postmaster to complain, but few measures appeared to have been taken to correct the matter.

Except Pace Lane lay a dozen blocks west of their house, in an older and slightly run-down section of town. Unless Paul held a completely twisted notion of U.S. postal routes, this envelope should have been handled by a different carrier altogether.

He found a pen in his coat pocket and scratched *Wrong address* above the addressee's name. He would swing by the

P.O. on his way home and leave it with a clerk, maybe speak to the postmaster face to face about his errant carrier.

He ate without tasting. The name on the rogue envelope ran through his head like a lyric. *Lucine Korth, Lucine Korth, Lucine Korth.*

There *was* something lyrical about it. Almost *magical*, he thought. Then he smirked at himself. What a load of bunk. Lucine could only be an old lady's name, generations outdated. Probably of Old-World origin. He'd never heard it before in his life.

He paid the check and left, eyes front and center to deflect the glares of the grumbling elders. When he'd made it safely to his car, he glanced through the window at the geriatric clientele and glimpsed a flutter of strawberry blonde hair at one of the tables near the restrooms: a single blush of youth in a white and grizzled garden.

Chapter Two

The post office lot appeared full, and he didn't want to wait in line with the rest of the yokels rushing to mail packages so they'd arrive in time for Christmas. He would simply drop the misplaced envelope in his residential mailbox, stick the flag up, and hope the incompetent mail carrier would find its proper home.

Paul found himself flicking on his blinker and turning onto William Street—half a dozen blocks ahead of his turnoff.

Just curious, he thought. *Just want to see what it looks like.*

He made the turn onto Pace Lane and rolled by the house marked 200. It was a two-story affair the color of goulash and rotten teeth. A sagging chain-link fence ran around a yard barely larger than the Jeske kitchen. He saw no lawn ornaments or discarded toys poking up from the scrum of snow. The only sign of life was a shoelace of smoke stringing up from the chimney. An old lady's home for sure, right?

Paul drove home in silence, chewing the edge of his lip.

He had the house to himself every other weekday morning. Michelle worked as a paralegal at the Parnell & Ostreicher firm on the other side of town, and the kids had school—Perry as a third grader and Jeannie as a preschooler. Paul worked at home as a freelance writer and editor. The gig paid better than expected, but it put a serious damper on the novel he'd been trying to hammer out over the last seven years.

Seven years, he thought, tossing his keys on the kitchen table. Had he really graduated from NCU so long ago? Could it be he and Michelle had just celebrated eight years of marriage last night? Perry had turned eight last October and Jeannie would be blowing out five candles come April. How terribly sly the passage of time could be—sometimes it makes you gasp.

Paul slung himself down before his PC, set on pulling up the blog he'd been assigned to copy edit that day—a thoroughly boring site devoted to botany—and found himself instead clicking on the desktop file labeled ROSETHORN.doc. He read the opening chapter, lips moving, before exiting out. There had been no need to save it; he'd made no changes. The novel would have to wait—Paul simply wasn't ready to move forward on it yet.

Give it time, he thought. *You'll get to it.*

Yeah, except it had been nearly a decade since he'd created the file for the book he intended to call *Rosethorn* and he'd only made it to the halfway point. If that. The excuses he contrived were numerous and varied. He needed to flesh out the characters, he needed to expand the plot, he needed to *world-build*. Or his personal favorite: The market for a genre-bending tale of a beautiful witch named Ethel Parks terrorizing the small Old West town of Rosethorn, Nevada had yet to present itself. Anything to put off admitting the truth, which was, of course, that Paul Jeske simply wasn't cut out to write novels. He'd told himself that hundreds of times, but Michelle insisted he keep at it. It was no *Wuthering Heights*—their shared favorite novel of all time, ever since reading it in the Brit lit class they'd taken together at NCU—but the chapters she'd read were, to use her term, "approaching brilliance."

Of course she'd say that, though; it was practically etched in their wedding vows. *Stroke husband's needy little literary ego at every turn, in sickness and health, till death do us part, I do.*

Feeling depressed, Paul pulled up a fresh browser and got as far as typing the first five letters of the botany blog when inspiration struck. He backspaced and conjured Google instead. He dug the envelope out of the mail, rested it against his monitor, and typed "Lucine Korth" in the search field. No results. He tried again after removing the quotation marks and had a little luck, but after reviewing found nothing that could be associated locally.

Disappointed, he opened the blog and prepared to edit text about the taxonomy of peonies. He opened the music streaming app he favored and clicked on his easy listening playlist. Soft hits of yesteryear turned out to be the only music he could work to. It helped him concentrate while other genres simply distracted.

For the next two and a half hours, Paul cut and pasted, nipped and tucked to Sam Cooke, Joni Mitchell, and Bob Seger. When he'd gotten the text to a readable state, he hit POST and went to fix lunch.

Michelle came in and tossed her purse on the table as he flipped the grilled cheese sandwiches in the skillet. She kissed his cheek. "Smells good."

"Want soup?"

"I'll get it," she said and dug a can out of the pantry.

"I didn't know if you wanted bacon on yours."

"Are you crazy?"

"I take that as a yes."

"Smart man."

"Good. Because I loaded yours."

"*Very* smart man," his wife amended, stirring a can of milk in with the soup concentrate. "How's your day going?"

Paul sighed. "Same as ever."

"What's today's topic?"

"Flowers."

"Really? Fucking *flowers*?" she asked, sticking a thumb in her mouth to lick off a dollop of condensed tomato.

"Fucking flowers," Paul confirmed with a protracted sigh.

"Next you'll tell me you're assigned to write about lady's lingerie."

"Jesus, don't jinx me."

"Aw, baby, don't worry. I'd help you research," Michelle said with a laugh and pinched his ass on the way to the refrigerator.

"So. Did you talk to Parnell about a raise?"

"Not yet. After lunch. Never ask a man for anything when he's on an empty stomach." The microwave beeped and she hauled the soup out with an oven mitt. "But I know what angle I'll work. I've been with that company six goddam years and I've only gotten a pay increase once. They owe me. They fucking *owe* me."

Paul raised his hands. "Hey, you don't need to convince me."

"Yeah, but I'm worried I'll have to give old Parnell a hand job if he resists."

"Whatever it takes, babe. I'm here if you need practice."

She threw the mitt at him. He laughed and pulled her into his arms, kissing her deep.

"Holy shit, I'm seeing stars," she said when they disengaged.

"You are such a practiced liar it steals my breath away," he told her, slapping the sandwiches onto paper plates.

"Oh, hey. Don't forget. Perry has soccer practice."

7

He had forgotten already. "Who plays soccer in *winter*?"

"Your son, that's who. Tuesdays and Thursdays through March. It's first day, so stick around and cheer him on, okay?"

"What am I supposed to do with Jeannie?"

"Leave her home with a pack of matches and a loaded gun."

"I'm serious, Shelly. Jeannie gets bored unless she has something to do."

"I don't know, let her play on your phone or something."

"Yeah, all right. What time'll you be home, the usual?"

"Unless Parnell has me stay late for a little overtime," she said, running her tongue up the crust of her sandwich.

"You're a sick, sick woman."

"Why else would you have married me?" she said.

Chapter Three

After Michelle had returned to the office, Paul tried to work on his next assignment but found himself distracted. Not even the soothing backbeat of The Foundations' "Build Me Up Buttercup" could focus him. He paced his office, bouncing a Nerf ball off the wall.

"Fucking fuck," he whispered and went to use the toilet. As he relieved himself, something occurred to him, and he hurried back to his PC.

This time he Googled "Lucy Korth."

"Bingo, bitch," he breathed. Nearly 300 results bounced back. Social media pages, professional profiles, pictures. Could any of these belong to the woman whose mail he'd received in error? He clicked the first link and found a Facebook account for Lucy Korth.

It had a flower as its profile picture. A pink hyacinth, to be exact, as he'd learned through working on the fucking botany blog. Nothing hinted at Lucy's geographical location. He scrolled through the timeline, searching for any clue of the user's identity, still uncertain as to his motives. Why did he care?

Writers are naturally curious, he thought, but it felt like a hollow excuse. Truth be told, Paul didn't know why he felt compelled to investigate the addressee of the rogue envelope … or refused to admit it to himself.

Admission would come in time.

The page seemed entirely on lockdown. Paul nearly gave up, deciding the name Lucine must indeed belong to an old lady—who named their kid Lucine these days? But then he stumbled on the only item of interest under the Photos of Lucy tab. A second photo had been posted by a user named Viola Datsun, tagging Lucy in it. Viola was also an old lady's name and he thought at first he must have stumbled onto a nursing home bridge club, but the picture she'd posted did not depict a geriatric person. The woman in the image purporting to show Lucine Korth was shockingly beautiful. The finish looked grainy, as if it had been taken with some prehistoric camera phone, but Lucy Korth's splendor transcended texture. Paul had to avert his eyes; it bordered on painful to behold her.

"Jesus Christ," he muttered when he found it in him to peek again, and then he couldn't look away. He had never seen a more attractive person—of this he was certain.

This couldn't be the Lucy Korth from Lake Winona. Not the same person who lived a few measly blocks away. No way. He'd know. This Lucy Korth probably lived in New York City or Rome or Milan and her feet must be blistered raw from all the runways she'd walked.

Without being able to glean anything further from the profile (aside from the erection in his jeans), Paul did the next best thing and clicked on Viola Datsun's page. Viola, unlike her dazzling friend, seemed to be an open book. Everything had been made public, from her constantly updated statuses to roughly a hundred photo albums to her birthdate, workplace, alma mater (NCU, wow small world!) and hometown.

Which she had listed as Lake Winona, Illinois.

"Holy shit," he whispered.

With a kind of manic, panicked frenzy Paul clicked through Ms. Datsun's albums in search of a picture in which she'd posed with her friend Lucy. Viola was a cutie, no doubt about it, with chestnut hair in springy curls that seemed to hover around her head like a cloud. Her teeth were as white and bright as polished piano keys. The dark eyes peering from the screen shimmered with capricious ambiguity, as if Viola Datsun hadn't a single care in the world. Yes, Ms. Datsun would be considered a catch for anyone, but she held no comparison to Lucine. Who, Paul discovered with deep disappointment, failed to appear in any of her friend's albums.

He glanced at the clock and nearly fell out of his chair. Jeannie was due to be picked up from pre-school at 2:00 and somehow it was already ten till. The fucking school was across town. Paul cursed and snatched for his coat. He dialed the school as he drove and explained he would be late picking his daughter up.

The teacher at least tried to sound understanding when he arrived. "We all get preoccupied sometimes," she said.

"I wasn't preoccupied," he said. "Car wouldn't start."

"'Tis the season," the teacher said, a hint of accusation trailing in her tone. Paul stepped around her to Jeannie, who had busied herself piecing a puzzle together in a corner of the classroom.

When she saw him, she leapt into his arms. "Daddy, guess what we had for snack today!"

"Don't tell me. Cheese cubes and applesauce."

She goggled. "How did you know?"

"I can smell it on your stinky breath," he said. Truthfully, he'd checked the snack schedule tacked to the lobby bulletin board as he did every day.

"My breath's not *stinky*!" she screeched.

"Not as stinky as your feet, at least."

"Daddy!"

He got her bundled up and thanked the teacher again before leading his daughter to the car. Jeannie babbled about her day—they'd made snowmen out of cotton balls and learned a new song—while Paul drove without hearing. When he made the turn onto William Street, Jeannie stopped speaking and looked around.

"Why are we going this way, Daddy?"

He blinked into the rearview mirror. "We're taking a shortcut, June Bug."

"We are? What about the longcut?"

Paul laughed, a forced, humorless sound. "The longcut's too long."

"Oh. Guess what Mrs. Landon said we should do every time we washed our hands?"

But Paul had stopped listening again. He rolled by the house belonging to someone named Lucine Korth, squinting at the windows. Thick drapes covered them. Smoke no longer crawled from the chimney. The place appeared deserted and for some reason this dropped Paul into a mild depression. If the woman from Viola Datsun's picture in fact lived here, he wanted her to be present and accounted for.

When they got home, he offered to make her grilled cheese, but Jeannie wrinkled her nose. "I want pizza. Mrs. Landon says a pizza has all five food groups."

"There's five now? When I was your age, we only had four."

She ticked them off on her fingers, proud of herself. "Fruits and veggies, protein, dairy, grains, and sweets."

"Sweets?"

"Like chocolate."

"You kids don't know how good you've got it these days."

"So can I have pizza?"

They compromised on a hot dog, cut into pieces and dipped in ketchup. "We need to pick your brother up in a little bit. Then I want you to lay down for a quick nap, okay?"

"We rested at school, Daddy."

"Did you sleep?"

"I was too busy coloring."

"Well, I'd like you to close your eyes for a while after we get your brother."

"Perry has soccer practice after school. Mommy said."

Soccer practice. He'd forgotten already. "All right, then after practice."

"It'll be suppertime by then," Jeannie whined.

She had a point. The kid wouldn't be getting a nap today, which could make for an interesting evening. A tired Jeannie usually equaled a grouchy Jeannie.

After lunch, they played with matchbox cars and read a storybook. Then they hauled on their winter gear and drove to McKinley Elementary where they waited for Perry, who came bounding through the doors with his backpack dragging the ground and a soccer ball beneath his arm.

"Dad!"

"Hey, Pear. How was your day?"

"Great! Sarah Haney threw up at lunch."

"That's too bad," Paul said. "So tell me about soccer practice. Where do we go?"

"Mommy didn't tell you? It's at the one place."

"It's not here at school?"

Perry shook his head. "It's at that other place."

"Which place?"

"The one big place. I can't 'member what it's called."

Fucking perfect, Paul thought. He'd assumed practice would be here, in the McKinley Elementary gym. He scrounged out his phone. "Okay, everyone into the car."

Behind the wheel, he leaned his head against the cold glass and closed his eyes. "Shell, it's me. You failed to provide the location of Perry's practice."

"It's at the field house, Paul. We talked about it last week."

"The field house? Jeez, that's five miles out of town."

"Yeah, hon. Through the Park District, remember?"

He did now. He must have been half-asleep when they'd discussed soccer. "Okay, we're headed over there."

"Don't forget his shin guards."

"Shin guards? They're only practicing."

"He needs shin guards, Paul."

"Where the hell are they?" he said, more forcefully than intended.

"Daddy said the H-word!" Perry called gleefully.

"What's the H-word?" Jeannie asked.

"Watch your language," Michelle said in his ear. "The shin guards are in his backpack."

"Okay. I'm sorry."

"Can I talk to the kids?"

Paul passed the phone to his son who again reported Sarah Haney's unfortunate exhibit in the vomiteria.

"I wanted to talk first!" Jeannie squawked. Yep, she would be a terror without her nap.

"I saved the best for last," Paul said with a wink in the rearview mirror.

"I heard that, Dad," Perry said, handing the phone to his sister.

Paul backed out and drove toward the field house. Jeannie was describing her school snack to Michelle in exquisite detail and bemoaning her father's denial of a pizza lunch. Paul rubbed his temples and cracked his neck. His head pounded.

"Hand the phone back, June Bug," he said.

"Mommy, guess what?" Jeannie said. "Daddy was late picking me up and we tooked a shortcut!"

"Jean Susan Jeske, hand it over."

"Bye, Mommy. I love you. See you at supper." She blew exactly six kisses into the mouthpiece and then dropped the device into Paul's palm.

"You were late picking her up?" Michelle demanded.

"Five minutes. I got sidetracked."

"What, the flower thing?"

"Yes, the flower thing."

"Did they charge you? If you're late picking up, they charge you extra."

"They didn't say anything. Look, it was only a few minutes. She was having the time of her life in the puzzle corner."

"And what's this shortcut you took?"

"Jeez, Shell. What's with the third degree? I cut down Pierce instead of Center. Traffic was heavy."

"Okay. Other than those hiccups, how's the rest of your day?"

"Groovy, baby," he said, pleased at the change of subject. "What about you? Get the raise?"

"I'm not sure, but Parnell definitely did."

"Ha, ha. You sick puppy."

"You wouldn't have me any other way."

That much was true. He wouldn't. Michelle was unique. Never a dull day—nay, never a dull *moment*—with her.

What in the world could Paul complain about? Nothing. Not a single damned thing. He lived a charmed life.

Chapter Four

Soccer sucked. Perry seemed to have no intention of following the coach's instructions. When she tried to put him through passing drills, the kid had no control over how hard he kicked. Twice the ball sailed over the sideline, narrowly missing an observing parent.

Jeannie, as predicted, became a monster. For the first fifteen minutes, she raced back and forth to the drinking fountain, giggling with glee, face dripping, until she got too close, and water shot up her nose. Then, catastrophe. Nothing Paul did could calm her. He carried her outside so her squeals wouldn't aggravate anyone, which only worsened the situation.

"*Daddeeeee* it's *cold*!" she shrieked. "My face is gonna *freeze*!"

"Just calm down, June Bug," he said, bouncing her on his shoulder.

"I'm not a bug!"

"I know you're not. It's a nickname."

"Well, I don't wike it." The L's in her words regressed to W's in times of distress.

"You love that name," he said, knowing full well the futility of reasoning with a napless toddler. "And don't say 'wike,' June Bug. It's 'like.'"

"I want to go home. I want Mommy."

"As soon as Pear finishes practice."

"I want to go home *now*. I want Gussy."

16

Gussy. Her favorite stuffed animal. She'd gotten the damned thing before she'd even been born—a baby shower from Michelle's mother. To this day, half a decade later, he still didn't know if Gussy was supposed to be a cow or a zebra. Michelle insisted it was a giraffe. Whatever, Gussy was the only thing on planet Earth that would calm Jeannie when she got in a tizzy. He should have known better than to leave home without it.

"Gussy's in your bed resting. Like you should be," he said. A mistake. Jeannie screamed so loud Paul thought she'd burst blood vessels in her face. He took her to the car and slung her into her seat, then climbed in and keyed the ignition. He found his iPod, scrolled to the Kid Tunes playlist, and hit PLAY.

"I want *Frozen*," Jeannie said between hiccups.

Paul thumbed the movie soundtrack on, then leaned back and closed his eyes. He couldn't wait for this day to end.

While his daughter belted out "Let It Go," not quiet but at least no longer sobbing, Paul dialed up Facebook on his phone, and found Lucy Korth's profile again. Should he send her a friend request?

You fucking idiot, what are you thinking? his mind whispered. What *was* he thinking? Did he seriously want to put his name and face out there to some stranger? Was he lacking something that felt he must attempt to introduce himself into this woman's world? With her profile on lockdown, she obviously valued privacy.

Then inspiration struck. He knew what he could do.

"Honey, Daddy's going to go get your brother. I'll be right back," he said into the mirror, but Jeannie wasn't listening. She was too busy harmonizing about rising like the break of dawn.

The coach took her time dismissing the fledgling soccer stars. Paul fidgeted on the sideline. He shouldn't have left Jeannie alone in the car, but he didn't want her making another scene. And besides, he'd left the heater running and locked the door with the fob—she'd be safe enough for five minutes. Except five minutes turned into seven. Then ten. The coach seemed to making some kind of motivational speech to her young charges.

They're fucking school kids, not World Cup challengers, Paul thought bitterly.

Another soccer dad noticed him huffing and twitching. "You all right there, chief?" he asked.

"I thought they were supposed to be done by now."

"You in a rush?" the guy asked. He had a nose like a crooked turnip and might have been an amateur boxer a decade ago. He had that kind of build. That kind of demeanor. A deep-simmering hostility buried beneath his North Face parka and Old Spice aftershave.

"Yeah, I left my daughter in the car because they were supposed to be done by now."

"You left your daughter in the car? In this weather?"

"The heater's running."

"You know that's illegal, right?"

Paul looked at him blankly. As a kid, his folks had left him in the car to run quick errands all the time. "It's illegal?"

"I ought to call Family Services," the guy said.

"That's not necessary. As soon as I get my boy, we're leaving."

"What's your name, chief?" the guy asked, pulling his cell from his pocket.

A whistle shrilled and kids rushed the sideline in a burst of shouts and shenanigans. The man's son threw himself around his father's waist and said, "How'd I do, Dad? Did you see the goal I scored?"

"You bet I did, pal," the man said, stroking his son's hair. To Paul he said, "You get a free pass today because you didn't know better. I hear you left your kid in the car again, I won't bother with Family Services. I'll go straight to the cops."

"Sure. Thanks. I appreciate it, really."

The guy gave him a lasting look, then led his boy out. Paul scanned the field for Perry who was looking earnestly up at his coach while she spoke with him face-to-face. Then she dismissed him, and he hustled over.

"What was that about?" Paul asked.

"Mrs. Coach was telling me about trying to keep my feet under control. They got a little wild, I guess."

"You'll get there, kiddo. Get your coat on, okay?"

"Hey, where's Jeannie?"

"In the car. Let's get home. I'm starved. How about you?"

"You bet! Can we have pizza tonight?"

"That seems to be the consensus," Paul said.

The *Frozen* soundtrack had moved from the fun sing-alongs to the orchestral arrangements, which had Jeannie sobbing uncontrollably. Perry buckled himself into his booster before covering his ears.

"Make her stop, Dad," he called.

"Jeannie, it's time to calm down," Paul said, an edge in his voice.

She tried to stammer something out, but her heaving lungs forbade it.

"I know, sweetheart, it got to the part you don't like. I'm sorry it took so long. Let's go home and order pizza," he said, hoping this might at last quell the tears. Nothing doing. Paul turned off the music and sat patiently until his daughter caught her breath. When she quieted, he tried again. "Sweetie, I said I'm sorry about the music—"

"I'm not crying about the music, Daddy," she said, gulping air. "I'm crying about the man."

Paul watched her in the mirror. "What man?"

"The man outside the car. When you were inside a man stood outside my window and wooked at me. He scared me, Daddy. He scared me *so bad*."

"What did he do?" Paul asked, craning in his seat to look at her. His pulse had quickened to a telegraph staccato.

"H-he … he-he …"

"Take a deep breath, Jeannie."

She did and tried again. "He was wearing a mask."

"Like a Halloween mask?" Perry asked.

She shook her head vigorously. "Like the kind Daddy wears when he shovels the driveway."

"A ski mask?" Paul asked. He pulled his from his coat pocket. "Like this?"

She nodded miserably.

"And what did this man in the ski mask do? Did he scare you?"

"He wooked at me."

"How do you know it was a man if he had a mask on?" Perry put in.

"He looked at you? What else?" Paul demanded. He could feel himself growing agitated with his daughter. Not because she'd done anything wrong, but because he was scared. Why had some guy been staring at his daughter?

Then he knew. The son of a bitch who'd threatened to call Family Services. "How tall was he, June Bug?" he asked.

"I don't know, he—"

"Was he taller than Daddy? Shorter?"

"I don't know, Daddy, he wooked at me—"

"Say '*looked*,' goddammit, not '*wooked*!'"

Both kids froze. Their father rarely raised his voice and never swore at them. Then Jeannie burst into fresh tears while Perry sat white-faced and watchful. Paul dropped the car into gear and pulled out of the field house lot.

Chapter Five

Jeannie had calmed by the time they got home, a thumb stuck in her mouth to pacify. Paul got her set up on the sofa with Gussy. He put Disney Junior on the TV and she seemed content enough to watch Mickey and pals cavort around their clubhouse.

Perry sat placidly at the kitchen table, staring out at the backyard. "When's Mom coming home?"

"Half an hour," Paul said. "Listen, I'm sorry about what I said in the car. I've had a lot on my mind, Pear."

"It's okay with me, Dad," he said. "I think you ought to tell Jeannie, though."

"You're right. I will, once she's rested a bit."

"Who do you think it was looking in at her?"

"Don't worry about that, son. Probably just someone passing by."

"It's weird, though," Perry said. He had always been older than his age and could sense the peculiarity of his sister's claim.

"It *is* weird," Paul conceded. "But it's behind us now. Water under the bridge. Understood?"

"Yes, Dad."

"There's something else I hope you understand."

Perry waited, eyes wide and wary.

"We should keep this between us, okay? No need to worry your mother for nothing."

"Don't tell Mom about the man looking at Jeannie?"

"That's right. You know how Mom gets. She'd be up all night. She's been trying to get a raise at work and if she goes in restless, she might not get it."

"She might fall asleep at her desk?" he asked, a grin at last surfacing.

Paul grinned back. "That's right. She might fall asleep at her desk. Or worse—what if she fell asleep at lunch and plopped her face right in her spaghetti?"

Perry guffawed and Paul thought he'd made things right with his son, at least. His daughter would be another story. He hoped the poor thing hadn't been traumatized. But if it had just been someone glancing in as he passed by, how traumatizing could it be? Surely her perception of the situation had been amplified by exhaustion. He went to where she lay, working her thumb for all it was worth.

"Hi, June Bug," he said, placing a hand on her head. She jerked at his touch—something she'd not done before. "Hey, are you all right?"

Slowly her eyes glided to his. "I was just ascared, Daddy. I'm awright now."

"There was nothing to be scared of, sweetheart. Just someone looking in at your beautiful face, that's all he was."

"I think Perry was right about something, Daddy."

"What's that?"

"I don't think it was a man."

"What do you mean, Jeannie?"

"I think it was a woman."

The pizza arrived right before Michelle did. When she saw it steaming on the counter, she gave her husband a look.

"Pizza, Paul? Really?"

"I was outvoted."

"I had chops thawed."

"We'll have those tomorrow. Come on, I'll pour some wine."

The kids had already taken their seats, napkins tucked dutifully into their collars. Neither looked worse for the wear.

Paul clapped his hands. "Okay, pie-slingers. Choose your weapons."

The meal had been going splendidly—Michelle had gotten her raise and without having to lay a hand on old Parnell's nether realms, she discreetly informed her husband—until she asked the kids how their days had gone.

"Someone looked at me," Jeannie said between bites. Paul froze. At least she hadn't said *wooked*.

"Someone looked at you?" she asked, glancing at Paul for explanation.

He took the reins. "A man walked by her car window and peeked in at her. It startled her, that's all."

"We don't know it was a man," Perry supplied.

"Paul?"

"He had on a mask," Perry said. The boy seemed to have forgotten their nondisclosure agreement or perhaps thought Jeannie bringing the matter up negated it. "A ski mask, like Dad wears when he shovels."

"Paul?" Michelle prompted again. This time her voice had an edge in it, something that typically signified impending conflict.

"It's nothing," he said with a little laugh, trying to lighten the tension building in the room like heat. "Jeannie didn't get her nap, she was over-sensitive, and she reacted to someone glancing in the window. That's all, end of story."

Michelle seemed to accept the anecdote until Jeannie said, "I wouldn't have been scared if Daddy hadn't left me alone in the car."

World War III exploded after they got the kids to bed. Michelle's glare could have fused atoms.

"How could you leave her alone in the *fucking car*?" she seethed. "Do you know how many children are kidnapped every year because of shit like that?"

"Shelly, listen to me. It was only two minutes. She was flipping out because she didn't get her nap. People were staring."

"I don't give a damn if she was puking pea soup—you don't leave a child alone in a car."

"My parents left me alone all the time."

"We don't live in the same world anymore, Paul, *Christ*. We can't let our kids out of our sight for a minute. Not these days."

"This idea that the world is more dangerous today than it was in our time is ridiculous. It only seems that way because we're constantly bombarded with bad news. This is the Information Age, Shelly. Everywhere you look, we see something bad has happened. It's exactly the same as it was when we were kids, only we were too dumb then to know it."

She stared him down, arms crossed. "You broke a law today. Whether you knew it or not, you broke a law."

He smiled, trying for a truce. "You gonna report me to the cops?"

For her part, Michelle at least put up a strong front before the dam broke. She jabbed a finger into his ribs. "You do something stupid like that again and you're goddamn right I will."

She let him pull her into an embrace. He apologized into her hair. For the next half hour, she forgave him.

The next day was Friday. No preschool for Jeannie. After he'd seen Michelle and Perry off, Paul spent part of the morning playing with his daughter. Jeannie seemed fine. Part of him had expected her to wake up screaming with bad dreams overnight, but she'd slept as soundlessly as a newborn: the lone advantage of her napless day.

They put together puzzles, ate a snack of cheese and crackers, and marked important dates on next year's calendar.

"You're going to be in kindergarten come August," he said as they flipped the pages. "How exciting is that?"

"I'm scared of kindergarten."

"Scared? Your big brother's been through kindergarten and lived to tell about it."

"Perry said you have to get shots to go to kindergarten. Shots, Daddy. More than one."

Thanks a lot, Pear. "Well, that's true. But the shots make sure you don't get super-duper sick."

"But they'll *hurt.*"

"Just for a sec. Quick, like a bee sting."

"A *bee* sting?"

Smooth, Paulie. "Well, not exactly a bee sting. Like a little pinch. That's all. Then we go get ice cream."

Her face lit. "We do?"

"Two scoops, June Bug, whatever flavors you want."

"That's not so bad then."

"Not bad at all. What should we do now?"

"Can I watch *Care Bears*?"

"One episode of *Care Bears*, coming up," he said, flipping the TV on. Once she engaged with the show, thumb in her mouth and Gussy at her hip, Paul stepped into his office to get some work done.

Except he didn't pull up that day's assignments. He pulled up the Facebook profile for Lucy Korth. In all the hubbub, he'd nearly forgotten about her. Nearly. The woman in the coarse pic could never fully be forgotten, he now understood. Her image had been implanted in his brain as thoroughly as if it had been done via a surgical procedure.

When he'd studied the image long enough (could it *ever* be long enough?), he logged into Twitter and ran a search of her name. One profile with protected tweets. No picture. Of course.

"What are you hiding, Lucine?" Paul whispered.

He half-heartedly ticked through his day's assignments until lunchtime. When he went to find out if Jeannie was hungry, he found her asleep on the sofa. Poor kiddo.

"Hey, June Bug," he whispered, touching her elbow. "You ready for lunch?"

She woke reluctantly and he carried her into the kitchen. "What're we having?"

"Well, it's a cold day out there. I thought something to warm our bones might be in order. Soup?"

"What kind?"

"Cream of celery, tomato, or minestrone?"

She made a face. "I don't like minestrone. Tomato?"

"Tomato it is." While he prepared it, Jeannie sang a snatch of song she'd learned at school—something about sticky-sticky-sticky bubblegum. Michelle called at the same time the microwave beeped.

"Hey, babe, you coming home for lunch?" he asked.

"Parnell's got me working through," she said. "I guess because he gave me a raise he felt inclined to make me earn it."

"Weird how that works. You want me to drop something off?"

"No, that's okay. We're ordering takeout from that new Chinese place."

"Ooh, save me an egg roll."

"In your dreams."

"Spoilsport."

"How's Jeannie?"

"Fine. We're having lunch."

"Daddy-daughter date. So stinking cute."

"I figure it's the least I can do for yesterday," he said, reluctant to bring it up again, but feeling compelled to make sure the subject had been put to bed for good, so to speak.

"Water under the bridge, big guy," Michelle said.

"Maybe I can have another helping of last night later?"

"There you go dreaming again."

They said good-bye and Paul dished up the soup. He and Jeannie sat elbow to elbow spooning it up.

"I was dreaming when you woke me up," she said.

"Oh? What about?" he asked offhandedly. His mind had already returned to Lucine.

"The man from yesterday. Only in my dream, it wasn't a man. It was a … "

"Woman?" he finished for her, but she shook her head.

"It was a monster."

"You know that was only a dream, right? The person who looked in the window yesterday was a person."

"I know, Daddy," she said, but sounded doubtful about her father's assertion.

"I want you to rest after lunch, okay?"

"But I already did."

"I still want you to try. I'll check on you in twenty minutes and if you're awake, you can get up. Okay?"

"Okay."

Jeannie wound up sleeping another ninety minutes. It was more than enough time for Paul to create fake profiles across all major social media sites.

Chapter Six

He was still busy filling in the details of a Twitter account under the name Susan Moll, a graduate student from his alma mater of North Central University, when Jeannie started screaming. Paul jerked in his seat and rushed to the sofa.

"What's the matter, sweetie?" he asked, pulse thudding. Gussy had fallen to the floor, forgotten.

"The monster! It came back!"

He hauled her onto his lap and rocked her against him. "Jeannie, honey, it was just a bad dream."

"No, Daddy. I saw it! It had dark eyes, just like the eyes in the mask."

"The man with the ski mask had brown eyes?" He tried to recall the eye color of the guy with the mashed nose who'd threatened to call Family Services for leaving Jeannie unattended in the car.

"Not brown. Not black. *Dark*."

"What's the difference, honey?"

"It's … it's … I don't know, Daddy. I can't say it."

"Okay, June Bug. It's okay. Only a dream. How about some Mickey Mouse?"

"Yes, Daddy." His daughter quieted, her thumb creeping back into her mouth, and for that he was grateful.

With Jeannie set up in front of her cartoons, he returned to his PC. Creating fake profiles now seemed incredibly juvenile and potentially dangerous. He logged out of each, vowing to delete them later. Had he really meant to try deceptively inserting himself into Lucine's social media circles? They had a term for that: cyberstalking. A crime, one step below live stalking. Paul Jeske may not have been perfect, but he certainly was no criminal.

He worked on an auto parts blog for half an hour, then went to check on Jeannie. She reclined in the same position in which he'd left her, eyes marking the antics of Mickey and friends. She didn't glance his way, so he let her be. The poor kid seemed all right now.

Michelle called to find out how the day was going.

"Very productive."

"Jeannie behaving?"

He considered telling her about the nightmare but didn't want his wife to worry. "Like an angel," he said.

"What did you do about lunch?"

"Tomato soup."

"Two days in a row? That must be a new record for you, Paulie. You're a man who appreciates variety."

"'Tis the spice of life," in a hideous attempt at a British accent he already wished he'd skipped.

"I'll have some spice for you tonight, if you're a good boy the rest of the day."

"Yummy," he said without emotion. *If you're a good boy.* He hated when she treated him like a child, as if he might be

Jeannie's slightly less intelligent sibling. "Hey, listen, I've got a lot on my plate, so I'll see you tonight, okay?"

"Okay. Sure. See you tonight."

She hung up hard, the office phone practically dropped into its cradle. Not a great way to leave things. Michelle was the type to let things fester, to build up into something larger than it had to be. A mountain out of a molehill type person. Paul doubted there would be any spice tonight. That was fine by him; he hadn't felt less like touching his wife in as long as he could remember.

Fuck it, he thought, and logged in again to Susan Moll's Twitter account. He searched for Lucine Korth's profile and clicked FOLLOW. A message popped up informing him his request was awaiting approval from the user.

Thirty seconds later, he got it.

The profile contained no information once he clicked on it. Simply her name and a single tweet. When Paul read it, though, something twinged in his belly. It said:

When at Last I Find You.........................

"What the hell?" he muttered. The line seemed creepy on the surface, but Paul recognized it as a lyric from the Beatles song "I Will." His and Michelle's song. So Ms. Korth was a Beatles fan. A coincidence, surely. But not really. The Beatles had millions of fans all over the planet of all ages and backgrounds.

Lucy Korth followed no one and had only one follower: Susan Moll, aka Paul Jeske. The tweet had been posted August

15th of the previous year. Obviously Ms. Korth was not a huge Tweeter. Then why had she approved his request so quickly?

Another coincidence. That seemed the only logical explanation. He had just happened to send the request from the phony profile at the same time Lucine had logged on. Things like that happened. Even more likely if she had her settings set to send her a text whenever she got a new request. Her phone had blipped, she'd seen a new follower, and had approved it.

"Yeah, that's it," Paul whispered. Unfortunately, there wasn't much to see here. He needed access to her Facebook account. Something more tangible, with real information. He wanted to learn what made this girl tick. It would seem obvious if she got a friend request so soon after the Twitter one, so he'd have to wait. At least a day. And it couldn't be from Susan Moll. Now that Paul really studied the name, it seemed too make-believe. Plus, he'd have to make the phony Facebook at least appear lived-in. He'd have to add some friends, post a few status updates.

He signed into the fake Facebook and updated the name to Linda Lopez. He Googled images of women, found some of an attractive thirtysomething with black hair and pearly teeth, and poached them for his profile. Then he added some basic information. Linda had studied at North Central University, major in psychology, minor in history. She worked as an adjunct professor at Winona Valley College—giving her a little local flavor would make her more authentic and relatable, Paul reasoned. He listed her as divorced with no children. Family lived in San Diego.

He added random friends—whoever the site recommended. When a few had accepted, he interacted with them, posting pleasantries on their timeline. A few minutes in, Linda Lopez received a private message from a user calling himself Igrekx Ingko (clearly a name as fake as it was unimaginative) which read simply: *Do u like big ones?*

Paul grinned. These fucking perverts were all the same; Michelle received no fewer than half a dozen similar solicitations every month. He'd play along. This could be fun.

Linda: Do I like big what?

Igrekx: U kno, big ones.

Linda: Ice cream cones?

Igrekx: U kno.

Linda: Why? You gay? I'M A GUY.

No response came for several minutes, and Paul had already moved on to adding another bevy of friends when his messenger flashed.

Igrekx: If I find u ur dead faggot.

Paul blocked the user. The level of anonymous aggression unnerved him, he admitted. He wondered how women put up with it all the time, every day. Oh well. Water under the bridge, as his mother-in-law had a fondness of saying. He moved on, as was his privilege.

The final friend request he sent belonged to Viola Datsun. He—Linda Lopez, rather—would gain instant cred with Lucine if one of her good friends in real life showed up on her mutual friends list.

"Daddy?"

Paul jumped. He'd completely forgotten about Jeannie. "Hi, June Bug. What's up?"

"What are you doing?" she asked, toddling into the room.

"Just finishing up some work."

"Who's that lady?" she asked, indicating the picture of "Linda Lopez."

"She's a friend."

"She's pretty."

"Not as pretty as you," Paul said, switching off the monitor.

"Can I have a snack?"

"You betcha. What'd you have in mind?"

"Some Oreos? Five of them, with milk."

"We'll have to see about that," Paul laughed, taking his daughter's hand. Together they went to the kitchen to find a snack.

They picked up Perry and came straight home. His son talked about his day, the highlight of which being the learning of two new words. When Paul asked which words they were, Perry only shook his head and said he'd heard some bad boys say them.

"You can tell me, Pear. You won't be in trouble."

"I don't want to. They're naughty."

"Care to spell them?"

His son swallowed. "I heard Danny call Marco a D-A-M-B-I-C-H."

Paul covered a smile with his fist and cleared his throat. "Well, Danny doesn't seem to think too highly of Marco. And those words are spelled D-A-M-N and B-I-T-C-H."

"What do they mean, Dad?"

"Don't worry about what they mean. You'll learn soon enough."

"Does Mommy know what they mean?" Jeannie wanted to know.

"She does indeed."

"I'll ask her," Perry said.

"Don't you dare. Mom's been under a lot of stress. She doesn't need her son swearing at her to fan the flames. Promise me you won't mention it."

Perry promised, then they all played a game of *Chutes & Ladders* before Paul started supper. Michelle came home a time later with a glint of something sinister in her eye.

"What's up?" Paul asked, a pang of guilt flashing through his gut. Had she figured out what he had been doing online?

Get a grip, asshole, he thought. *No way she could know.*

"Oh, nothing much," his wife replied. She reached into her purse and pulled out a bottle of Champagne. "Except that tonight we celebrate."

"What are we celebrating exactly? You already got your raise."

"This is better than a raise. Do you remember the seminar I signed up for in Denver?"

"The one about re-enrolling in college after a lapse? I thought we decided it would be too expensive?"

"This is one of the best seminars in the country, Paul. It gives you all the tools you need for a seamless transition."

"But the money. I mean, I know you got a raise but let's not go crazy here."

"Stan's covering it. All expenses paid, round-trip, last weekend in March."

"*Stan?* It's not old man Parnell anymore?"

"He insisted I call him by his name."

"Okay."

"Well, Stan's footing the bill. Well, the firm will reimburse us. Whatever. The point is, I get to go. Isn't that great?"

"But you already have a college degree."

"In *Sociology*."

"I don't get it. You're a certified paralegal. What more education could you possibly need?"

Paul became aware of the kids studying their parents intently, their heads moving from one to the other as the conversation volleyed.

Michelle set the bottle on the table. "That's the best part. Stan says I have the drive and temperament to become an attorney."

Paul gaped. "You're putting me on, Shell. Do you know how long it takes to earn your law degree?"

"Stan and Ted said they'd help get me through it."

"Do you know how much it *costs*?"

"They're willing to reimburse up to five thousand dollars per semester, assuming I stay on with the firm once I pass the bar."

"Five grand won't cover a semester, Jesus."

"Near enough. And by the time I'm a practicing attorney, we'll pull in three times that. Hell, four."

"Mom said the H-word," Perry announced. No one paid him any mind.

"Michelle, look. I think we should talk this through before we make any decisions."

"We're talking it through now."

"I mean in private," Paul said.

"We will, honey. Tonight, after we've tucked the little ragamuffins in."

"I'm not a ragamuffin!" Perry cried indignantly.

"What's a ragamuffin?" Jeannie asked.

"Never mind," Michelle asked. "What's for supper? I'm starved."

Paul didn't reply. He was thinking ahead to the last weekend in March.

Chapter Seven

The talk didn't go well. Paul thought Michelle applying to law school bordered on absurd. He didn't appreciate her lecherous (in his mind's eye, anyway) employers putting delusions of grandeur into her head. Their tuition reimbursement offer sounded too good to be true, and he'd want to see it in writing and have it reviewed by an attorney outside the firm.

"Don't worry, Paul. It will all work out."

"I just don't think we should rush into anything."

"I know it seems like a lot to think about. But I really want to do it. I've paid my dues. And I think I'd make a drop-dead sexy lawyer, don't you?"

"Can't argue with that," he conceded. "Can we at least sleep on it?"

She poured another glass of Champagne. "Of course, love. Just so long as you say yes in the morning."

He opened his mouth to say something and that's when Jeannie shrieked from upstairs.

They found her sitting up in bed, facing the wall, cradling Gussy to her belly.

"Jeannie, what's wrong?" Michelle called, shouldering past Paul into the room.

"What's the matter, June Bug?" he said, pulling up behind his wife on the bedspread. They each took one of the child's shoulders.

Jeannie wept into Gussy's weird antlered head.

Just what is that fucking thing, cow or zebra or giraffe? Paul wondered for the millionth time.

"I saw it again," she cried.

"Saw what again, baby?" Michelle asked gently.

"The thing with the dark eyes."

"Paul? Do you know what she's talking about?"

"I forgot to tell you. Jeannie had a nightmare during her nap. About a man with black eyes."

"It isn't a man, and it isn't black eyes," she whined. "It's a *thing* with *dark* eyes."

Michelle stared an accusation at Paul as if somehow this whole thing was his fault and drew Jeannie away from him onto her lap. But the whole thing *was* his fault, wasn't it? His daughter was having nightmares about the jackass from the field house. He was going to have words with that son of a bitch come Tuesday.

"Everything's okay, sweet pea. You can sleep with Mommy tonight."

"Where am I supposed to sleep?" Paul asked. The queen-sized bed barely fit the two of them comfortably, let alone a little one.

"There's a vacancy here," Michelle said, her tone acidic.

Paul watched her lead their daughter down the hall, jaw working, then heard the door shut. He flopped back onto the tiny bed, kicking a drift of stuffed animals over the footboard, and tried to get comfortable.

Michelle woke him at 7:45, before she left for work. "Hey," she said.

"Hey yourself."

"I want to apologize for last night."

"Don't worry about it. Best sleep I've had in years," he said, pleased to be having this bump in the road smoothed over.

"You're a terrible liar," she said, patting his sleep-skewed hair.

"How's Jeannie?"

"She's fine. Slept straight through. She and Pear are eating breakfast."

"I hope this doesn't become a thing."

"Me, too," Michelle said. She cocked her head. "Paul, do you think that guy who looked at her through the window … God, do you think he did something worse?"

"Like what?"

"Like, exposed himself or something?"

"It was fifteen degrees outside. There'd be nothing to see."

"I'm serious."

He sighed. "I don't know, Shell. I don't think so. I think some guy walked past, peeked in, maybe made a goofy face, probably had on a pair of dark sunglasses, and her mind translated it into something monstrous."

She studied him, nibbling a nail. "I hope that's all it is."

He pulled a teddy bear from beneath his rump and tossed it aside. "It'll blow over, trust me."

But it didn't blow over. In fact, it got worse. Jeannie woke from nightmares every time she slept alone, whether overnight or during her nap. It got so bad Michelle finally made an appointment with their pediatrician.

"Do you really think that's necessary, Shelly?" Paul asked as his wife got Jeannie ready to go. "I mean, she's missing school today for this? You're going in late to work?"

"I want to hear what Dr. Copple has to say. This isn't normal, Paul."

"Well, Jesus, let me take her at least. You don't want to miss time so soon after getting a raise." He made a point not to mention the other considerations Parnell had offered his wife; he was still far from sold on them.

"I want to be there," she replied. Translation: *You'll just fuck it up.*

"Fine. I'll take Perry to school. Let me know how it goes."

They shared a peck on the lips, then went their separate ways—Michelle towing Jeannie by one hand (with Jeannie similarly towing Gussy by one hoof) and Paul packing Perry's backpack.

Paul was sorting through the gaggle of Linda Lopez's new friend requests (both those he'd solicited and the bevy of men soliciting her) when Michelle called.

"What's the verdict?" he asked.

"Dr. Copple says she's suffering from night terrors. While it's not exactly common, it's perfectly normal in kids her age."

"That's a relief," he said. Something occurred to him which surprisingly hadn't earlier. "You didn't tell him I left her alone, did you?"

"Are you crazy? He'd have called DCFS so fast his speed dial would've broken." A pointed pause. "I still can't believe you did that."

"I won't again," he said through gritted teeth. She was going to drag this punishment out. Mercifully, she let the subject lapse. For now, at least.

"Did Perry get to school okay?"

"Yep. He was bummed that the weather was too cold for outdoor recess until I reminded him of soccer practice after school. That boosted him a bit."

"Good, good," Michelle said in a distracted tone. "Listen, I'm going to drop Jeannie off with you and head to the office. We'll be there in fifteen minutes or so. Would you do me a favor? Would you make her a peanut butter and jelly sandwich?"

"It's only ten," he said, checking the PC's clock. "She's not going to preschool?"

"No. I called her in sick. Please, Paul? Let's make her feel really special for a while. Maybe that will help her sleep better. PB and J is her favorite."

He closed his eyes. "What kind of jelly does she like?"

"If you don't know by now, I'm not going to tell you," Michelle replied. Oh, she was enjoying this punishment, all right.

"Right. See you when you get here."

He knew Perry preferred strawberry, but couldn't remember if Jeannie's was raspberry, apple, or grape. Jeannie let him know in no uncertain terms.

"It's *grape*, Daddy," she said with a scowl of contempt.

"Yeah, Daddy, it's *grape*," Michelle echoed. A flicker of a wicked smile fluttered on her lips.

Paul glared at her.

"Oh, Jesus, where's your sense of humor?" she sighed, flicking his rump with her purse.

"Aren't you going to be late?"

"I'm already late. I'm going to be later. Fix me a sandwich, too."

"Are you serious?"

"As menopause. Crunchy with apple. On honey wheat, not white."

"Daddy, I don't like crunchy peanut butter," Jeannie whined.

"I made yours with creamy," he said. He'd remembered that much, at least.

"I'm sleepy," Jeannie commented and yawned hugely.

"You and Daddy can rest on the couch after your snack," Michelle said.

Paul said, "Daddy has to work this morning, Mommy. Remember?"

"Daddy can spend an hour with his daughter who hasn't been sleeping well," she retorted.

"Sure. Screw deadlines."

"Language, dear. Deadlines come second to family."

"Tell my clients that."

"You tell them. Then you spend an hour on the sofa."

"Yes, master." He made the sandwiches without bothering to cut the crusts off his wife's as she preferred. Let her snatch them off herself.

"All set, June Bug?" he asked. He'd gotten her set up on the sofa with her pillow, Gussy, and Mickey Mouse on the tube.

"Will you lay with me, Daddy?"

"Daddy has to work, honey."

"Mommy said you had to."

Paul flared his nostrils. "Mommy's not the boss of Daddy, okay? Daddy's a very busy man."

"Okay, Daddy."

"You'll be all right, yes?"

"Yes, Daddy."

"I'll just be right in my office. Look, you can see the door from here," he said, which was true if she crawled to the other end of the sofa and craned her neck.

"Yes, Daddy," she said, already resigned. The thumb went into her mouth and Gussy to one hip. She surveyed the TV with glassy eyes. He noted a tiny smear of purple preserves on the corner of her mouth.

Paul kissed her forehead and slipped into his office to sort through his new friend acceptances. One of them, he noted with elation, turned out to be Viola Datsun.

He devoured Viola's profile for any scent of Lucine. To better conduct such an endeavor, he put on his heavy metal playlist. Napalm Death bludgeoned through his earbuds.

Paul scrolled through Viola's timeline with one hand and drummed furiously on the top of his desk with the fingers of his other. His blood was up, like a hunter on the trail of a fox. Or a wolf. He didn't know yet just what kind of animal he could compare Lucine Korth to, but he would find out, by God. A slinky mink, perhaps.

After fifteen fitful minutes of futility, he hit pay dirt. Deep in one of Viola's photo albums, this one titled Oct-Nov 2014 he found a pic of Lucine Korth. With a hungered frenzy he usually reserved for the brief moments preceding sex, he clicked the image and watched it balloon to full size. Embiggen, in internet nerdspeak.

Painted in full-color 1050 x 1680 resolution, Lucine Korth came to life. Glorious, ethereal life. The scratchy black and white pic of her had been nothing compared to this. She looked askance of the camera, but her eyes blazed a fierce aquamarine ringed with gold, surely the work of contact lenses or Photoshop; if not, they must be a mutation, for Paul had never beheld eyes of such a hue. Not even Mother Nature painted with such a glorious palette. Her skin appeared flawless, a perfect deep bronze. Again, he couldn't determine if the tone was natural or filtered. Her hair hung in a braid over one shoulder so black it appeared blue in the sunlight. Her lips resembled twin tulip petals, dewy and perfectly pink. She wore cutoff shorts and a blouse opened to the top of her cleavage and tied above her navel. Her breasts sacked in her shirt like a pair of overripe grapefruits. She wore no bra and a spritz of sweat adorned the valley leading into her shirt.

Napalm Death had given way to Cannibal Corpse, the drum and bass thrumming in time with his erection. For the better part of five minutes, he could not pull his eyes from the screen. He studied every detail of Lucine's face, her trunk, and her supple, muscled legs where they disappeared above the knee at the bottom of the frame. She was utterly hypnotic.

"Holy Christ on a Christmas tree," he muttered, dimly aware his mouth had filled with saliva and sweat had sprung on his brow.

"Daddy?" Jeannie called from the doorway. It was clear she had been there for some time, but he hadn't been able to hear her over the volume of the music.

Paul snapped back to reality. He shut down the death metal and thumbed off the monitor, unable to bring himself to close the image on his screen—it would seem a betrayal to Lucine to take such drastic action.

"Hi, June Bug. What're you doing up?"

"Someone's knocking."

"Knocking?"

"At the door."

He jumped up and lurched into the living room, wishing his dick would get out of his way. Jeannie followed, wearing a quizzical look on her angelic face.

When he got to the door, he glanced through the shades first. The stoop stood empty. Paul hauled the door open, but their caller had gone. He turned to his daughter.

"Did you see who it was, kiddo?"

Jeannie shook her head. "Mommy told me to find a grownup if someone knocks."

The ever-resourceful *Mommy* strikes again. "She's correct. You did the right thing."

"Can we have lunch?"

He glanced at the wall clock and was shocked to find nearly two hours had passed since he'd set her up on the couch with Gussy and cartoons. "Sure thing, June Bug. Let's go."

♀

Jeannie shrieked awake from her nap. Paul cursed and dragged his jockey shorts up, kicking his chair aside. He tore open his office door, member throbbing (but swiftly softening), and stepped into the living room.

Jeannie rocked on her haunches, Gussy hugged to her cheek. "I saw it again, Daddy. The thing with dark eyes."

Paul crouched and took her by the shoulders. "Jean Susan, listen to me. There's no man with dark eyes. You have to understand that. It's only a dream you're having."

"I know, Daddy, but I can't help it. I keep seeing the eyes wook at me."

He shook her. "Stop saying *wook*, for Christ's sake."

"Daddy, you're *hurting* me."

Paul took a deep breath and released her. He paced, scrubbing a hand over the stubble on his jaw. If they'd had a family pet, he might have kicked it now.

"Daddy?"

"What?"

"Don't we have to get Perry now?"

He checked the clock. Ten to three. What the fuck had he been doing? *Get it together, Paulie. Don't lose it over some fucking chick you saw online.*

Except Lucine Korth wasn't just some chick. She was perfection incarnate, Helen of Troy or perhaps the goddess Athena herself. How she lived in his town and had escaped his detection eluded him. Well, she wouldn't now. Not anymore.

He got Jeannie into her coat, and they went to pick up Perry.

Chapter Eight

Jeannie behaved much better at her brother's soccer practice that day and Paul thanked the powers that be she'd gotten in a full nap before the nightmare had awaken her. She played happily with an errant ball, kicking it back and forth along the bottom row of bleachers.

He saw the guy with the mashed nose and ambled over. "I need to talk to you," he said, more confrontationally than he'd intended.

The guy arched his eyebrows. "Mr. Family Man," he said. "What can I do you for?"

"What do you mean by staring in at my daughter and scaring her half to death on the way to your car the other day?"

The eyebrows dropped. "Say again?"

"My girl said you looked in at her on the way to your car. She's had nightmares ever since." He considered, then added: "And, no offense, but I see why."

"Listen, pal. I don't know what your kid told you, but I didn't look at nothing on my way to the car. You think I'm some perv? Some pedophile or something? That what you're suggesting?"

Paul backed off a step. "She said someone matching your description stared in at her. You have no business doing something like that."

"Maybe you got no business leaving your kid unattended in a vehicle in the middle of winter."

"This isn't about that," Paul said. "Don't you ever let me catch you looking at my kid again."

"Or what?" the guy said, squaring his shoulders.

"Or I'll be the one calling the cops."

The man took a step closer. His breath smelled of sausage and onions through yellowed teeth. "You threaten me again and I'll knock your head off your shoulders right in front of your kids. You hear me, you son of a bitch?"

Some of the other parents glanced over, whispering. Paul felt their stares and took another step back. He opened his mouth to say more, then closed it again before stalking away to the far end of the field.

They waited in the car for the guy to usher his son out. Paul pointed at him.

"Look, Jeannie. Is that the man with the dark eyes you saw looking in at you the other day?"

Jeannie craned to see. "No, Daddy. He's too short."

"Take a really good look, kiddo. That's him, right? See, he's wearing sunglasses."

Jeannie shook her head. "Nope. The thing I saw had dark *eyes*, not *glasses*."

Shit, Paul thought. He'd been so sure it had been the guy who threatened to call Family Services.

"Dad, can we go home? I'm hungry," Perry said.

Paul didn't answer. He peeled out of the lot behind the guy's Range Rover.

"Where are we going?" Perry asked when his father drove past their turnoff.

"I just want to see something," Paul said absently.

Perry, ever sharp, said, "Are we following him?"

"Who?" Paul said, glancing in the mirror, on guard now.

"The man who looked in at Jeannie."

"It wasn't a man," Jeannie reaffirmed.

"The guy from soccer practice. Are we chasing him?"

"We're not chasing anyone, Pear. I just want to see something."

Paul kept three car lengths back but got caught at the light on Greenville and watched the guy with the misshapen nose cruise away. Thursday. He'd get him Thursday. Paul made a right onto Shade Tree Drive and looped around to Pace Lane.

"Where are we now, Dad?" Perry asked.

"Heading home, buckaroo."

"What did you want to see?"

Paul blinked at the mirror. "Oh. They're building a new pizza parlor up that way, and I wanted to see how it was going."

"Pizza?" the kids cried together.

"No pizza tonight," he said.

He put leftovers on when they got home while the kids played in Perry's room. They rarely played together, being of different genders and with the age gap, so when they did it made Paul happy. He turned the chops in the skillet, then went in to snap a few pictures of the kiddos.

"Whatcha playing?" he asked, thumbing on his phone to pull up the camera. If the kids answered, he didn't hear them. He never got as far as finding the camera app either. He had a new Facebook message—or rather Linda Lopez did—from Viola Datsun.

He hurried to his office and eased the door closed, then called up his messages. He ignored those from desperate men looking to make a quick love connection and opened Viola's.

It said: "Do I know you?"

Paul's mind cycled feverishly. What could he possibly say in reply? He remembered she'd attended North Central University and had her major listed as Anthropology. It would be a start, anyway.

He typed: "If you're the Viola I remember, then we went to college together. I think we took a few of the same anthro classes."

A minute ticked by, two. Then the message window indicated his message had been read. Fifteen seconds later, it reported Viola was typing. A message popped up: "Oh, Linda. NCU, right. I'm sorry, it's been a few years, but I think I remember you now."

Heart thudding, Paul typed: "I've been trying to catch up with college friends and your name popped to mind. In fact, I'm a little embarrassed to say this, but you actually helped me on a couple projects."

Message read. Pause. Then: "LOL that's right! How are you Linda? Are you still doing the whole psych thing?"

Psych thing? What psych thing? Paul thought before remembering he'd listed Linda Lopez's major as psychology. So Viola had glanced over his fake profile. Good. He typed: "Yup! In grad school now, working toward my doctorate."

Another pause, this time almost three whole minutes. Then: "Congrats, girl! Proud of you!"

51

Paul wrote: "Thanks. How's anthropology treating you?"

She replied: "Oh I dropped that gig years ago. I'm a server over at Cabana Girls now."

Cabana Girls. A Hooters nightclub knockoff on Lake Winona's north side. The glitzy side, if this town had one. He'd never been, but he'd make a point to now. Maybe Lucine would even put in a cameo.

He wrote: "Nice! I've heard good things about that place."

Then nothing. He waited for Viola to reply, but she didn't. A sharp, shrill tone stuttered from somewhere, startling him. It took him a second to place it, but when he did he ran for the kitchen.

The chops had burned. Black smoke roiled from the range. He slapped the burner off and flipped on the exhaust fan. The smoke detector bleated. He grabbed the skillet and tossed it, chops and all, into the sink and turned on the water. He spun and saw the children crowded shoulder-to-shoulder in the doorway, terror etched on their faces, hands clapped to their ears. They were screaming something, but he couldn't hear them over the blatting of the alarm. He stood on tiptoe and pried the bastard off the wall, tore off the back, and clawed the batteries out.

Jeannie's shrieks replaced the alarm, matching it to the decibel.

"Stop that, Jeannie," Paul said, but she never slowed. She hadn't even heard him. "I said stop that noise, Jean Susan." His daughter cried all the harder. Paul lost it. "I said stop that *goddamn noise!*" he bellowed, taking three stomping steps toward his children.

Perry pulled his sister into a protective hug and backed away. Paul blinked at the new fear dawning on their faces—no longer from the abrupt alarm tone, but because of *him*. Jeannie had even quit crying to regard him in mute wonder.

"Oh. Oh, kids, hey. Listen. I'm sorry. Daddy didn't mean to yell." He took another step toward them, gentler now. They backed away, Perry's arms still locked around his sister. "Hey, you two. It's okay. Everything's okay."

The door opened and Michelle stepped inside, the satisfied smile of another completed workday slipping from her face as she surveyed the scene. She took in her children grappled together, her husband hunched over them like some fairy tale troll, the stench of burned food and the miasma of smoke.

"Paul?" she said. "What the hell is going on here?"

Chapter Nine

That night Paul's exile from the bed wasn't caused by Jeannie's night terrors. He slept on the sofa where he'd left his daughter that day because Michelle claimed she'd simply had enough.

"I don't know what the fuck is going on with you, but you had better get it together," she said after tucking the kids in. "Stat."

He hated when she said "stat." God, that pissed him off. "Look, I got busy with a project and burned dinner. It's not the first time it's happened in this world, and it won't be the last."

"This stuff has been happening too often lately," she said. "I honestly don't know what's gotten into you. You were fine on our anniversary. The next day, bang, you're acting like a maniac. Our anniversary was the last nice day we've spent together."

"I know. I'm sorry. I'm going to withdraw from some projects, maybe that will help reduce some stress." He hated when he sounded like a kid wheedling his way out of trouble.

"Oh, sure. Bring in *less* money. That's always a recipe for reducing stress."

Blood rose in his cheeks. "I'm trying here, Michelle. What do you want me to do?"

"What do I want you to do? *Try harder*. And in the meantime, it would probably be best if you slept elsewhere."

He nearly brought up the Tom Rood affair then. Nearly. But he held off, because he thought he'd need to save that trump card for later. The fling Michelle had had with her ex-boyfriend during the time Paul was courting her had never fully fled his mind, even though he'd said he'd forgiven her. No, he'd save good ol' Tom Rood for when these waters became *really* troubled. It was as good as a Get Out of Jail Free card. Instead, he gathered his pillow and an extra blanket from the closet.

"Pleasant fucking dreams," he said and tromped downstairs.

Paul flipped on the tube and surfed until midnight, finding little of interest. He tried to sleep, knowing he'd have a lot of work to catch up on tomorrow after missing nearly all of today, but only tossed and turned. Finally, flinging the blanket aside, he padded over to his office.

Linda Lopez had a cache of new friends and twice as many requests. He checked the dialogue box, but Viola had not yet replied (though the timestamp indicated she had seen his last message at 6:27 p.m.). Linda had half a dozen messages from mediocre-looking men wearing eyeglasses and argyle sweaters or shitty goatees and bad toupees. Most of them were like the user called Igrekx Ingko, offering subtle or not so subtle sexual innuendos. One sent a marriage proposal and another a picture of his glistening miniscule erection.

"Fucking perverts," Paul muttered. What was the matter with his side of the gender spectrum? What were they missing in their lives that made them so needy, so aggressively offensive? Had they always been this way or was it merely a symptom of the globalization of communication?

A thud from somewhere sounded, but he barely heard it. He scrolled through the messages, responding to some, deleting others (including Mr. Pinky Penis), then returned to Viola Datsun's. Should he send something inviting her back to the conversation? No, it would be better to wait, at least until morning. Restraint, not desperation.

The thud came again, louder now. Paul glanced up. It sounded as if it had come from the front of the house. He recalled Jeannie reporting someone knocking and got up to check.

They kept no guns in the house at Michelle's insistence — not that he'd ever really wanted one either, but he'd been more open to the idea — but he kept a police-issue baton in his office closet. He'd picked it up at the Army-Navy surplus store downtown and not even Michelle knew he had it. It wouldn't hurt to take it with him now, in case someone might be trying to break in. What if the busted-nose guy had looped around and followed *him*?

"Bring it, bitch," Paul said aloud, surprising himself. He'd never been violent by nature and had, in fact, never been in a fist fight with anyone other than his kid brother twenty years previously.

He crept to the front windows and peered through a gap in the curtain. The street appeared empty. Same with the stoop. He listened.

Thud.

It had come from outside, near the garage. Paul toed into his sneakers and eased out the front door.

The chill bit deep. Snowflakes drifted out of the darkness; their minute bodies held in harsh relief beneath the streetlamp. Paul squinted toward the garage but could make out nothing in the shadows. A crushed paper cup scraped its way along the curb. A dog barked a block over. Nothing else.

He'd made up his mind to return to his office when the noise came again, except out here in the dark it sounded more like a wooden *thunk*, reminding him for some reason of the rigging on a pirate ship striking the hull. Something moved near the garage. Paul released his breath in a plume and shook his head—one of the decorative window shutters had come loose and banged the wall when the wind gusted. He'd have to fix it in the morning, he decided, and turned to go back inside.

A shadow standing in the doorway flushed adrenaline through his system.

"Paul? What are you doing out here?" Michelle asked, her bathrobe cinched closed at her throat with one hand.

"Shelly. Thank Christ it's you."

"Who did you expect? The Elephant Man?" She eyed the baton, then cut her glare back to him. "What is *that*? Is that a fucking *billy club*?"

Paul moved to step around her, but his wife held her position. The adrenaline did nothing to warm him. "Let me in, Shell. It's freezing."

She did not move. "What are you doing outside with a billy club?"

"Let me in and I'll explain."

"You can explain from there."

You vindictive bitch, he thought. She loved this punishment she'd been dishing out of late. Oh yes, she *loved* it. Through gritted teeth, he said, "I heard a noise, so I came out to make sure Jeannie's black-eyed boogeyman wasn't trying to get in. It's just a loose shutter. I'll fix it tomorrow. Now let me in."

She crossed her arms. "And the club?"

Paul's grip on the handle tightened. For one horrifying instant, he saw himself slamming the business end into his wife's face, shattering her lovely high cheekbones, her orbits, and her petite bitchy little nose. He clenched his jaw and said, "You don't let guns in the house, so I chose a weapon that might better adhere to your specifications. Now let me in the *fucking house*."

She stood aside and he pushed past.

"Speaking of Jeannie's boogeyman," she said, slamming the door, "she had another nightmare. We had a pretty interesting talk once I got her calmed down."

"Oh yeah? She mention her boogeyman breathe fire or sprout antlers or some shit?"

"The talk wasn't about the boogeyman. It was about you, Paul."

He turned to her fully, the club still in his fist. He felt its deadly weight. God, it would be glorious to strike something with it. Slowly, deliberately, biting off each word, he said, "What about me?"

"She said she came into your office this morning and saw a pretty lady on your computer screen."

"Yeah, and?"

"Care to explain that?"

"Jesus, Shelly. I was probably reading an article on the *New York Times* website."

"Somehow I doubt that."

"Does every time you view a picture of a man online mean you're having an affair with him?" he demanded, holding the club parallel to his thigh. It felt good in his hand, like an extension of his body—an extraneous limb on some ancient god, perhaps.

"So you'd be okay with me checking your browsing history?"

"Knock yourself out, my love," he said with saccharine sarcasm. *Or maybe I'll knock you out.* Why should he care if she checked his history? He set up all the phony profiles in incognito mode, so none of it had saved anyway.

Except ...

Except had he closed down Linda Lopez's most recent session? He couldn't honestly recall. If Michelle stepped into his office and discovered he'd registered a profile under a woman's name and having conversations with complete strangers, he wouldn't be able to talk himself out of that hole. What could he say? They'd be in divorce court next week.

She gave him a lingering look, then marched into his office and tapped the mouse to kill the screen saver. Paul peered over her shoulder. Just his desktop, with the icons for the Recycle Bin, the anti-virus software, and the file labeled ROSETHORN.doc.

Michelle dropped into his chair as if she owned it and called up a fresh browser, going straight for the History button like an ape at bamboo shoots. The only thing she found worth noting turned out to be a healthy dose of visits to a sports betting site.

She eyed him, clearly disappointed in finding nothing of substance, but she wasn't about to let it go. "Gambling, Paul?"

"I check football odds from time to time."

"Why?"

He shrugged. "They fascinate me. The idea some lug out in Vegas is sitting in a dim office wearing a visor and plugging numbers into a computer is intriguing. I mean, what a job. Right?"

Michelle stood. "I'm going back to bed. If I don't see you in the morning, don't forget to send Perry's permission slip to school for his field trip on Friday."

I'll see you, all right, Paul thought as his wife made her way upstairs, though he had no idea what it meant. He returned to the sofa, slid the club beneath it, and dropped into an uneasy doze.

Chapter Ten

How his wife slipped past him in the morning, Paul didn't know. He must have slept harder than he'd imagined. He'd been in the middle of a dream in which he ran through a maze of streets in a nameless metropolis, looking for a way out. None of the signs made any sense, as though written in an alien language. Perry shook him awake at 7:30.

"Dad, wake up. Jeannie's crying."

"Where is she?" he said, sitting up.

"In your bed. What are you doing on the couch?"

Paul blinked around. "Worked late last night. Guess I didn't quite make it to bed. Where's Mom?"

"She left. Are you and Mom fighting?"

Why did she leave so early? he wondered.

He slugged the boy playfully in the ribs. "Fighting? Heck no. We're fine, kiddo. Let's go see about your sister."

They found her cuddled beneath the sheets with Gussy covering her eyes. Paul lifted her into his lap and asked her what the matter was, but he already knew.

"I woked up and Mommy was gone, but the thing with dark eyes wasn't. It was right in Mommy's spot," she said, pointing to Michelle's side of the bed without removing the stuffed animal.

Paul looked. The impression of his wife's body remained in the mattress. "Oh, sweetie, look. That's where Mommy slept.

See? That's all. She left for work this morning and the mattress hasn't had time to puff up again."

"I saw Mommy leave and tried to go back to sleep. When I opened my eyes, it was laying there wooking at me."

A vein twitched in Paul's temple, and he rubbed at it with two fingers. "It was only a bad dream, June Bug. Remember? We talked about that."

"It didn't feel like a dream."

Paul smoothed her hair back and kissed her forehead. "That's the funny thing about dreams. A lot of times they seem very real. In fact, I was having a dream just as your brother woke me up."

"You were?" she asked. "What was it?"

"Yeah, Dad. What was it?" Perry chimed in from where he stood at the foot of the bed.

"You know what? It's already fading from my mind. That's another thing about dreams. They disappear once you let them go."

"They do?" Jeannie asked.

"Sure do. So what I want you to do, while I fix breakfast, is let your bad dream go. Just let it float away, like a feather in the wind. Can you do that for me?"

"I'll try, Daddy."

"Good. Now how about some Frosted Flakes?"

"Yay!" Jeannie said, transforming instantly from sorrowful gnome to bright cherub.

Paul walked his kids to the kitchen and got out the milk. Michelle had left no note wishing him a good day or saying she loved him. There'd been a time, not long ago, when she would have left one every morning—which got him wondering again: Why had she left so early?

♀

While the kids ate, Paul stepped into his office. No more fucking around today—he had to get caught up on work. The bills wouldn't pay themselves.

Well, maybe a little fucking around, he thought, Lucine Korth rising through his synapses like hypnotic hallucinogenic smoke. But business first, play second.

He pulled up his assignments and stopped, fingers hovering above the mouse. Where he'd had a dozen pending jobs only yesterday, only one remained—a 500-word SEO optimization article paying a meager $25.

"What the hell?" he muttered, clicking on his inbox. Eleven messages awaited, all clients who'd withdrawn their offers and all because he'd failed to meet the expected turnaround time. "Shit. *Shit*."

Paul thought he'd had at least another day or two on each of these, some of them up to a week. He opened the original proposals, one by one, and realized with shock each delivery date had expired. How the hell had he gotten so far behind?

But he already knew the answer. Lucine. He'd been preoccupied with her, he admitted to himself. Except "preoccupied" didn't quite cover all the bases, did it? No, a closer term would be obsessed. Paul had been obsessed with the woman. And, Christ, not even the *woman* but an *image* of her. He'd missed out on over $500 in revenue because of a fucking *picture*.

Well, he'd just have to play catch up. He browsed the list of offered jobs and submitted proposals to five ghostwriting projects, six proofreading jobs, and half a dozen in copyediting. He lowballed the bids to make the offers more attractive. If even half of them bit, he'd be back on track by the end of the week. Until then, if cash came in short supply, they would have Michelle's raise to fall back on.

While he waited for the fish to come nibbling, he pulled up Linda Lopez's profile and scrolled through new friends and messages. Still nothing from Viola. He was in the middle of formulating a plan to sneak over to Cabana Girls when he caught motion in the hall.

"Dad?" Perry stood in the doorway. "I'm ready for school."

Paul looked at the clock. 8:12. God, he was losing it. "Okay. Let me get dressed. Help your sister get her coat on."

"Dad, we're going to be late."

"No, we won't. Do as I say, Pear."

Paul kicked his slippers into his closet, hauled on the first pair of pants he could find, and stepped into his sneakers. By the time he got to the living room, Perry had succeeded only in getting his sister's hair caught in the zipper of her coat.

"Ow!" Jeannie cried as Perry yanked the zipper up and down.

"Let me," Paul said, moving his son's hands away. But the girl's hair remained stubbornly stuck. *Fucking shit.* "Perry, get in the car. We'll be right there."

No matter how he tried to work it, the hair wouldn't come loose. Perry and the zipper had worked a number on it.

"Daddy, it *hurts*," Jeannie whimpered.

"We'll have to work on it when we get home. Your brother's going to be late." He carried her into the garage and strapped her into the car seat. Her head rested nearly on her shoulder because the trapped hair pulled it down at an angle.

"*Daddeeee.*"

"Hang tight, June Bug." They backed down the driveway and into the street, Jeannie sobbing all the way. They got to school with a minute to spare, and Paul kissed his son and sent him off. By the time they got home, Jeannie had grown hysterical.

Paul tried to work the hair free with a comb but failed. After fifteen minutes fighting with it and his daughter wailing in his ear, he finally got the shears and clipped the stubborn lock free. He hadn't thought it would be easy to spot, but when Jeannie raised her newly-freed head, the deficit became clear. He groaned. Michelle was going to kill him.

He called the salon where Michelle took the kids for haircuts, but they had no openings until Thursday afternoon during the time Perry had soccer practice. Jeannie had preschool prior to that. Perfect.

At least Jeannie's mood had improved after she'd discovered her reflection in her mother's hand mirror. "I look silly! Silly-Billy-silly-Billy," she sang.

Paul found one of Perry's Chicago Cubs hats and planted it on her. It would cover the flaw while they ran errands. "Come on, June Bug, back in the car. Daddy has a few things to do downtown."

They drove to the bank, where Paul checked the balance of both savings and checking—so far, they'd remained clear of dire straits. If he didn't land at least a few of those jobs, though, they might find themselves smack in the middle of them.

Next stop: Citgo station. Paul paid at the pump because he didn't want to drag Jeannie inside and the thought of leaving her alone in the car—even for a minute—chilled him. He'd been stupid to do it the first time and Michelle had every right to be furious. He still wondered why she'd left so early and decided a drive by Parnell & Ostreicher might be in order. Perhaps he could surprise her with lunch.

Only that would mean bringing Jeannie with. Jean Susan Jeske: she of the horrifically hellish hairstyle. To say Michelle would flip out should he drag Jeannie in with her mutilated locks would be an understatement.

"Hey, that's where Mommy works!" Jeannie proclaimed from behind him.

"That's right, kiddo."

"Can we see her?"

"Not right now," Paul said, slowing as he drove by the office so he could peer inside. The blinds covering the window of her compartment (not quite big enough to be called an office, too large for a cubicle) were closed. He caught shadowy motion near the reception area, but nothing more. A wash.

He drove north and rolled by Cabana Girls. Could Viola Datsun be working now? Probably not, the place didn't appear to be open yet. Surely the peak business hours for such an establishment wouldn't start until after dinnertime. Paul pulled into the parking lot and right up to the front door to check the hours.

"There's a naked lady on the sign," Jeannie giggled from the back seat.

"It's just an outline of her, June Bug. You can't see anything," her father replied absently. Cabana Girls opened at 4:30 and closed at 2:00 Sunday through Thursday, an hour later on weekends. Good to know.

He backed out and had turned onto the highway when his cell chirped. Paul snatched it out of his coat pocket and checked the ID. Michelle's work number.

"Hey, babe," he said.

"Hi. Are you at home?"

"Yeah. Why?"

"You didn't drive by a few minutes ago?"

"Drive by what?" he asked, careful to keep his tone level.

"The office."

"Nope."

"Because Sandra swears she saw you and Jeannie go by not ten minutes ago."

"I guess Sandra was wrong," he said. "Anyway, would driving by my wife's workplace be a capital crime?"

"No, but it would odd."

"Why's that?"

"Well, why wouldn't you stop in and say hello? What could possibly bring you out this way except for a surprise visit?"

"I didn't go that way."

A pause, calculating. "How's the baby? Can I talk to her?" Michelle always referred to Jeannie as "the baby" during times of stress; it was a subtle nuance Paul had picked up on when Jeannie was still a newborn.

"Napping." Paul looked at his daughter in the mirror and held a finger to her lips. Jeannie giggled into her cupped hand: *We're tricking Mommy!*

"Okay. Did you get the shutter fixed yet?"

"After Jeannie wakes up. I don't want the banging to disturb her."

Finally, the guarded tone she'd taken with him the past few days seemed to soften. "I'll see you tonight, then. How's Chinese sound for dinner? I'll pick it up from Chiang's on the way home."

"Chinese sounds delightful."

"Chicken chow mein?"

"With extra soy," he said.

"'Kay. Kiss the kiddos for me."

"I will."

"Paul?"

"Yes?"

"I love you."

"Love you, too," he said and ended the call before she could say more.

Chapter Eleven

When they got home, he fixed lunch, and then put Jeannie down for a proper nap. She fell asleep within moments, Gussy tucked beneath her chin. He watched her for a time, working her thumb with her tongue, her mangled hair mussed, and felt such an indescribable love it brought tears to his eyes. Paul eased her door closed and stepped into his office.

He called up his recent bids and stared in shock. None had been accepted. Not a single one—something which had not happened in his freelancing career. He called up his profile and found the reason why. All the clients who'd withdrawn in the past day had given him one-star reviews. Each shared the same general complaint: Contractor failed to meet guaranteed delivery date. One client even said she had added him to her blocked list. In the span of 24 hours, his carefully curated reputation had crumbled. It would take another four years—if not longer—to rebuild it on this site. It didn't matter how many positive reviews he'd received. Even one negative review (let alone a pack of them all at once) would call his credibility into question.

"I'm fucked," he told his unsympathetic monitor. Paul knew of a few other freelancing sites, but none as prominent or prolific as this. This one often paid big. The others he'd encountered paid only fractionally by comparison, but they might be the only choice he had now. Paul spent the next two hours creating profiles (with his real name and information this time, not Linda Lopez's or Susan Moll's) and started bidding on projects. He kept his bids low to attract the fish. By the time Jeannie woke from her nap, though, none had bitten.

His daughter wandered in, rubbing her eyes. "I'm hungry."

"Hey, June Bug. Let Daddy finish up and we'll get a snack. How'd you sleep?"

"Fine."

"No bad dreams?"

"No dreams at all."

Thank God for small favors, he thought, pulling her into his lap. She sat attentively by as he submitted a few more proposals. He asked, "Sweetheart, why did you tell Mommy you saw a picture of a pretty lady on my computer?"

Jeannie blinked owlishly. "She asked."

"She what?"

"Mommy asked if I ever saw anything on your computer."

"What kind of things did she mean?"

"She asked if I ever saw any ladies. Naked ladies, like the one we saw on the sign today."

That bitch, he thought. *Why would she ask their daughter such a question? What is the matter with her?*

"I told you, honey. The lady on the sign today wasn't naked. It was just an outline. Like a drawing."

"Okay."

"Listen, I don't want you telling Mommy you saw that today, all right?"

"But why not, if it was just an outline?"

"Because it will upset her. And I want you to do something else for me. If Mommy ever asks you any more questions like that about Daddy, I want you to tell me. Can you do that?"

"Yes, Daddy."

"Good girl. Let's go see about that snack."

After they picked up Perry (the boy cracking up at his sister's unfortunate hair), Paul checked his proposals on the new sites. Still nothing. Shit.

At quarter past five, the door opened. "Soup's on!" Michelle sang. Paul went out to greet her, his prepared speech ready to launch on his tongue, but his eagle-eyed wife had already spotted the Cubs cap askew on her daughter's head. She didn't understand at first, thinking the child had decided on a new favorite accessory, and actually laughed. It was a sound he'd not heard her make in nearly a week and it would surely be short-lived.

Michelle turned to him, two paper sacks with *Chiang's Chinese Cuisine* printed on them and gave him a genuine smile. "I see you've finally converted our daughter," she said, not unkindly. His wife came from a family of diehard White Sox fans.

"Not exactly," he said and before he could even begin to explain Jeannie jumped up, flipped the hat away, and cried: "Ta-daaaa!"

A look of horror replaced the look of playful poutiness on his wife's face, and she actually dropped the takeout bags to clap her hands to her face. The effect might have been comical had it happened under other circumstances.

"Oh my *God*," she whispered, any trace of mirth gone. "What happened to her *hair*?"

"Before you get mad, just know I made an appointment at the salon for them to fix it tomorrow afternoon."

"What did you *do* to her?" Michelle demanded, rounding on him.

"Her hair got stuck in her coat zipper. I couldn't get it loose."

She gave him a glare of such naked spite that he took a step back. Michelle scooped her daughter up and examined the shortage, whispering reassurances.

"Jesus, Shelly, it's just *hair*," he said, feeling more than ever like a boy caught with his hand in his pants. "We've been talking about getting her a pixie cut anyway."

"I like it," Jeannie said. Her use of "like" instead of "wike" at least reassured Paul. Maybe she'd gotten through her traumatization.

Michelle stared him down. "A pixie cut can't fix ... *this*."

Paul opened his mouth with no clue how to counter when Perry came to his rescue. "It was my fault, Mom. I was trying to help her with her coat and zipped her hair into it."

"That's sweet of you to try to cover for your father, but not necessary." Michelle shot her husband an *I'll deal with you later* look and carried Jeannie upstairs.

"Is Mom mad at me?" Perry asked.

Paul crouched beside his son. "No, she's mad at me."

"But I'm the one who did it."

"I'm the one who held the scissors. I should have known better."

"Are you going to get a divorce?" he asked, eyes shimmering.

"Where did you hear that word?"

"Benny Gehant, from soccer practice. His mom and dad are getting a divorce. He said that means his dad won't live with them anymore."

"No, your mother and I aren't getting a divorce," he replied and thought *I hope*. "Look, I don't want you to say anything to your sister about that, you hear?"

"I won't."

Paul shooed his son off to the kitchen, then picked the takeout sacks up off the foyer tiles. Soy sauce had leaked out of one of them, looking like black blood on the grout. He soaked it up with a fistful of paper towels, stripped the saturated sack off the chicken chow mein, and sat alone at the table to eat.

Michelle emerged a time later. Paul had found a basketball game on TV, though he paid it no mind. He watched his wife descend the staircase. She regarded him if not with forgiveness at least without rancor.

"I think I fixed her hair for school tomorrow," she said. "Fastened with a barrette, it looks kind of cute."

"Glad to hear. What are they doing?"

"Playing in Perry's room. They're getting along better than ever these days." And by *these days* she clearly meant the past week in which Paul had become a world-class fuckup.

"I put your food in the fridge. Didn't know if you still wanted it."

She sat on the sofa beside him. "I'll eat in a bit. I want to apologize for the way I've been treating you. I know you've been under stress about this whole seminar thing."

He waved it away. "I think it could be good for you. For us."

Michelle took his hand in hers. "Do you mean it?"

He inhaled deeply and pulled his eyes from the meaningless ballgame to find hers, inwardly thrilled he had found such an easy way to bridge the gap between them. "Absolutely," he said. He put on his biggest goofball grin and tried some levity. "Way I see it, it can't get much worse."

When she laughed, it sounded genuine, and she leaned into him. "I know this has been a rough patch for us, but I'm still as in love with you as the day you proposed. More, even."

"Likewise, Shelly," he replied. "Want me to warm up your egg drop soup?"

"Would you?"

"You bet. What'll the kids want?"

"Perry's campaigning for ravioli. Jeannie wants pizza."

"Jeannie *always* wants pizza," he said. They shared a laugh. To Paul it felt like a homecoming of sorts. "I'll see what I can find to appease our little highnesses. Feel free to change the channel. This game sucks."

Michelle found the remote and flipped to *History's Mysteries*. Paul stepped into the kitchen, the smile slipping from his face.

Chapter Twelve

For the first time since Jeannie's night terrors began, Paul slept in his own bed. It felt good to be back in a familiar environment, not surrounded by black-eyed stuffed animals or sprawled out on a back-breaking sofa. He found the place on the mattress which his body had carved out after years of use and dropped into an easy doze.

Michelle finished in the bathroom and lay beside him. She whispered his name.

"Mm?"

"Paul, look at me."

He opened his eyes and found not his wife in bed beside him, but Lucine Korth. She wore the same clothes from Viola Datsun's picture, the neck of her blouse open in a plunging V. Her nipples protruded from the cloth like pencil erasers. Her hair flowed over her shoulders like black water and her eyes marked him with ravenous frenzy. Except they weren't that unique aquamarine any longer: now they appeared as black as her hair.

Not black, though. Black was a color, or rather the culmination of all colors, and these orbs bore nothing remotely along the color spectrum. They were simply *dark*.

Paul cried out and clawed the bedside lamp on. When he looked again, Michelle sat beside him with her robe clutched at her throat. He could smell wildflowers from the lotion she'd applied to her hands and face.

"Jesus, Paul, are you all right?"

"What happened?"

"You had a bad dream. You screamed."

He shoved the heels of his hands hard against his eyes. "Fuck. How long have I been out?"

"All of five minutes. You were awake when I went into the bathroom and started bellowing like a stuck sheep when I sat down on the bed."

Paul pulled his wife to him. She let him, which was good. If she'd resisted, he'd know she still felt spiteful toward him and the thought of that would send him reeling toward despair. He wanted things to be right again between them. Needed things to be right between them.

They lay in one another's arms for another half hour until Michelle rolled one way and he the other.

He woke to the smell of waffles and coffee. When he'd used the bathroom and made his way downstairs, the kids, dressed and groomed, had already dug in and Michelle dripped batter onto the iron for a second round. The clock stood at 7:42, a detail he'd remember for the rest of his life.

"Good *mooooorniiiiiing*!" the kids chimed. He kissed them each on the top of the head. Michelle was right: the barrette made Jeannie's disfigured hair invisible.

"This is a lot of fuss for a workday," he commented, wrapping his arms around his wife's waist from behind. "What's the occasion?"

"I wanted to do something special for my family, that's all," she said, craning to kiss his cheek stubble. "Belgian waffles are your favorite."

"You know me well," he said, stabbing one onto a plate and filling the crevices with syrup. "This is awful kind of you, Mrs. Jeske. How do you imagine I could ever repay you?"

"Oh, I'll think of something, Mr. Jeske," Michelle promised. "Likely involving your hands on my feet."

Paul stopped chewing. "Wasn't the place I imagined my hands in this scenario."

She laughed and swatted him on the chest. "Go eat with the other children, you bad boy."

He took his plate to the head of the table. The morning paper had already been unrolled.

"Your son was kind enough to retrieve your paper," Michelle called across the breakfast bar.

"Is that right?" Paul asked his son, ruffling his hair.

Perry nodded dutifully. "I even put the Sports section out for you first, the way you like."

"Did I ever tell you you're my favorite son?"

Perry giggled and stuffed another bite into his mouth.

Jeannie said, "Am I your favorite daughter?"

Paul walked his fingers across the table. When they reached the edge, he jumped them to her ribs and tickled. She squealed. "You are absolutely my favorite daughter, June Bug."

"I'm your *only* daughter!"

"And you're also my smartest daughter." She beamed at him, her face a mess of butter and syrup. "Hey, no bad dreams last night?"

"No dreams at all," she happily reported.

He held up a palm. She slapped it. "Atta girl. I knew they'd quit before long."

Michelle joined them, but with only a mug of coffee.

"Not hungry?" he asked her.

She checked her watch. "I had a half. I should get going."

That reminded him. "Hey, I was going to ask—why'd you leave so early yesterday morning?"

Her face grew taut. "I just needed time to think. I drove around a while before heading to the office."

"And now that you've thought?"

Her million-dollar smile resurfaced. "I've thought about how much I love my family and how there's no other place in the entire universe I'd rather be than with you three love bugs."

Spontaneously, as though of one mind, each member of the Jeske clan reached for one another's hands. The Lucine dream tried to rise in his mind, but Paul wouldn't let it. Not now. This moment in time had nothing to do with Lucine Korth, and he banished her fully from thought.

Paul savored that moment, but not for long enough; he would remember it to his dying day as the last truly happy one of his life.

With the kids dropped off (Mrs. Landon commenting on how *cuuuute* Jeannie looked with her hair done up), Paul returned home to try to salvage something of his career. Marriage Road may have been smoothed over for now, but if Michelle found out most of his clients had block-listed him, it would likely grow potholes large enough to swallow them whole.

Except his career seemed beyond salvaging. Overnight, four additional poor reviews had appeared on his page like virtual cold sores. It didn't take long to make the decision to start over with a completely new profile. Paul got to work.

"Linda Lopez" looked even better on the freelance website than she did on social media. Her credentials gleamed as bright as her smile. Paul dug up some of his past work samples and added them to Linda's online portfolio. Then he applied for jobs until he could find no more matching his skills, cutting the bids to the bone.

At lunchtime, he ate at his desk while the offers poured in. He was back in business and Michelle would never have to be any the wiser.

His mistake came when he clicked the button to accept his—Linda's—first assignment. The website prompted him to complete and submit a W9 for tax purposes, and Paul Jeske instantly learned the limitations of anonymity on the internet. It only went so far before real life intervened.

"Fuck," he said. A whole morning wasted on setting up this fake bullshit. "Fuck this in the *ass*."

He kicked his chair backward and slammed a fist into the bulletin board hanging beside his desk. The cork split. He punched the board again and felt the drywall behind it collapse.

Paul stood for a minute, breathing through his fury, then found the car keys and went out.

Walmart did nothing to soothe his mood. The aisles were clogged with oblivious holiday shoppers who bustled their carts along with no more consideration for their whereabouts than the weather. Paul made it to the home office section, selected a corkboard, and returned to check out.

The lines extended back nearly to the mouths of the aisles, and he selected the one which appeared shortest. He stood with his single item beneath his arm, scanning the rows of fashion magazines. Lucine Korth ought to be on every last cover. Every single issue would sell out. When he reached the impulse items by the register, he added a pack of spearmint gum, a Bic lighter, a prepaid phone card, a pair of 1.5 magnification reading glasses, and a three-pack of miniature LED flashlights to his order. Impulse items indeed.

The girl at the register flirted a little, but he barely realized it. He had more important matters to consider.

Cabana Girls was closed at this hour, but Paul drove out to it anyway. He parked, got out, and cupped his hands to the glass door. The place appeared deserted, although an ancient Buick Regal sat in the last slot. Paul tried the door. Locked.

He'd climbed behind the wheel and keyed the engine when an enormous guy wearing a striped sweater and cable-knit cap came out. It seemed unlikely he'd fit in the Buick.

"You want something?" he called through the windshield.

"Just checking your hours."

"Were you here the other day?" the guy hollered.

Jesus, when did the world get so watchful? Paul unrolled the window. "Might have been."

"You didn't think to check the hours then?"

"Guess it slipped my mind," he said, pulling his hat lower and dropping into reverse. He certainly didn't want this guy remembering him. It might cause trouble down the road.

The bouncer—if that's who he was; he certainly held the physical stats to qualify for the position—watched him drive away. Paul kept an eye on the rearview until the nightclub disappeared.

Chapter Thirteen

Next stop: William Street. He parked and got out. The wind hushed up at him from the pavement and Paul hunched deeper into his coat. He checked the street and found it empty. The rows of rundown houses showed no glimmer of life. Paul plucked a ski mask from his pocket and drew it over his face. Then he walked to the corner of Pace Lane and took it, feeling a little like Batman. Batman of the 'Burbs. He liked the title.

Lucine's house stood half a block up. No smoke from the chimney, same as the last time he'd been by. Could she have gone on vacation? The idea depressed him, he was shocked to discover.

He reached her walk and strode by without slowing, subtly turning his head to scan the windows. Nothing. No movement. Paul checked the street again, but nothing stirred. The sun had vanished beneath a curtain of ironed-on clouds.

He turned around and tried the decrepit gate closing off her walk, found it unlocked, and pushed it in. It squealed on rusted hinges. He strode confidently up the five wide steps to her meager front porch, drawing the misplaced letter which had started this whole fiasco in motion from his pocket.

The mailbox nailed to the wall beside the door was a simple tin block painted black with the numerals 2-0-0 pasted on in reflective lettering. Paul flipped the lid, meaning to drop the letter inside and walk away, but hesitated. The mailbox overflowed with envelopes and one small package in brown cardboard.

He risked another look at the street, then reached into the box and dragged all the mail out and stuffed it under his arm. The mask made him invincible. Paul Jeske ambled back to his car, not hurrying, not dallying. If anyone noticed him, they gave no sign.

To label Lucine Korth's mail stash a treasure trove would have been a gross understatement. After sifting through fashion catalogs and credit card solicitations, Paul at last came to what he thought of as "the good stuff."

First up: a Discover bill. Paul slit it with a letter opener and scanned the contents. $279.28 at Lowe's. $595.07 at Menard's. $2,682.88 at Home Depot. All home improvement stores. Nothing for groceries, fast food, or takeout. The only oddball item on the invoice was for a place called Eve's Garden, something Paul had never heard of. He ran a quick web search and felt his face color.

"Holy shit," he muttered. Eve's Garden appeared to be an adult online supercenter, specializing in everything from your run-of-the-mill porno vids to high-end lifelike sex dolls. The amount itemized on her bill was listed as $1,451.21. Hardware and hardcore all on one invoice. He needed a beer for this.

Paul didn't drink much—a glass of wine here and there with supper and the occasional Friday night out with the boys—but today he felt he could use something. He knew he had to pick Jeannie up in ninety minutes (setting his cell phone alarm accordingly so as not to show up late again) but thought he could squeeze in two brews and pop a stick of gum without anyone being the wiser.

On the trip to the kitchen, something slammed against the side of the house, and he screamed. The fucking shutter. He'd fix it later. There were more important issues at hand. Paul scrounged a Heineken from the crisper and jogged back to his office.

The stolen mail made a mild drift on the desktop. He snatched up the next piece—a lavender envelope smelling of lilacs—and tore into it. Flowery stationery greeted him: an actual honest-to-God handwritten letter. Did people still do that? It seemed archaic, from another age entirely, but stirred a feeling of deep nostalgia within him. Paul read it, lips moving:

> *My Dearest Lucy,*
>
> *It seems an eternity since Paris. I stayed at the Mandarin in the Royale Suite, but it simply wasn't the same without your elegant presence beside me. To think I had to seduce a bellhop just to get what I needed! I think I ruined the poor garçon. Not that he minded. Ha! Ha!*
>
> *In all seriousness, my love, I should have wished it had been you instead—males are so fragile in both mind and body and to think you could have given me what I needed (and vice versa, of course!) made me set this pen to paper. I wish to see you again as soon as possible. Say it may be so or say naught to me again.*
>
> *Forever and ever in my thoughts,*
> *E.J.G.*

"She's a lesbian," Paul said, feeling punched. Whoever this E.J.G. person turned out to be, she was obviously Lucine's lover. But it also said something about seducing the bellhop, so maybe Lucine swung both ways. That could be interesting down the road. He still couldn't get around to thinking of her by the diminutive "Lucy"—it somehow sounded older and frailer to him than her given name had initially, like a 50s sitcom housewife.

The next envelope carried another handwritten note, though not nearly as detailed as the original. A simple rectangle of white cardstock bearing a brutish masculine script said:

> *L—Meet me in Rio. You know time and place.*
> *Don't make me beg, because I will. Please?*
> *-D*

Could that be where she was now? In Rio, with this "D" guy? A lake of fire opened in Paul's belly, a jealousy so incendiary it shook him. He didn't know exactly when he'd begun to think of Lucine Korth as *his*, but he had.

Six or seven similar envelopes had been addressed to the resident of 200 Pace Lane, but Paul couldn't bring himself to read them. He grabbed the small package, ripped it open, and upended it.

A pink vibrator, not much larger than a lipstick tube, rolled across his desktop. A leaf of onionskin paper fluttered after it. Paul pinched it up and read a single sentence: *You left this in Miami, love.* No signature and no telling whether a man or woman had written it.

"She's a hooker," Paul said. That had to be it. A high-end call girl who traveled the world to meet clients. The idea made him sick with some blend of emotion he couldn't identify or make sense of. Jealousy, certainly. Possessiveness. Greed. Lust. He wanted Lucine Korth all for himself.

That's fucking ridiculous, champ, his mind whispered. *You're a happily married man.*

But was he, though? If someone had asked him a week ago, Paul would have shouted it from the rooftops. Michelle was his one and only, his true love, his soulmate. Except one week is plenty of time to change. Circumstances shifted every day. People fell out of love.

"I haven't fallen out of love with my wife," he said aloud.

And then, as if conjured, the front door opened and Michelle called, "Paulie? You home? I brought lunch."

The front door stood twenty paces from his office, and he had as many seconds to straighten things up.

Paul swept the stolen mail into the space between his desk and the wall. The beer bottle went on the floor in the kneehole beside the network router. He jumped to his feet and met his wife at the office door.

"Hey, babe. What a nice surprise. What'd you get?"

"Is everything okay, Paul? You're flushed."

"Fine. Just finished up a little exercise."

"When did you start exercising?"

"Oh, it's a little pre-New Year's resolution. You can never start too soon." He fired off a few half-hearted jumping jacks to illustrate.

"Well, come on in the kitchen, Schwarzenegger. I brought you a burger."

Paul laughed, hoping it sounded natural. "A burger sounds great."

"Sure it won't ruin your physique?"

"Ha fucking ha."

She set his sandwich on a plate, garnished it with a heap of fries, and asked, "How's work? Staying busy?"

"For sure," he said, easily enough. "More clients than I know what to do with."

"That's good news," she said. "I'll need you to deposit two hundred into checking from your escrow."

Paul paused mid-bite. "How come?"

"Looks like we're going to be a little short this month. License plate sticker renewal on the Corolla and Jeannie's preschool tuition are both due the same day."

He chewed without tasting. He had more than $200 in his freelance escrow account, but not much. Transferring it to their joint checking account would practically wipe it out and he liked to keep a cushion, just in case. Failing to accrue new assignments would stretch them thinner than he felt comfortable with. Checking proposals today would be top priority.

"So will you do it?" Michelle asked.

"Not a problem. After lunch."

She smiled. "Thanks, love. Now tell me all about this new workout regimen."

After his wife returned to work, Paul deposited the requested sum. His escrow balance now stood at $89.23 and likely wouldn't rise anytime soon. He confirmed this by checking his proposals and finding no new bid acceptances, not even for Linda Lopez.

He retrieved the dumped mail from beside the desk and stuffed it into a plastic bag, minus the envelopes he'd slit open. Those were placed in a separate bag, tied off, and dropped in a gas station dumpster he passed on the way to get Jeannie.

His daughter took a peaceful, dreamless two-hour nap, which Paul spent bidding on jobs until all his credits had dried up. To bid further, he'd need to upgrade to a Premium account—ten bucks a month he had debated paying many times but now could no longer afford.

With no work, though, he could play. Retrieving the lukewarm beer from beneath the desk, Paul logged into Linda Lopez's Facebook account and checked for messages from Viola. Nothing. No problem. He'd be seeing her soon enough. At least she hadn't deleted Linda Lopez from her friends list.

He accepted the two dozen friend requests (all from men) and liked all the greetings on her timeline, even commenting on a few of the less lecherous ones to add credibility to the profile's authenticity.

When he could stand it no longer, Paul locked the door, pulled up the color pic of Lucine, dropped his pants, and relieved himself into the trashcan.

Chapter Fourteen

No way would the squash-nosed man get away after soccer practice this time. Paul blew two amber lights and squeaked through a red to keep pace.

"Are we in a race, Daddy?" Jeannie asked, breathless.

"Nope. Just taking a little drive."

"It feels like we're chasing someone again," Perry said.

"We're not chasing anyone, Pear."

"What about the man from practice?"

Paul glanced at his son through the mirror. "What man?"

"He's Benny's dad. The one who's getting a divorce."

"What about him?"

"I saw you talking to him the other day. Is he the one we're chasing?"

"We're not chasing anyone."

"Home is the other way."

Paul gritted his teeth; Perry was getting too smart for his own good. "I know, son. I just want to check something."

Mercifully, the kids fell silent.

Benny Gehant's father pulled into the driveway of a two-story house on Hyacinth Lane, a cul-de-sac in an almost affluent neighborhood. Paul noted the address, turned around, and drove to Jeannie's hair appointment.

"She looks absolutely gorgeous," Michelle gushed when she saw her daughter's new 'do. "Look, we can brush it this way or that way. Put a little curl in it. Tuh! It would look great with pink ribbons, don't you think, Paul?"

"Absolutely," he remarked from the sofa without looking. He had other things on his mind.

Michelle came over and put a hand on his. "What's wrong, love? Is it the haircut? Because you did a fabulous job describing what we wanted to the stylist."

"Hm? No, it's not the haircut. Jeannie looks like an angel."

"What is it then?"

"Nothing." He looked up at her. "It's nothing, really. I think I'll try to get a little work in this evening."

"Good idea," his wife said. "I'll start supper."

How long would Mr. Gehant live on Hyacinth Lane? Perry said he was divorcing his wife and would be moving out. How long did Paul have to finish things with the man? He'd have to expedite matters. That is, if he planned to go through with them. The alternative would be to let it go, but he couldn't let go the idea of Gehant scaring his daughter like that.

You know it wasn't Gehant, his mind whispered. Jeannie had said as much, but what did kids know? And anyway, the bastard had threatened physical harm to Paul. That wasn't something he could abide, whether the man had been in the right or not.

"I'm gonna get you, Mr. Gehant," Paul whispered in the silence of his office. "No one scares my daughter and gets off free."

He pulled up a browser and got to work.

Christmas came and went. Santa visited and the kids went nuts. It took all day for them to come down from the holiday high, but when they did they crashed hard. Jeannie hadn't had a night terror in a week and Michelle hoped they'd seen the last of them. So did Paul, but that didn't mean he let Gehant off the hook.

The squash-nosed man had moved out of the Hyacinth house to an apartment downtown above a Mexican restaurant. Perry had been right about them getting a divorce, or at least separating. One step at a time. By then, Paul had an accurate read on Mr. Gehant's movements. The man ran a tight ship. He worked as an insurance broker Monday through Friday, 8:30 to 5:00, taking lunch at quarter past twelve on the button. Every other weekend he saw his son on a supervised visit. It seemed he'd had a little Family Services investigation of his own. Investigation for what, Paul hadn't yet determined. He would in time.

But Mr. Benjamin Gehant Sr. was Paul's secondary project. His primary project took pole position.

He still had not requested Lucine's friendship on Facebook, but he had gotten himself in place to do so and would make the move soon. Viola Datsun had resumed their conversation after gentle prompting on Linda Lopez's part and Paul had gotten her to fully believe they'd taken anthropology courses together. He'd researched all the professors who'd taught in that department during the time Viola would have spent at the university and naming them had boosted her confidence in the veracity of Linda as an old classmate. Viola had personally invited Linda to an exclusive VIP event at Cabana Girls, which Linda had politely declined since Paul couldn't well very show up in her stead.

But he had made plans to visit the nightclub on his own. Michelle had decided to take the kids to her parents' house downstate for New Year's Eve. They missed Grammy and Pop-Pop and Michelle missed the extravaganza her affluent parents threw at the close of each year. Paul had valiantly offered to stay behind to guard the homestead.

"But Mommy will miss Daddy," Michelle had pouted, running a finger from his chest to his crotch on Christmas night after the kids had passed out in their post-present euphoria.

"Daddy will still be here when Mommy comes home."

"Well at least give Mommy something to remember Daddy by," she said, yanking his sweatpants to his ankles. He granted her request.

Finally, fucking *finally*, they left on morning of the 27th with plans to return on the third day of the New Year. An entire week to himself. He loved his family, but he needed the time off. And Michelle and the kids could stand some time away from him as well. Paul knew he hadn't been the best husband and father in the weeks since finding Lucine Korth's letter mixed in with his mail. Maybe this week would give him time to get it out of his system. Same story with Mr. Benjamin Gehant.

He kissed his family goodbye and waved them out of the driveway, watching as they puttered up the street and out of sight. The sun shone bright but cold. The wind scattered snow along the walk like spilled hourglass sand. A cardinal landed on the neighbor's birdbath and watched him with black pill eyes. Otherwise, the world held still. Paul turned to go back inside when something banged like a shotgun.

The shutter. He still hadn't gotten around to fixing it. Well, it could fucking wait. He had business to attend to.

He cracked a beer first. 7:30 in the morning seemed the perfect time of his vacation to start drinking. He hadn't had a drink this early since his senior year at NCU, though getting drunk was not his directive. Not now, anyway. Paul needed something to take the edge off. To prepare himself for what he meant to do. He drank tipped back in his office chair with his feet up on the desk.

He opened a second bottle, slugged it, then unlocked the bottom drawer of his filing cabinet and dug the bag of Walmart impulse items from behind the hanging folders. It rested atop Lucine's stolen mail. No need to lock up again for now; he had a whole week to leave it wide open.

Upstairs, he laid out one of his two suits. The black one with pinstripes. Red tie. Yes, it would better fit today's agenda. He stripped and stepped into the shower. After toweling off, he shaved, dressed, clipped his cuffs with silver links, knotted his tie, and stepped into black wingtips. He combed his hair, gelled it, and dabbed cologne on his throat.

In the bag of impulse buys, he found the reading glasses and tried them on. They changed his face completely. Along with the suit, Paul no longer appeared as the grizzled freelancer, but a Wall Street investment banker.

"Showtime," he told his reflection before stepping downstairs to the Corolla, backing out, and driving to church.

♀

Paul Jeske had been raised Lutheran and Michelle Methodist, but neither practiced any longer. They had decided to allow the kids to determine their own beliefs as they grew older—both felt early indoctrination to organized religion synonymous with brainwashing.

The church Viola listed on her profile was called Haven Revival Chapel on the southern edge of town. The opposite side of Viola's risqué workplace, as though she'd prioritized keeping them apart. The church seemed to cater to an offbeat sect who worshipped through music and full-immersion baptism. All were welcome to "join in an energetic service with a practical message to help the attendee know and grow closer to God," per their website. The Lake Winona chapter had opened only last year, but already had attracted quite a following. Like, perhaps, a pitcher plant attracted flies.

Paul guessed he'd grab a pew near the exit in case he wished to make a hasty getaway. Truthfully, he only wanted to glimpse Viola with his own eyes, make sure she was real. And if it turned out Lucine attended the same church, well hell, all the better. He wouldn't hold his breath on that count, though; Lucine Korth seemed like the last person on earth one would spy taking the Holy Spirit to her impressive bosom.

On the drive, he detoured down Pace Lane. Her house still looked empty and unlived-in. Two packages rested on the porch and envelopes propped the mailbox lid open. He made a mental note to make another withdrawal this week before she got home. *If* she got home. What if she'd moved in with one of her copious lovers? What if crummy old Pace Lane in boring Lake Winona, Illinois had simply gotten too much for her and she'd pulled up stakes to go live in the South of France with one of her wealthy johns or janes? Unthinkable. Unconscionable.

He found Haven Revival and parked near the lot's exit. There weren't many other spaces anyway; all but a few had been claimed as worshippers moved toward the entrance. Paul felt self-conscious as he joined the throng, slipping into the last pew as planned. No one seemed bothered by his presence or even to notice him at all.

Above the stage—for a stage is precisely what dominated the head of the nave instead of a chancel—hung an enormous crucifix suspended by translucent cables. A giant halo of gold neon encircled the Christ's head. The stage itself lay littered with musical instruments of all variety: guitars, banjos, bongos, something resembling a lute, a ten-piece drum set and an honest-to-God full-size harp. Paul had never seen one in real life.

The congregation buzzed with pre-sermon restlessness. All told, he guessed greater than three hundred souls had gathered in this place of worship. No clergy or deacon appeared in evidence. Paul scanned for any sign of Viola but without a higher vantage there simply could be no sure way to spot her. He'd have to see about catching her another time.

Paul stood and excused himself through the tail of the crowd, heading for the door. Then he stopped. A curtained archway stood to the left. A plaque beside it read Staff Only Please. He loitered, gazing at bulletin board notices reporting chili suppers and coat drives, until he had the lobby to himself, then ducked behind the curtain. What would be the worst that could happen if someone caught him? Splash him with holy water?

A carpeted staircase led upward, and he took the risers slowly. It opened on a media booth with a soundboard to equalize the stage instruments, currently unoccupied. From this perspective, the whole chapel sprawled beneath him, and he spotted Viola Datsun at once, near the back. It could be no one else. She sat a little apart from those around her, attending today in solitude.

Paul studied her for the duration of the sermon, from which he took away only that God lived in each and every member of the congregation and that He alone could save them from the Lake of Fire. At odd intervals, someone would flop into the aisle and blabber nonsensically for several embarrassing moments while random shouts of "Amen!" punctuated the scene. Though he'd never witnessed it personally, Paul realized these displays were devotees speaking in tongues. It looked utterly maniacal. He watched to see if Viola would partake in this strange ceremony.

But she didn't. In fact, she barely moved during the entire sermon as if she'd been coerced to sit through it. When the pastor dismissed his flock, she was first to flee. Paul followed her to the lot with the idea of tailing her home but lost her in traffic. No matter. He'd find her again soon enough.

Chapter Fifteen

Michelle accepted the glass of wine her mother handed over and sipped greedily. Her father had the kids entertained in the front room with one of his infamous clown routines; their giggles permeated the kitchen despite the heavy door dividing the rooms. She was just happy to have them away from their house, in a healthy environment, and once her mother had gotten through lamenting Michelle's brother Chad being unable to attend the New Year's party due to work, she was more than happy to listen to her daughter's woes.

"Gracious, child, take a breath," Darlene said. "Is it really so bad?"

"I think he's seeing another woman," Michelle forced herself to say. She'd refused to speak it aloud before now for fear it would bring her deepest dread to light. If she didn't say it, maybe it wouldn't be true. Faulty logic, she knew, but it comforted her. But now she'd said it to the one person in the world she knew she could trust, and it sounded realer than ever.

Darlene Craycraft clucked her tongue. Before she got married, Michelle couldn't wait to move on from her maiden name, but now it didn't seem so bad. "You don't really think so, do you?"

"I don't know, Mom. He's just been acting so *strange*. We had a great time on our anniversary, then boom—he's on this weird man kick."

"What's he doing? Talk me through it." Darlene ticked a patient, polished nail on the stem of her glass, ready for girl talk. Ready to *mother*.

Michelle polished off her wine and poured more. "He almost forgot to pick Jeannie up from school. He got her hair stuck in her zipper and then instead of working it out, he cut it off. He—"

"I happen to find Jeannie's new cut adorable."

"That's not the point, Mother. Follow along."

"I'm listening," Darlene said, refilling her own glass. "So far it sounds like he's simply being a man."

"He left Jeannie in the car once. Alone."

"Goodness, for how long?"

"Only a few minutes, but—"

"Oh, sweetheart, we used to do that with you and your brother all the time."

"Yeah, back when the world was safe."

"The world was *hardly* safe then."

"Then some creeper peeked in at her and scared her to death. She had nightmares for weeks."

"But she's better now?"

"Well, yeah." Michelle ticked a fingernail against the lip of her glass, unconsciously mimicking her mother, and trying to conjure another of Paul's recent lapses. She found it and snapped her fingers. "He said he'd fix a broken shutter on the house. It's been almost a month and that goddamn thing is still banging away. Probably like he's doing right now in some slut's bungalow—"

"Michelle Elizabeth!"

"Pardon my French, Mom, but really. He's a completely different person. I can't figure out what's going on."

"Have you tried talking to him?"

"Of course."

"And?"

"He seems fine. A little distracted, maybe, but fine. But I'm not worried about what he says. It's what he does that's got me simmering."

"You did the right thing in coming here. Perhaps he simply needs a little breathing room. He's got the kids all the time, taking them to school and soccer practice on top of all the work you say is rolling in. This break will be good for everyone."

"Maybe you're right," Michelle said and gusted air between her lips.

"Mark my words. Everything will be set right when you get home."

"How did you get so smart?"

"Mothers know everything, dear. Haven't you learned that yet?"

"I guess not."

"Well, you're young yet. You'll get there. More wine?"

Darlene's reassurance settled her, at least long enough to enjoy the rest of the evening with her family. Her mother was right—Michelle needed a break from Paul. So did the kids. It was healthy, she told herself. And she had New Year's Eve to look forward to. Some of her friends she'd not seen in years were coming to celebrate and bringing their kids so Perry and Jean would have playmates. Yes, all would work out fine.

After getting them tucked into the twin bed in her old room and wishing her parents goodnight (they turned in at 8:30 sharp as they had since her girlhood), she stepped into the kitchen for another nip of vino. She found her phone, tapped it against her thigh for a moment, then dialed her husband.

It rang eight times before voicemail picked up.

Michelle slept in the guest room adjacent to her old bedroom, though to say she slept would be misrepresentative of the word. She dozed. She tossed. She kicked at the daisy-patterned comforter. Around midnight, a brief but potent nightmare unfolded behind her eyes.

In it, Michelle was hiding in the closet of the master bedroom of their house in Lake Winona. Someone had broken in and lurked around the main floor. Paul was nowhere to be found. She knew the kids were safe because she'd left them at her parents' house. Slowly, someone climbed the stairs to the second story. Michelle could hear each deliberate step as it came and then nothing for a long time. Then the creak of their bed as someone lay upon it. *Paul, thank God,* she thought in her dream. Except the creaking increased in frequency until the headboard banged the wall. When she found it in her to peek, she discovered Paul rutting against a gorgeous woman on their bed. Both her husband and his mistress stared straight at the place where Michelle crouched hidden as if they could see through the doors and straight into her soul. Both wore maniacal leers. And when they climaxed simultaneously, they began to laugh.

Paul seemed to shrink as his orgasm escalated, and she realized his muscles were wasting away, like footage of a corpse in time-lapse photography. When it was over, Paul had become nothing but a blackened skeleton which the woman shucked aside before standing to face the closet and for the first time Michelle realized the interloper's beauty: full of breast and hip with wrists and ankles delicate as necklace links. The triumph she wore nakedly made her features gorgeous while Paul's pearly seed dripped down her thighs.

Somehow worst of all, though, were the woman's eyes. As she watched, they filled with darkness like the shadow of smoke.

In the morning, Michelle considered telling her mother about the dream but refrained. She knew what Darlene would say—the dream had been a subconscious manifestation of her daughter's fear of infidelity. And Darlene would be right.

Only it hadn't felt like a dream.

"A lot of dreams are like that," she whispered to her reflection in the bathroom mirror and almost believed it.

The kids had already stormed the breakfast table and were face-deep in a stack of "flopcakes"—her father's term, and one she'd always found somehow a touch repulsive—by the time she got there. Michelle took a seat beside Jeannie and let her mother serve her. She knew Darlene missed mothering.

"The kiddos tell me they slept like the dead last night," Darlene said with a splinter of disapproval. "Their words."

"Paul's been letting them watch too much TV."

"And how did *you* sleep, my dear?" Darlene asked, placing a plate of eggs and flopcakes before her daughter.

"Not like the dead, that's for sure."

"Well, it can be difficult readjusting to old environs," her father put in, pinching her cheek with weathered fingers.

"Stop, Dad," Michelle said, swatting at his hand.

"Ah, you love it. You can't fool this old goat."

They ate, making small talk, discussing the kids' schools. Michelle made no mention of her dream. Nothing good could come of it. Best to let it go.

But she couldn't. Not after she'd seen the woman's eyes and the way Paul had seemed to diminish as he spent himself inside her. She needed to call him. Not after lunch. Not this evening. Now.

She excused herself from the table and stepped into the guest room to dial.

He answered immediately. "Hi, babe. How's it going?"

Michelle had half-convinced herself he wouldn't answer—surely he would still be in bed with his mistress.

"Hi," she said, a little breathlessly. Her dream recurred, full force. "Things are great."

"Glad to hear it. Kids behaving?"

"As well as can be expected." She laughed, feeling foolish for worrying. Everything was fine; she'd be able to hear betrayal in his voice, she felt certain. "What's new?"

"Work, work, work."

"Well, make sure you take some time to play this week. Did you make New Year's Eve plans?"

"I think Jerome, Sean, and I might grab a few drinks. Some of the nightclubs are having all-you-can-eat buffets."

"That sounds nice," Michelle said and meant it. She looked forward to seeing her childhood friends at the party but throwing back a few cold ones with a buddy at one of Lake Winona's watering holes sounded like more fun at the moment. She changed gears casually, no longer worried but curious, nonetheless. "So what did you do last night? I tried calling but got your voicemail."

"You did? Huh. No calls registered in my history."

"Ugh. We *so* need new phones."

"Tell me about it. I wonder how many client calls I've missed."

They chatted a few minutes longer. Michelle asked if he wanted to talk to the kids, but he said he'd catch them before bedtime as he had an important job which had just cropped up and required his immediate attention. He hung up without saying *I love you* or even a tepid *Good-bye*.

Chapter Sixteen

After losing Viola, Paul had driven home more determined than ever. No more fucking around: It was Go Time. He'd added enough friends and made enough interactions that it was time to shoot for the main prize (at least virtually).

He clicked on Lucine Korth's Facebook profile and hit Add Friend. Then he waited. He chewed through a ham sandwich methodically without tasting, watching for his notification icon to trigger. When it didn't, he puttered around, thinking he could fix the shutter—it would take all of two minutes—but simply couldn't find the motivation. He drank a few beers. He opened a few more pieces of Lucine's mail but found nothing of interest. He jerked off to her picture, imagining the way her nipples would feel against his chest. By dinnertime, when he still had received no confirmation, Paul decided to take a drive.

The house on Pace Lane remained desolate, the chimney a dead stone throat. The mail had not been touched. No footprints leading up the walk in the fresh snow which had fallen overnight. He turned around and parked half a block up so he could study her house discreetly. The entire street seemed asleep. No stray pet prowled the sidewalk. Nothing moved except the bare elm branches shadowboxing with the wind. No light aglow in a window. As darkness overtook Pace Lane, an unsettling feeling struck Paul. He imagined quite clearly a neighborhood of corpses, as if this part of town had suddenly been stricken dead by some unnamable force.

Paul fingered the keys dangling from the ignition with the clear intent of driving straight home—the only cure for the heebie-jeebies which had jangled his nerves—but then let his hand fall away.

"It's the perfect time," he said aloud to his reflection. "If there's some kind of blackout going on, now's the perfect fucking time."

He took another glance around, noticed no one, and got out of the car, snatching up the canvas bag he'd brought along. Then he pulled the ski mask down over his face.

The mail lay thicker on the porch than was discernible from the street. If she'd gone away for an extended time, why hadn't she postponed service? Something occurred to him. What if she hadn't gone on an extended vacation? What if Lucine Korth lay dead inside her meager abode, like everyone else on the block seemed to be? The idea disturbed him, and he did what he'd come to do now out of a sense of duty. Or so he told himself.

No key lay hidden beneath the mat, nor behind the porch light fixture. There wasn't one taped beneath the mailbox, but it turned out finding a spare didn't matter because the door was unlocked.

Almost as if our Ms. Lucine was expecting company, he thought and shuddered. Behind him, the street remained dark, and Paul resolved blame must certainly lie with a power outage.

"Hello?" he called into the shadowed foyer. "Anyone home?"

Silence, the same he'd receive as if he'd called a hail into a tomb. He stuck his head over the threshold feeling somehow like a convict settling in beneath the guillotine. He detected no odor of decomposition which would be evident in the shut-up house.

"Don't mean to intrude, but I happened by and saw mail. Wondered if you might want some help bringing it in."

Nothing.

Paul stepped in and eased the door closed behind him. The darkness seemed oppressive now that it had been disconnected from the brisk outdoor air. He tried the switch and nothing happened. A-plus on the outage theory. Paul dug in the bag until he found one of the impulse-buy flashlights and clicked it on, dragging the beam along the walls. A painful hard-on pulsed in his pants like a forbidden curse.

The foyer led straight ahead to a kitchen with a living room opening to the left and an ascending staircase to the right. The place was furnished in fashions more common two decades previous but nothing overtly offensive. A Felix the Cat clock ticked above the refrigerator. Paul inhaled, trying to detect discernible feminine scents: perfume, body lotion, Vidal Sassoon shampoo. Nothing. Only stale air cut with dust.

In fact, nothing on the ground level categorically defined the house's occupant as female. The fridge held nothing but steak sauce and a jar of pale pickles, the freezer only two pounds of unidentifiable ground meat mummified in cellophane. The cabinets were bare save for a can of Carnation condensed milk and a few unlabeled jars of spices he couldn't readily identify. A cordless telephone of the sort he'd not spied since adolescence hung on the wall.

The living room contained a threadbare sofa, mismatched loveseat, and an actual console television set similar to the one his grandmother had owned. A fireplace full of cold ashes took up most of the east wall. Above it hung a picture depicting Christ bleeding at wrist and ankle.

"She's a fucking Jesus freak, too," Paul said. But one hell of a photogenic Jesus freak.

A battered coffee table held only a month-old copy of the Lake Winona *Sun* and a layer of dust. No main floor bathroom. A locked door stood between kitchen and living room, probably to the cellar where a battered washer and dryer set would rest, perhaps as mismatched as her furniture. Maybe he'd have better luck upstairs.

The steps had been carpeted in a thick gray shag, adhering to the house's passé flavorings. Three doors stood at the top: one left, one right, one dead center. All closed. Paul approached the middle and stood listening. Nothing. He turned the knob and the door opened onto a small bathroom. The medicine cabinet over the sink was empty except for a travel-size fold-up toothbrush standing in a glass. No toothpaste, makeup, or medicine bottles. The shower floor bore rust stains but was otherwise clean and dry. No shampoos, conditioners, or soaps. No traces of hair in the drain. The single towel he found balled up in the corner turned out to be coal black—nothing floral or frilly.

The bedroom to the left had been converted to a storage area. It contained a bed, but it was covered in cardboard boxes, all sealed with packing tape. The bed itself had no sheets or quilt—only a stained bare mattress. More unopened boxes had been stacked in the closet.

Behind the final door he finally hit pay dirt. Lucine Korth's bedroom could not have been more different from the rest of the habitat. Easily the largest room in the house, it contained a four-poster bed with a canopy and curtains like something out of a Charles Dickens novel. The curtains hung closed, their braided cords dangling.

Anyone could be in there, Paul thought and the more he considered it, the more he became certain. Lucine Korth or perhaps a lover had been deeply asleep when he came in and had only awakened when he'd entered the room. Now the person—or people—had roused and hunched poised, ready to strike down the intruder. Maybe they would shoot him right through the curtain, targeting the flare of his flashlight.

He listened, but the only sound came from the wind slipstreaming beneath the eaves outside the high window. Paul held his breath and took the distance between doorway and bedframe with slow, measured steps, his face hot and damp beneath the mask. Batman no longer, merely a common criminal. He reached toward the curtain with one gloved hand, becoming ever-more certain someone else occupied the room. A type of contained energy sparked in here, a low-wattage life force dissimilar from the spare indifference of the rest of the house.

His fingers brushed the hanging velvet, closed around it, and yanked it aside to reveal an empty bed. At the same moment his cell phone rang, and he screamed.

Dropping his gloves, he fumbled his phone out. Michelle.

Perfect fucking timing, babe.

She'd have to wait. He let it go to voicemail, deciding he'd call back as soon as he'd made it back to the car. His job here was almost done anyway, at least for tonight. Two things remained to check: the closet and the towering chest of drawers opposite the bed.

The closet held only empty wire hangers dangling from a crossbar. The flashlight beam picked out a small trapdoor in the ceiling with a pull cord. The last thing Paul wanted to do tonight was shuffle along a dusty rafter crawlspace, so he changed direction to the bureau.

The varnished mahogany oblong stood nearly as tall as he, like a monolith, with eight tiers of drawers. The hardware looked to be made of gold encrusted with tiny gemstones. It appeared positively ancient and while he was certainly no antiquarian, Paul estimated it to have been hand-crafted nearly three hundred years ago. It must be worth a fortune. Who would possibly use such a piece to house their unmentionables?

Lucine Korth, that's who, he thought, dragging out the top drawer. Bras and panties littered it, hundreds of each, and Paul's already-throbbing erection seemed to burn hotter against his belly. He moved to the next drawer. Shirts. Below that, casual pants. Next, dress slacks. The remainder of the drawers were empty. Not a pair of socks or shoes in the place. What kind of woman didn't keep a battery of shoes in her house?

Only what if this wasn't her permanent residence? What if it merely acted as a Midwest stopover for all the other destinations to which she traveled? Based on the evidence, such must be the case. Someone who possessed Lucine's aspects would never have to pay for a thing in her life; people—men *and* women—would throw money at her anywhere she went just for the chance to be near her.

The cordless telephone in the kitchen shrilled. Paul jumped and took the interruption as his cue to exit. Before he did, he grabbed an empty box from her bedroom floor. On the porch, he piled the packages and mail inside while the phone rang on and on behind him. He packed the car with the stolen goods and drove away. Not home, though. Not yet.

Chapter Seventeen

Cabana Girls did a pretty good business on Sunday nights if the number of cars in the lot proved anything. Paul found it harder to find parking here than at church this morning and wound up having to use the overflow lot across the street. He couldn't imagine what a Friday night here must be like.

He wore the same suit from his foray at Haven Revival but ditched the glasses in the glove compartment; the slight magnification gave him a headache if he wore them too long.

A bouncer greeted him at the door—thankfully not the same man who'd questioned him before, though this guy seemed no friendlier.

"ID," he said.

Paul handed over his driver's license. The bouncer scrutinized it so long Paul finally asked, "Is there a problem?"

The bouncer stared at him with deep-set piggish eyes. "Not unless you make one."

"Great. So are we done here?"

"We're full up."

"You're full up," Paul repeated, as if to a slow child.

"Yeah. Capacity's five hundred. I let you in, you make five-oh-one. Against the law."

"There were still plenty of spaces in overflow," Paul said, thumbing the air over his shoulder.

"I guess folks carpooled."

Paul regarded the man, fury igniting his brain. "Listen, man. I came here to spend money and stare at pretty ladies. Either you let me in, or you can explain it to your boss."

The giant crawled off his stool and popped his knuckles. "I guess we gonna have a problem," he said.

Paul held his ground, opening his mouth to offer a retort that likely would have been slammed back down his throat, when the door opened and Viola Datsun herself stepped out. Paul froze like a kid caught shoplifting. He could smell her perfume from where he stood.

"What's going on, Ty?" she asked the bouncer, her voice low but commanding and dragging with it an accent she was carefully trying to mask. Something foreign, maybe east African. She eyed Paul up and down.

"Jokerman here giving me lip."

"Well, let him by and he won't."

The guy swung his head from her to me. "I don't like the look of him."

Incredibly, Viola said, "Well, I do. Let him by. He's with me."

"You're lucky my friend Vi likes you," he grunted as Viola took Paul's hand and led him around the guy's girth.

The place boomed. Music shuddered through hidden speakers. A DJ spun on a stage roughly the same size as the one at the church. The bouncer had been right about one thing — the place looked full beyond the municipal fire code capacity. Many of the servers wore half-shirts and skirts barely covering their thighs. Viola was no different and when she pressed him into a quieter corner, he got a full look at her.

"Are you following me?" she demanded. "Because if you're a creeper, I'll take you right back outside and let Tyrone have his way with you."

"Excuse me?" Paul asked, both mystified and terrified.

"I saw you at church this morning."

He recovered quickly. "Oh. I'm new in town and I'm trying to get a lay of the land. You attend Haven Revival?"

"Wouldn't think it to see me now, would you?"

"How a person makes her living makes no difference to me. Besides, as you pointed out, I was in church this morning, too, and now here I am."

"Yes. Here you are. What's your name, creeper?"

"I'm not a creeper," he said, and it almost sounded convincing in his ears. He considered giving an alias, but if she demanded to see his ID the game would be over. All his plans and plots down the drain. He stuck out a hand. "My name's Paul."

"Hi, Paul. Viola Fredrick." As she took his hand, her grin became more genuine despite lying about her surname. Paul wondered what would happen if he asked to see *her* ID.

"Pleased to finally meet a friendly local."

"Make yourself comfortable. I'm waiting section six, toward the back. What can I bring you?"

"Oh. I guess I'll take a club soda."

She laughed. "We don't serve that here unless it's watering down vodka."

"One of those then. Whatever is best in house."

"Coming up," she said and vanished in a swirl of her skirt.

He found a table and waited. Everything seemed to be happening too quickly. He didn't much care for the fact she recognized him from Haven Revival—he hadn't even seen her glance his way and he'd been watching her like a wolf watches a wounded rabbit. The bouncer who'd questioned him the other day sauntered by, still wearing his cable-knit cap, but didn't notice Paul. Good. He didn't want any more questions.

Viola appeared with a tray and a wink. She placed his drink on a paper napkin and said, "I'm off in a few. Want to buy me a drink?"

"Sure," he heard himself say.

"Good deal," she said, highlighted curls bouncing on her shoulders like springs. "Don't creep away now, creeper."

He didn't creep anywhere.

By the time Viola's shift ended, Paul was drunk. He hadn't meant to be—had, in fact, purposely paced himself to avoid it. Nonetheless, here he was, watching the world slew sideways. Two club kids got into a fistfight nearby and someone threw a bottle, which smashed on his table, splattering him with warm Budweiser.

He bellowed and clambered to his feet, meaning to find whoever had done it and lay him flat. But then Viola appeared and touched his wrist.

"Don't worry about them," she said, her breath a warm curl in his ear.

"You know how much it's gonna cost to dry clean this suit?"

"Honey, hush," she said, pressing a finger to his lips. Viola was no Lucine, but still she was gorgeous. And in possession of a tender touch. He calmed instantly. "Let's go someplace quieter."

Paul let her lead him through a door marked PRIVATE, past a warren of dressing rooms, through an enormous backroom overhung with red velvet drapes that could have housed another 500 patrons, and out back. The late-December air nipped at his eyes but seemed to clear his head. A little.

"Where are we going?" he asked.

"To my place," she said, searching his eyes. "If that's okay with you."

Paul considered a moment through his shimmery brain and determined it was.

Paul caught sight of himself in the bathroom mirror when he went to pee. His hair stood in angry, oily corkscrews. Bags hung beneath his eyes where before there weren't any and crows' feet etched the edges. His lips appeared peeled and chapped. He looked like he'd aged five years overnight. Was that the price of adultery?

He'd never cheated on anyone before, least of all his wife. Not even when they were courting during their North Central University days when he'd had ample opportunity. Not even after the Tom Rood affair, which had given him clear authorization (at least in his mind) to do it. So why had he slept with Viola Datsun? Why had he spent the night and now hoped to sneak out before sunrise? Why had he not once thought of Michelle during the entire course of his betrayal?

"I'm a horrible fucking person," he told his reflection. His reflection made no attempt at rebuttal.

He crept back to Viola's bedroom, where she slept with her back to the door. The dimples above her rump resembled smiling eyes as he gathered his clothes. One of his socks had gone missing in action, but he didn't want to hang around looking for it. It would be better to escape unimpeded while the chance remained.

Paul rushed up the street at a fast walk and ordered an Uber along the way. It picked him up at the corner of Seventh and Bell Village Road. His car waited in Cabana Girls' overflow lot—it hadn't been towed, thankfully. Paul paid, then hurried to his car, peeling out of the lot. He never wanted to see Cabana Girls or Viola Datsun again, as if denying their existences would absolve him of matrimonial treason. But it couldn't. Nothing could.

"Why'd you do it, you sleazy bastard?" he asked the rearview. "Because you were drunk? Because Viola is hot piece of ass who cleans up nicely on the Sabbath?"

No, a voice deep in his gray tissue murmured. *You did it to get closer to Lucine.*

It was true, he knew. But how exactly had he gotten closer to her? He'd laid her friend. He'd slept in an apartment Lucine had undoubtedly visited. But how did those things get him nearer his ultimate goal? They hadn't. He'd accomplished nothing but betraying his wife, his kids, and himself. His ego may have received a welcomed boost, but egos are for losers who care only for themselves. Is that what he'd become? An egomaniacal loser?

No. He still loved his family more than he loved himself. Of that he was certain. It would be best to chalk last night up as a mistake and move on. Forget it ever happened. Steer clear of Haven Revival on the south end of town and Cabana Girls on the north. Stick to the middle, where he belonged. And if he ever bumped into Viola while out running errands, he'd simply duck her. She knew his face, sure, but she'd seen him only in a Sunday suit (and his birthday suit, of course, don't forget that). If he dressed like he normally did, casually, maybe don dark glasses and a baseball cap like a celebrity avoiding the paparazzi, he might be all right.

Paul wheeled into the driveway, happy and relieved to be home. He brake-checked, though, when he got a look at the place. The front door stood ajar.

Chapter Eighteen

N othing appeared to be missing. Paul walked the place, room by room, but noted nothing out of place. The only oddity, aside from the door standing open, was the illumination of his desk lamp as if someone had been hard at work all night and had only now decided to take a break. Had he left it on? He couldn't recall. Guilty thoughts of infidelity departed. Paul came back to the living room and turned a slow circle, surveying the violated vicinity again. He inhaled deeply, trying to pull some olfactory evidence into existence.

Nothing.

He checked the street before hurrying the stolen mail from the car to his office. He dropped into his chair with the intention of getting to work on the first package when his phone rang.

Michelle. He could put her off no longer without rousing suspicion, if he hadn't already. He answered as casual a tone he could muster: "Hi, babe. How's it going?"

After a few minutes of idle chat, in which he determined she suspected nothing (or if she had, his easy speech had put her off the scent), he made an excuse about work and hung up.

Then he got down to the business of opening Lucine's mail. The packages all contained some form of sex toy, from enormous dildos to Ben Wa balls to a pair of incredibly lifelike inflatable dolls, one male and one female.

"What the fuck is with this chick?" Paul wondered aloud. He shouldn't wonder, though, with her having friends like Viola who dressed in her Sunday best for church in the morning and fucked her patrons by night. Hell, she hadn't even made him wear a condom. In fact, she'd *protested* when he'd offered.

"And I want you to finish inside me, baby," she'd purred in his ear. "Unload all you got, sugar."

For the love of all things holy, he *had*. He'd spent himself harder inside her than he could ever remember doing before. For the ten thousandth time since sneaking out of her building, he wondered what the hell he'd been thinking. That was it, though, wasn't it? He *hadn't* been thinking. Christ, for all he knew he'd contracted some disease from her. He'd need to schedule an appointment to get tested and started to call the clinic before realizing that wouldn't work. The visit would show up on their insurance bill and Michelle would question it. Maybe he'd go to the county walk-in clinic, then. Later.

But first breakfast. Food hadn't crossed his mind, but now that it had he realized he was ravenous.

He cracked three eggs into a skillet and dumped in cubed ham, cheese, and veggies that still smelled fresh. When the omelet was finished, he ate it out of the pan while standing over the sink and staring out into the yard. The ticking clock from the living room provided the only sound. Paul set the dishes in the sink, popped a beer from the fridge, and settled into his office chair. He logged into Linda Lopez's Facebook to check her messages but was greeted with only a single notification.

Lucy Korth had accepted the friend request.

For a time, he could only stare at the screen. His mouth dried and he wetted it with brew. Any thought of getting an STD test vanished. With a not-quite-steady hand, he clicked on her profile.

Full access granted him the ability to review her status updates, what she liked, her personal information (precious little on that front), and most importantly her photo albums. All fifty-two of them. Yes, he counted.

Paul gave the textual portion his initial attention, wanting to save the best for last. According to her profile, Lucy had been born in some unpronounceable village in Georgia. The eastern European nation, not the American state. Google Maps revealed her birthplace to be on the western shore of the Black Sea.

No listing for current city.

No listing for workplace.

No listed political or religious affiliation.

No relationship status.

Paul scrolled her timeline. A few statuses stuck out at once.

Her most recent, a week old, read: "Thank you, Paris, for your hospitality. As always, XOXO." Paris? The city or someone she knows? No one had liked or commented on it.

A month earlier she had posted: "Houston, you're up. Be ready." Again, did she mean the location or a friend? Be ready for what? No likes, no comments.

In October, a post which seemed to simply be a series of seemingly unrelated numbers cropped up: "021 476 0907 8779 1215 4798 1818 1314." Nothing more. A handful of users had liked it, including Viola, but again no comments.

In September, she had posted only a winky-face emoji which had garnered greater than fifty likes. No comments.

Then, nothing. Her timeline was blank all the way back to the date she registered her account in May of 2012.

Private girl. Not much of a social media butterfly, I guess, Paul thought. That was fine by him; he wanted to get to the good stuff anyway.

Licking his lips, Paul opened the first album. Before he let himself look, though, he pulled up his music streaming app and hit PLAY on his electronica playlist. He wanted this to rock. He also wanted another beer, which he procured before settling in.

The albums couldn't have thrilled him more. In them, he found Lucine Korth in various stages of undress. Nothing lewd. Just enough. Lucine in a string bikini on a beach. Lucine in a different bikini on a green-tended lawn that spanned the entire range of the photo. Lucine in tight cutoff jeans and midriff shirt staring the camera saucily down. Each image seemed jaw-droppingly better than the last. He cranked the volume and clicked through album after album. Before he'd made it even halfway through them, he'd entirely forgotten about finding his home invaded.

Paul stripped and stood staring at the screen, his erection bouncing free and still sticky with Viola. As quickly as he could, he tore the plastic off the female sex doll and blew into it until he was red-faced and out of breath. He dropped into his chair, gasping. When had he gotten so out of shape? He told Michelle he'd started exercising, but of course he hadn't. He'd never needed to work out; he had the type of body which seemed to resist fat, an ever-youthful tone to his muscles. But now, simply blowing up a glorified balloon had knocked the wind out of him.

"Settle down, kid. Just settle the fuck down," he murmured until his heart and lungs regulated. When he felt he could go on, Paul clicked back to his favorite image of little Lucine he'd yet found—her in a checked cowgirl shirt, hanging open to expose her cleavage and navel, with a pair of denim shorts unsnapped and showing a wedge of flowered panties—then grabbed the doll.

"Get ready to have your latex brains fucked out, bitch," he told its mannequin's face and readied himself for insertion. At that particular moment, though, the streaming service decided on playing The Beatles' "I Will." His and Michelle's wedding song. Somehow, through some gross oversight probably on his part, it had invaded his electronica playlist. Before the first verse had even begun, his erection had withered beneath the crushing weight of guilt.

"What am I going to do?" he asked the doll. She remained mum, her dead eyes obstinate. He waited out the song and when the final chiming notes dissipated, he picked up the phone to call his wife.

Chapter Nineteen

The house seemed too empty, so Paul drove to the lake and parked in one of the picnic area lots.

The sun sparkled off the water like strewn gems. He took one of the hiking paths encircling the water, hands shoved in his pockets, shoulders hunched. The temperature had dropped as the day wore on, but walking cleared his head.

Flurries fluttered out of the sky. Before he'd made it halfway around the two-mile circumference of the lake, he'd come to a decision. He would get tested at the county clinic in the morning. If the test came back positive for venereal disease, he would confess all to Michelle and suffer the consequences. But if it came back negative, he would never speak a word of his infidelity to anyone. It would die with him. And Viola, of course.

Either way, nothing would stop him from pursuing Lucine Korth to his final breath.

When he got home, Paul crashed on the sofa. He couldn't recall ever having felt so exhausted. His naturally fit frame felt as though it might fall apart any moment. A good, long snooze would fix him. Maybe he could sleep until midnight, then try to find some freelance work. He still needed to keep his end up somehow.

When Paul woke, though, morning sunlight slanted through the curtains. He jumped up and checked the clock: 10:35 a.m. He'd never slept past 9:30 in his adult life.

"Holy fuck," he whispered, scrubbing his eyes with his palms. The past fifteen hours had passed as if he'd been removed from them. His sleep had been marred by not a single interruption; he didn't think he'd even changed position. And the worst part was he didn't feel any more rested.

Paul stepped into the bathroom to relieve a bladder that seemed to weigh ten pounds. When he flushed, he turned to the mirror and stopped dead. The wrinkles crowding his eyes had deepened and the bags had gotten puffier. Patches of white hair had appeared at his temples. He looked as though he'd aged ten years.

"What the hell is happening to me?" he asked the mirror. The mirror, as usual, offered no opinion.

He decided there would be no visit to the county clinic today; today he had bigger bears to snare.

Paul found some of Michelle's face cream in her medicine cabinet and smeared the cold gunk around his eyes. It was supposed to smooth wrinkles and reduce eye bags. Forgoing breakfast, he drove to the drug store and bought hair dye close to his natural color, praying it matched.

At home, he showered and applied the dye. After checking his reflection carefully, he decided it would do. The cream seemed to have helped his eyes, too. Unless you knew to look, you couldn't see a difference. Everyone grew old, but not overnight. He wasn't about to look like those crotchety old timers down at Dot's Place at thirty fucking years old.

He checked both his real and phony accounts for new job acceptances, but both remained stubbornly empty. He needed money and in order to find money, he needed to find work.

Or did he? What would a bevy of unopened sex toys go for on the secondary market? The female doll was out, of course, but that was fine—he had plans for her. But the male doll and the cache of vibrators still in their packaging might fetch a cool mint.

After some research, Paul snapped pictures of the items and uploaded them to a website called SecondCumming.com—the porn world's version of eBay for all unopened and unwanted sexual miscellany. A link on the site even had a section for "gently used" items, but Paul wasn't going to touch that one. He set the auction time for three days so there would be plenty of time to get them shipped before Michelle and the kids got home. All told, he stood to rake in over 500 bucks, assuming they sold. And they would, he realized after half an hour—each item garnered immediate bids. Hell, he wouldn't even have to splurge on shipping supplies; he'd use the same boxes in which they'd been delivered to Lucine.

What else could he use from her? He thought of her house on Pace Lane sitting dark and disused and knew what to do. The stacks of boxes in the spare bedroom. No doubt they contained other products Ms. Korth's myriad amours had sent her.

"Looks like another drive is in order tonight," Paul said to the empty house. He sensed it somehow listening.

He ate breakfast, then went to peruse Lucine's Facebook profile again. She had posted a new status only fifteen minutes previously. It read: "Returning from abroad Friday nite—who's up for drinks???"

Already five likes and a comment from none other than Viola Datsun: "U kno it, girl! Same time, same place."

Cabana Girls. Lucine-fucking-Korth would be at Cabana Girls. That had to be the place Viola had referred to. Where else?

But he couldn't get hard just yet. He knew when Lucine would return and where she would go, but he couldn't just walk into Cabana Girls and offer to buy her a drink. Not with Viola there. Why had he ever fucked her? It could topple everything, from his marriage to his chances with Lucine. No self-respecting person fucked their best friend's lay.

I'll go in disguise, Paul thought. Of course. But how could he disguise himself so that Viola wouldn't recognize him and blow his cover faster than she'd blown his cock? He'd shave, for one. He'd dress casual and not like a church boy. Maybe bleach his hair. He actually snorted at that—Michelle would skin him alive if she came home to a towheaded husband. He might already be in for it if she detected he'd used dark dye. It would raise far too many questions.

So you're going to chase a mistake with another mistake?

"Damn right I am," he said aloud. The way Paul figured it, he'd been making mistakes ever since finding the envelope addressed to Lucine mixed in with his mail. Since then, nothing seemed to have gone right. What more could possibly go wrong? And now was his chance, with the family safely 250 miles away in the state capital. No matter the outcome, this was it. After Lucine, whether he failed or flew with her, he would settle down. This was nothing more than a quick seven-year itch which badly needed scratching. After he'd scratched, he'd quit forever. Be the good husband and father. The quiet family man. He only needed to get this one thing out of his system.

Except … except what if he *couldn't* quit? What if he slept with Lucine and he found himself addicted to her? Many stories of such infatuation-turned-obsession played on late night television—Michelle loved those kinds of shows. The shy neighbor stalking the schoolteacher. The vengeful girlfriend lopping off her cheating boyfriend's penis. It happened all the time.

"It's a chance I'm willing to take," Paul said. It felt good to speak aloud, as if Lucine might be lounging nude on his sofa, hanging on his every word and awaiting another steamy romp.

Hesitantly, he hovered the cursor over Lucine's status, swallowed, then clicked Like.

All the stolen items listed on SecondCumming.com had sold by 8:30 that night. The world was full of horny, impulsive people who couldn't seem to wait to indulge their fantasies. That Paul Jeske could be counted among their ranks never crossed his mind.

He sat drinking beer and relabeling boxes. All the postage was purchased online, so all he had to do in the morning was drop the packages at the post office. His PayPal account had bloated to greater than $725, more than enough to transfer into their bank account to cover whatever bills needed covering with some left over to play with. It made him think of Michelle, and he called to find out how they were doing.

Perry answered, his voice bubbling with excitement. "Hi, Daddy! We're playing *Clue* with Grammy, Pop-Pop, and Aunt Bert."

"Sounds like fun, Pear. You behaving yourself?"

"Uh-huh."

"Your sister, too?"

"Yeah, but she's been crying a lot."

"Why?" Paul asked, praying the nightmares had not returned.

"She's homesick. Babies get homesick sometimes."

"Don't call her that, Pear."

"Well, she is one."

"Put your mother on, okay?"

"She's not here."

The idea of Michelle's absence startled him. All too easily, he saw her driving north on the interstate at 75 mph to surprise him. If she came home with the house littered with stolen sex toys, it would—at best—unequivocally spell divorce. At worst, castration.

He cleared his throat. "Where is she, buddy?"

"I don't know. I think she went for a walk."

"Is the car in the driveway?"

"Lemme check."

"That's okay. Can you put Grammy on for me?"

The phone clunked on the table and his son called for his grandmother. Paul's mind raced. Darlene Craycraft picked up a minute later. "Hallo, Paul. How's my favorite son-in-law?" she said. It sounded like she might be two or three glasses deep into a nice Merlot.

"Doing fine, Darlene. Is my family eating you out of house and home yet?" he asked, trying to keep the tone light.

"Of course, they are, dear, but I would expect nothing less. Your children are growing like little piglets and anything they want, they get here at Grammy and Pop-Pop's."

Paul forced a laugh. Darlene loved dangling her wealth in front of anyone who crossed her path. He switched to Pretend Paul, a persona he often adopted around his in-laws. "Great,

great. Say, listen, Perry mentioned Michelle ducked out. Any idea when she might return?"

"She went out for the evening with a few old school friends."

"Without her phone?"

"Oh, you know how people are. Sometimes they just don't want to be found."

Paul entirely understood the notion. "Fair enough. If she gets in before midnight, would you have her call?"

"I won't be awake at midnight, dear. In fact, it's past my bedtime now. If it weren't for these delightful grandchildren you and your beautiful wife were kind enough to make, I imagine I'd be dreaming of bare-chested buccaneers carrying me off to grand golden galleons docked in some exotic port."

"I heard that, woman," Ned Craycraft called in the background. "You don't mind your Ps and Qs, I might just let them take you."

Darlene clucked her tongue. "That old goat doesn't realize the treasure trove he has before him. In any case, Paul, if Michelle steps in before I'm kicking my legs over Blackbeard's shoulder, I'll pass along the message. Would you like to speak to your younger offspring?"

Without awaiting a reply, the phone landed in Jeannie's plump hands. "*Daddeeee!*" she shrieked into the mouthpiece. Paul yanked the phone away from his head before any lasting damage could be done.

From a safe distance, he said, "Hi, June Bug. I miss you."

"I miss you, too, Daddy. I have to go. Miss Scarlet did it in the lounge with a candlestick!" Her voice grew muffled as she set the phone down, but Paul caught her asking, "What did she do with it, Grammy? Did she light a candle?"

He didn't wait for Darlene or—God forbid—Ned to come on the line. He pressed END, then got back to work.

Chapter Twenty

He couldn't carry out his new undertaking at home—it would take hours to move all the boxes—so after sundown he packed up his laptop, his phone, and an overnight bag and drove to Pace Lane. The homeowner wouldn't be home until Friday, if her Facebook status could be trusted, and he saw little reason why it couldn't.

Pace Lane glowed with cold white streetlights, the power outage evidently resolved, though nothing moved in the neighborhood. People in these parts seemed to keep to themselves, which probably explained why Lucine chose it. Paul simply walked right in. He waited ten minutes to ensure no looky-loo had decided to come investigate the masked man who'd entered their pretty neighbor's house (or who'd decided to call LWPD to do it), but when no one came he got busy.

The boxes did indeed hold packaged treasures of sexual healing. He was certainly no expert, but once he'd looked everything over he put a price tag of over $10,000 on the lot. He spent an hour snapping photos and another listing them on the sex site. In minutes, the bids began rolling in.

While they did, Paul decided to pick up takeout. He drove to Chiang's and ordered sweet and sour pork with two egg rolls, then drove back to his default parking space on William Street. Hauling the bags of food off the passenger seat, he drew his mask over his face, and rounded the corner onto Pace.

Only now Pace Lane no longer remained a hub of inactivity. Two police cruisers and an ambulance stood parked half a block up, their strobes painting the houses in a blood-red rinse.

I'm busted, he thought desperately. *They're inside her house right now, confiscating my laptop.*

But that wasn't true. The vehicles had been parked next door at 202 Pace. Paul moved cautiously, meaning to turn up Lucine's walk and be inside before anyone spotted him.

"Excuse me, sir, may I have a word with you?" Too late. Paul glanced around at a plainclothes cop hurrying his way.

"Good evening, officer. What's going on?"

"It's detective. Sanders is the name." Paul wondered how much shit the cop would get if he ever made colonel. "Do you live around here?"

"No. Actually, I was bringing dinner to my friend, but I may have wasted a trip—doesn't look like she's home."

"Who's your friend?"

He hesitated. "Lucy. Lucy Korth."

"And you say she's not home?"

"If I had to guess, she isn't. Not a light on in the place."

"You just happened to bring her dinner without calling first?"

"I was hoping to surprise her," Paul said and winked through the ski mask's eyehole. He was happy to have it now.

"Why'd you park around the corner?" the cop inquired.

Paul had anticipated the question and would use it to deflect the subject to something other than his presence on Pace Lane. He nodded to a street sign which read EMERGENCY SNOW ROUTE NO PARKING IF OVER 2 INCHES. "It's supposed to snow tonight. I hope it holds off until you're finished here. May I ask what happened?"

"Do you know Mr. Andre Diaz?"

Paul shook his head. "I'm afraid not. Is he hurt?"

"He's dead. His wife called it in."

"I'm sorry to hear it. Old age?" He still thought of this part of town as home to elderly residents due to its cemetery-quiet nature.

The cop shocked him by saying. "He was twenty-six."

"Oh, God. Do you suspect foul play?" The question was rhetorical, though — if they had a detective present, foul play must at least be under consideration. If he'd simply choked on a chicken bone, they wouldn't have bothered.

"We can't speculate at this point and couldn't divulge it in any case."

"I understand. Please give my condolences to the Diaz family," Paul said, turning up the walk to Lucine's house.

"Sir, do you mind if ask your name?" the cop asked behind him.

Paul never slowed. "Benjamin Gehant," he called. "Call me Ben."

"Do you mind if I see some ID? And maybe your face?"

Paul stopped halfway to the porch. "Am I being detained?"

"Of course not," the detective said with a snicker. "Just hoping to know exactly who it is I'm speaking with."

"Ben Gehant. I already told you. If I'm not under arrest, I'd just as soon get inside. It's damn cold out here."

"No problem, Mr. Gehant. I may be calling on you, though."

"Great. I'm in the White Pages." Paul flicked of a short salute. "Good luck with your investigation. I'm sorry to hear about Mr. Diaz."

"I thought you said your friend wasn't home," Sanders called.

"I've got a key," Paul hollered back, holding it up to be picked out in the streetlight. He let himself in, closed the door, and triple locked it. Then he peeled back an inch of curtain and waited as Detective Sanders moseyed back into dead Mr. Diaz's house.

♀

He knew it was risky to stay but didn't guess the cops would come knocking without a warrant. If they did, he simply wouldn't answer. Let them come back with a warrant.

Paul watched the bids tally up while working the pork over with chopsticks. The screen looked blurry, so he settled the 1.5 mag reading glasses on his nose. They helped. Christ, now he was going blind on top of gray. *Age sneaks up on you*, his father used to say. *One day you're fit as a fiddle, the next you're pissing blood*. Paul hadn't gotten that far yet, but perhaps such a terrible symptom lurked not far in the future.

Can't live forever, had been another of his father's gems. *Live it up while you can.*

Amen, Dad. Living it up is precisely what he planned to do with the remaining time he had to himself.

Each time an item sold, he sent a command to his home computer to print a postage label. In the morning, he'd collect them, return to Lucine's, and affix them to their proper package before driving them to the post office. A few hours' work and he wouldn't have to worry about finding contract work for a year. And by then he could have completely rebuilt his reputation on the freelancing sites.

Something creaked on the main floor. Paul froze, noodles dangling from his lips. He imagined the cop, Sanders, changing his mind and coming to insist "Ben Gehant" come downtown to answer questions. But no—Paul had locked the door. In triplicate.

Lucine, his mind offered. *She's home early.*

Paul dropped his chopsticks, slapped the cheap glasses off his face, and crept to her bedroom door, head cocked. Nothing. No sound. He waited, but the creak he knew he'd heard did not repeat itself. Just the house settling, then. All old houses make weird sounds, like a geriatric with heartburn. He wanted to know what lay behind the locked door on the ground floor. A cellar, no doubt, but why keep it locked? Hell, she didn't even bother locking her front door while she was away. So what sort of goodies did Lucine hide down there? More sex toys? Gold bullion? Dead bodies?

Paul returned to his meal. The bids trickled in. Some of the pervs had already transferred payment. Suckers.

Maybe he could find a key to the cellar door. Of course. She must keep a spare someplace. Paul finished his food and started searching. He'd almost given up when he struck gold—literally. A glittering gold key had been taped to the bottom of the kitchen's silverware drawer.

"Got to get up pretty early in the morning to fool this guy," Paul said, taking the key to the narrow door and socking it into the lock.

Only it wouldn't turn. It fit fine, but it simply wouldn't budge. He muttered a curse and stuck the key in his pocket. What the hell did it open, if not the basement door?

The creaking he'd heard came again, louder now. And closer. Much closer. Paul had heard people claim their blood froze when they felt fear, but this was the first time he'd experienced it. His feet rooted to the floor. His bowels went watery. The sound had come from the other side of the basement door, as though someone behind it had treaded gently upon a squeaky stair.

When he found the ability to move, Paul took a shaky step backward. Then another. Then a third. The thought of returning upstairs to retrieve his laptop seemed incredibly idiotic, but he couldn't leave it here. If Lucine came home early (or if she was already home, hiding for some reason in her cellar), he would be busted. He'd not be looking only at divorce but prison time. He must have committed a dozen felonies over the past forty-eight hours.

Paul took the stairs to Lucine's room two by two, snatched up his computer and fled downstairs again. He missed a step and tumbled to the landing, the laptop clattering away. Through the pain of a twisted ankle, Paul envisioned the cellar door creaking open and Lucine striding up to find him writhing on her foyer floor. He risked a glance toward the kitchen, but it remained dark and silent except for the Felix the Cat clock ticking over the fridge.

He collected his belongings, yanked open the door without bothering to close it, and raced to his car. The cops and ambulances had departed to deposit Mr. Andre Diaz at the Lake Winona city morgue. Paul pulled onto Pace Lane, eyeing number 200 as he whipped by.

Someone stood at the front window, looking out into the night. The same window he'd used to spy on the cops only hours before. Though he could make out no features of the watcher, he clearly saw the curtain drop back into place.

Chapter Twenty-One

Michelle couldn't recall when she'd had a better time that she'd been having at Sauce, the premiere nightclub in town. It had been years—not since college, she thought—since she'd come to a club to cut loose. Her days since then had been focused on her career. A career which, she hoped, would soon burgeon into something better. Parnell certainly had faith in her abilities and while she and Paul joked about ulterior motives, he'd never once put the moves on her, to her relief. Too many of her friends had fallen for sleeping their way to the tops of their professions.

Emily, for example, worked as vice president for a prominent Springfield firm. She'd admitted once how she'd broken the glass ceiling on her knees. Michelle had been shocked, but Emily had laughed it off. "If taking a shot in the mouth will earn me five hundred grand a year, I'd happily blow every man in town."

Michelle watched her friend now, flirting with a guy across the bar. They'd all agreed to leave men out of the picture tonight, but Emily had never been one to follow the rules. At least Heather and Danielle hadn't abandoned her yet.

She craned around in her stool, fingernails ticking on the stem of her martini glass, and marked them on the dance floor, gyrating to some electronica number. They'd tried to get her to join them, but Michelle hadn't danced since ... well, since her wedding night. There simply had been little inclination. She'd feel foolish to try it now, in front of her friends (not to mention total strangers).

Heather caught her looking and beckoned. Michelle shook her head, but Heather's face took a turn for the severe and Michelle reluctantly stood. She didn't want to be a Debbie Downer.

"It's like riding a bicycle," Dani hollered over the music.

"More like a unicycle," Michelle called back, but the music swallowed her words and they'd sounded better in her head anyway. But Dani had been right—Michelle found her old college rhythm soon enough.

Their fun was short-lived, though, as she knew it would be. A guy in tight jeans and cowboy boots wearing his hair too long strutted up and tried to break into their space.

Heather and Dani, bachelorettes who'd never fully given up their partying days and were accustomed to such intrusion, simply turned away without breaking stride. It left Michelle as the last opening, and Mr. Cowboy locked in on her.

Too late she tried to emulate her friends' cold-shoulder tactic, but by then he'd danced so close she could feel the crotch of his jeans against her thigh. Rough hands gripped her hips. She smelled sweat and Stetson cologne.

"What's your name, darlin?" the guy rumbled in her ear.

Michelle flashed the diamond Paul had given her eight years previous, relishing the way it reflected the pink and blue neon bar décor. She hoped it blinded him. "I'm married."

"That don't make no nevermind to me," Cowboy said.

"Well, it does to me," she said, hauling away from his touch.

"Hey, hang on a second, honey," he shouted. By then her friends had figured out the dilemma. They each gripped one of Michelle's hands and moved as a unit to their table.

"What a scuzz," Dani said.

"There's always one to ruin the fun," Heather added, like a mantra.

Emily, sensing something amiss, excused herself from her flirtations and returned to the table. "Asshole alert?"

"Code red asshole alert," Dani said.

"God, men are such morons, always thinking with their teeny wienies," Emily said, wiggling a pinky in the air. Michelle figured no one knew better than Em.

"Maybe he'll leave," she suggested, but her friends quickly dispelled that hope.

"They're like sharks," Heather said. "Once they get a whiff of you, they won't let you be until either they've had their way, or you tell them to fuck themselves."

"This isn't how I remember it working in college," Michelle said. Her friends laughed and swirled their drinks.

"Honey, college boys are pups. Cute to look at, fun to pet, but stupid as hell. It's when they grow up that you got to start worrying about them biting. If they don't get it out of their system young, you get guys like Shitkicker there," Heather said and for some reason, Michelle thought of Paul. He hadn't been a wild child in college, so could that be what he was that what he was doing now? Could he be taking advantage of her absence so he could "get it out of his system"?

No. Despite the terrible dream she'd had, Paul wouldn't cheat on her. She thought. They'd been down that slope before, about a year before their marriage, and she'd been at fault. It had been on a visit home, just like this one, during winter break of their senior year at the university. Paul had stayed behind to work on an assignment for his Advanced Essay course, even though she'd begged him to join her at her parents' for the holidays. He'd been adamant, though: "Shell, if I don't get this paper done—and done *right*—I can kiss a spring graduation good-bye." His insistence had seemed silly to her; Paul *always* nailed his papers. Straight-A student, Dean's List, all the bells and whistles. His refusal to spend the holidays with her had wounded her deeply.

Which may have been why she'd found the decision to jump in bed with Tom Rood so easy following a party at Emily's place. She and Tom had dated briefly in high school but had slept together only once. Perhaps that reason alone swayed her—it didn't really seem like cheating if she'd already traveled that road. That's what she told herself.

When she confessed her infidelity to Emily the next morning, her friend had come off as nonchalant about the affair. "On the one hand, it's not like he's some barfly you never met before," Emily had consoled, before adding, "But on the other, you're committed to Paul. Right? *Are* you committed to Paul, Shelly?"

Michelle had confirmed as much, the first errant tears springing to her eyes.

"Then again," Emily backpedaled, "It's not like you're married. I mean, cheating when you're just dating—and with someone you've already slept with—isn't the same as cheating when you're married. Marriage is the game-changer. I wouldn't spend another moment's thought on it, sweetness. What happens in Springfield stays in Springfield."

Emily would eventually adopt that credo as she slept her way through the upper echelon of the state capital's top law firm. Michelle couldn't, though, and on her first day back from break, had confessed.

Paul had taken it surprisingly well. No stomping or shouting or cursing her name. He simply nodded along with her story, her hands clasped in his, before sucking breath through his teeth and saying, "It's my fault, I suppose. I should have gone with you."

She had tried to make it clear the slip hadn't been due to his absence, but she determined he never fully accepted that. In any case, Paul had let the subject drop with a closing remark as ambiguous as Emily's response had been: "I'm going to say one last thing, Shelly, and then I don't ever want to talk about this again. I forgive you this trespass. But should the day come when I trespass, I expect equal forgiveness. Fair enough?"

Of course, she'd eagerly agreed, relieved to sneak past her error with such ease. But as the days turned into weeks and the weeks into months, she found herself displeased with the pact. He'd left himself an enormous out should he ever get a case of the seven-year itch. Maybe they wouldn't even make it seven years. Maybe she worried for nothing. Still, that last loophole had kept her up nights during those first few months of spring semester. Anytime he'd come home late from the library, she'd wonder if he'd really been out at a bar picking up some hussy. She regularly checked his shirt collars for lipstick stains, sniffed the material to pick up any hint of perfume. Each time, she found nothing incriminating. Even if she had, he couldn't be incriminated. He had automatic immunity. A one-time Get Out of Jail Free card. Because of the clause she'd gamely agreed to. In short, he had her up against the wall when it came to fidelity.

On their wedding day, a chilly afternoon in late December, he'd spoken his vows as though he meant every word. His piercing eyes gave away no hint he even remembered his bride's brief affair with a former beau. Maybe he *had* forgotten, she hoped. At that moment, as he finished speaking, she determined never to think of it again. Life was simply too short to live with such anxiety gnawing at the back of one's mind and when it came her turn to speak her vows, she did so with love and conviction.

They'd been happily married eight years and if any itch had bitten Paul, he'd given no indication. Clearly the dream she'd had of him with the dark-eyed woman had been her subconscious playing the role of a devilish trickster. Michelle put all of it out of mind: the dream, her long-ago infidelity, Paul's calm yet open-ended response. She had to focus on *now*.

Emily set a fresh martini before her, but Michelle had lost the urge to drink. She wanted to be home, safe beneath a familiar roof. With her children and her parents. She wanted to return to an uncomplicated life where drunk cowboys didn't flirt. Michelle envied her kids their remaining childhood. Maturity wasn't as fun as advertised.

After making a headache excuse, Michelle hugged her friends and promised she would see them at the New Year's Eve party. Emily walked her to the door.

"Don't let some horn-dog scare you off, Shell. We've got your back. We your girls."

"It's not that," Michelle said. "I'm thinking of Paul. Homesick, I guess."

"You're not still dwelling on that thing from, like, ten years ago, are you?"

"What thing?" she asked, playing dumb.

"Girl, please. The Tom Rood thing."

"I wish you hadn't brought that up."

"All I'm saying is, it's ancient history. It was one time. No big deal. God, if you knew half of what I'd done, you'd probably gag. I know I do if I think about it too long."

Michelle disengaged from her friend and hurried to her car. She hadn't had much to drink, so she'd be okay to drive. Driving wasn't what concerned her, though. Emily was wrong. It *was* a big deal. That one night years ago, those fifteen fleeting minutes, had changed the course of her life, she now realized. May have changed it for good.

And for bad.

Chapter Twenty-Two

As his wife reminisced on past regrets in a bar in her hometown, Paul Jeske sat at a stoplight which had gone green, staring in disbelief into the night. Someone behind him tapped their horn. Paul blinked, checked his mirror, and proceeded into the intersection.

"I'm fucked," he said. And he was. Or would be, anyway, once whoever had been in Lucine's house made his or her way upstairs.

He had left his cell phone behind. It wasn't in any of his pockets, nor in the bag with the leftover Chinese food. In fact, he knew exactly where he'd left it—on the comforter of Lucine's bed. It wouldn't take someone long to figure out to whom it belonged. In fact, lovely Lucy could at this very moment be calling the police on it to report an intruder.

She could be calling Michelle, Paul thought and found the prospect infinitely more terrifying than the cops.

He pulled a U-Turn right there on King Expressway and sped back with no clear agenda in mind other than to retrieve the forgotten phone. After parking in the usual William Street spot, Paul walked to the other side of Pace so as to have a clear vantage of the house, the ski mask snugly in place. Snowflakes skated out of the sky. Though dark had come on fully now, no light burned in her windows and no string of smoke blotted out the stars. Could he have imagined the twitching curtain? What about the sounds behind the cellar door? Nothing more than mice on the prowl?

What should he do? Bum rush the door, shoot upstairs, grab the device, and get out? He didn't even have a weapon; maybe he should drive home and get his club.

A *weapon*? What the hell was he thinking? First he invaded an innocent person's house, stole her personal belongings before selling them online. Now, after he was caught, he was considering breaking and entering again and adding a battery—and possibly a *murder*—charge? Christ, he was in deep. If he got out of this, he would never do another crooked thing in his life. Straight as a signpost, right hand to God.

Maybe he should try the back door. It would be less visible from the street. But what if it was locked? What if he snagged on the fence, got hung up by his belt? What if unknown obstacles—grills, landscaping, lawn gnomes—proved too difficult to stealthily navigate? No, the back wouldn't do. It had to be the front. He knew the layout. And he knew the door would be unlocked.

Quick, before he could rethink it, Paul jaywalked to Lucine's yard and took it with swift, purposeful strides, eyes locked on the window. No movement. His breath came hot inside the ski mask. The mask seemed to be his only true defense right now; at least it would protect his identity. Assuming that hadn't already been ascertained from his phone.

With a last glance at the street, Paul pushed into the house, looming dank and dark as ever. Still, he could detect no evidence of residency. The place felt like how he imagined the inside of a mausoleum must feel.

"Anyone home?" he called, his face burning with guilt beneath his mask.

No answer in the deathly silence.

"Um, I'm sorry to intrude, but I think I may have left something here."

Nothing.

"I hope you'll allow me to explain. My name is Benjamin Gehant. I mistook your house for someone else's. Perhaps you know my friend Andre? Andre Diaz? Well, I hadn't seen him since college, and I must've jotted down his address wrong."

Excuses didn't come any flimsier, he knew, but it was the only one he could muster. In any case, it didn't seem to matter—no one answered his hail.

Paul stepped hesitantly across the foyer to the staircase. He stared up the narrow passage, hoping to determine whether someone occupied the second story, but it remained as dark as the rest of the place. He took a breath and then rushed the stairs as quickly and quietly as he could all the way to the top.

At the landing he paused to listen but heard nothing. He swallowed thickly, wishing his heart would calm. Paul eased open the door to Lucine's bedroom, realizing he hadn't closed it on the way out, but knowing he had no choice but to try for the phone. It was his only chance.

The place seemed as though it existed beneath miles of bedrock or perhaps in outer space, so silent and lifeless it was. Without daring to turn on the light, he took three towering steps to the head of the bed and felt around, but the phone was gone.

Then he did feel something. Hair. Clumps of it lying on the pillowcase. Attached to a head as cold as clay. The head of a corpse.

Paul's bladder threatened to release. He drew his hand away in revulsion. A nerve twitched feverishly in one cheek.

She killed herself, he thought wildly. *After she watched me drive away, she came up here and killed herself*. How long did a body take to cool after it died?

He had decided to give up on the phone when it shrilled from where it had fallen to the floor, illuminating the room in sickly green.

Paul didn't think or hesitate. He grabbed it and bolted to his car without looking back.

By the time he got home, he'd allowed himself to consider perhaps everything would work out. He would lay low, scope the situation from a distance. Under no circumstance would he approach 200 Pace Lane again.

Paul showered and then, dressed only in boxers, tossed his old attire, including his coat, gloves, and balaclava mask into the washer, chased them with an inordinate amount of detergent, set it to hot, and sent it spinning. He wanted the laundry extra clean.

It wasn't until the washer had reached the spin cycle that he thought to check his phone. He was certain the caller who'd helped him find his phone would be Michelle, but it wasn't. He didn't recognize the area code. In fact, it didn't appear to even be national—it had too many digits. The caller had left no voicemail. Telemarketer, most likely. But who telemarketed this close to midnight? No matter—he wasn't about to call back. If it was important enough, they'd try again. Preferably after breakfast.

Paul discovered he was too exhausted for any further intrigue. The night had worn on him. He made his way to the bedroom and slid beneath the sheets.

When at Last I Find You

After slumbering fitfully through a bevy of bad dreams, he woke sometime before dawn with the distinct feeling he was no longer alone in the house.

Chapter Twenty-Three

Michelle Jeske tossed and turned through nightmares of her own, though thankfully no repeat of the woman with dark eyes. In one dream, a skeletal cowboy wearing torn denim and a checkered shirt boogied toward her, holding one bony hand out in invitation. If she accepted the dance, she knew she would die. She backed away but the corpse bopped onward, ever onward, until she could smell its fetid breath. *May I have this dance, darlin?* it rasped, one claw closing over her wrist and the other over her throat.

Michelle jumped awake. The clock read 3:26. She pressed her hands to her eyes, then climbed out of bed. After checking on the kids, who both slept easy, and replacing Gussy beneath Jeannie's arm from where the cow-giraffe-zebra thing had fallen to the floor, she went downstairs for a light snack.

Once she'd fixed a small salad, she hauled her phone out of the pocket of her bathrobe to catch up on social media. Before she could pull up an app, though, she noticed a missed call. Thinking Paul must have tried to contact her, she checked the history but found only a number with an international calling code. No voicemail. Some solicitor calling from what would likely be a less ungodly hour in their time zone.

She had finished her salad when the phone buzzed on the table beside her bowl. It was Paul. Why was he calling now?

"Paul? What are you doing up?" she asked. What he said broke her skin into gooseflesh.

"Shelly, tell me you came home early and are playing some kind of trick on me." His voice held a wedge of wild desperation.

"What are you talking about? Are you drunk?"

"Jesus, if it's not you who could it be?" he said, his voice edging dangerously toward a whine.

"Paul, calm down and tell me what's going on."

"Someone's playing games," he said. "Someone's really playing games with me."

"Will you just tell me what's happening, Paul? You're scaring the shit out of me."

He took a deep breath. "Okay. Okay, I'm sorry. I'm just freaked out."

She waited for him to continue. Wind rattled the kitchen windows and hummed through the crack in the screen door.

"I woke up and heard someone in the kitchen. It sounded like they were making something to eat, and I figured you must have come home early as, I don't know. A ... a surprise or something."

Michelle's pulse quickened, but she wouldn't let herself panic. "And then?"

Paul said, "I went downstairs. The kitchen light was on. I could see it under the door, from the top of the steps. And I could hear a woman humming."

"Jesus, Paul—"

"That's not the weirdest part, though. She was humming our wedding song."

"She was humming 'I Will'?" Michelle asked.

"It sounded just like something you would've done, I don't know, five or six years ago. So I crept up to the door and shoved it open, ready to jump in and holler 'surprise!' except when I did the kitchen was dark and there was no one inside."

Michelle allowed herself to feel relief. "Paul, honey, you must have been dreaming. That's all it was—a dream."

"Christ, Shell, don't you think I know the difference between being awake and being asleep?"

"There's such a thing as lucid dreaming. Remember what Jeannie was suffering from a few weeks ago?"

"This wasn't a dream, dammit."

Michelle let out a long, slow breath. "Okay, hon. I believe you. Now if the boogie monster isn't making an egg soufflé in our kitchen, I think you're safe to go back to sleep."

"There's more," Paul said after a short hesitation.

"What is it?"

"Every fucking cabinet door was open."

"*What?*"

"The fridge and freezer, too."

"Was anything missing?"

"Not that I could tell."

"Paul, you sleepwalked. That's all. You were having an incredibly vivid dream and you sleepwalked. Honey, you did that stuff yourself."

"I would think maybe you were right, but I found footprints on the floor."

"Footprints?" she asked, her panic-meter edging now toward critical mass.

"Bare footprints, caked in mud. About women's size nine."

Back in bed, Michelle sat with her back against the headboard, the covers pulled against her chin. She had told Paul she would leave for home the minute the kids woke, but he had told her not to. *Insisted* she didn't, mostly because of the impending snowstorm expected at the state capital but also because he said he could handle it.

Michelle had agreed, but only on condition he promised to call the police. Not in the morning, as soon as they hung up. Paul promised he would.

Now it seemed foolish to just sit here and let him deal with it on his own. She loved her husband, but recently he seemed increasingly distracted. Nearly forgetting to pick Perry up. Leaving Jeannie alone in the car in a public place in the dead of winter, not to mention cutting off a hank of her hair. Something was happening with him, she knew, but hadn't the slightest clue what it could be. And now someone had broken into their home on top of it. The world had slewed sideways over the past month.

"Everything's going to be all right," she told her old house, as if the walls had ears. They didn't, but they did have memories. Happy, secure childhood memories. Maybe those memories could hear her. Maybe they could console.

Michelle rolled over on her side, staring into the darkness, and at last closed her eyes.

She told her parents about Paul's pre-dawn call while the kids ate breakfast in the other room.

"Lady footprints, eh?" Ned said. "You sure your guy isn't dancing in someone else's disco?"

"Daddy, jeez."

"Pay no attention to your father," Darlene said, sipping from a tall glass of orange juice Michelle suspected may have been spiked with vodka. She knew her mother's penchant for mimosas. "If Paul says he has it under control, he has it under control. He's a good man, your husband."

"Why don't you call him back and find out what the police had to say?" her dad suggested.

"I tried calling three times already. Goes straight to voicemail."

"Well, the best thing to do is relax. There's no time to worry until it's time to worry," Darlene said. "Here, let me fix you breakfast."

"I couldn't eat a bite, Mother."

"Nonsense. Never a Craycraft existed who could refuse a hot breakfast, isn't that right, dear heart?" Darlene asked her husband, patting his belly.

"She's got a point, Shelly," Ned conceded before launching into another Ned Craycraft patented saying. "Come on, I could eat a horse. Neigh, I could eat the whole stable."

Darlene and Michelle offered their usual groan at the Ned-ism and went into the kitchen. Michelle picked at her pancakes—*flopcakes*, her father corrected, when she misspoke—with her phone resting beside her plate.

Chapter Twenty-Four

Paul had no intention of calling the police, of course. After his brush with Detective Sanders, he'd had enough with cops for a while. He moved room to room, looking for any barefoot woman who may be hiding. He even checked the attic crawlspace. The house was empty. It didn't add up. If not for the muddy prints staining his linoleum, he might have thought he'd dreamt it, as Michelle suggested.

That was the other thing: the prints started at the kitchen door and ended at the stove. No mud tracked through from either the front door or back. As if the intruder had simply appeared in the kitchen and disappeared when she'd heard him coming.

Paul found his phone, opened the camera app, and snapped some shots of the prints. Just in case. He flicked through them one by one in hopes of picking up something in them he couldn't see with his naked eye. He hadn't consciously considered this to be anything paranormal, but it couldn't hurt to try. The try turned out to be in vain. They prints appeared exactly in his phone's gallery as they did in reality.

He was about to shut down the gallery when he noticed an image which hadn't been there before, stuck between one of Jeannie attempting to twirl a baton and the first of the footprint images. Paul tapped it and could only stare.

The image was dark and grainy from being snapped sans flash, but it was clear enough. It was a photo of him, taken from behind, as he walked down the stairs of Lucine's house toward her kitchen. Enough detail had been picked out in the glow of his flashlight to confirm it: the wood banister, the shag-carpeted steps, the back of his dyed hair in sharp relief. Someone had stood behind him on the landing and snapped a picture with his phone.

The thought of the hair attached to the cold head recurred. Paul shuddered. Maybe whoever it was hadn't been dead. But who had it been? Certainly not Lucine—she was still out of town until Friday (or so she'd claimed). So who could it have been? A house-sitter? If so, where had she been while he'd been uploading photos of sex toys?

Paul deleted the picture. He got out a bucket and filled it with water and Mop 'n Glo, cleaned up the muddy tracks, and dumped the contents down the toilet. Then he checked all the doors and windows to ensure they were locked. Nothing out of place. Not a damned thing.

He decided he was hungry enough to finish off his egg roll. Something occurred to him as it heated. The microwave dinged, he grabbed his food, and carried it to his office.

A pile of shipping labels lay stacked on the printer's tray. Hundreds of dollars' worth, already purchased via his PayPal account. That took most of what he'd earned through the first batch of stolen toys, and he couldn't get at the ones he'd left behind in Lucine's house. Going back would simply be too risky.

"Son of a bitch," he growled, reviewing his gutted account. The balance now stood at $129.53—barely enough to cover the water bill.

He sat staring at the screen as he chewed through the egg roll as if willing the money back into his account. When he finished, he looked for a way to cancel the postage but found no means by which to do so. Wasted money.

It wasn't your money to begin with, that little voice in his head commented. *You're nothing more than a common thief.*

Paul fired the food wrapper into the trashcan and returned to the kitchen, fuming. He dug out the fortune cookie and cracked it open, half-expecting the message inside to say something like *The foolish man winds up in sheep dip* or *Man who plays with matches will always burn fingers* or even a simple *You're fucked*. But the message he received seemed more optimistic, at least on first blush: *Something wonderful is going to happen*, it read.

Yes, and the something wonderful was going to be returning to his life as he'd known it before Lucine Korth. No more stalking with phony profiles, no more breaking and entering, no more one-night stands. He'd lost his grip, he understood that much, but now it was high time he found it again. He needed to rebuild his online reputation, needed to find steady work, needed a return of familial stability. He merely had to forget Lucine Korth existed. All his problems solved.

Easier said than done, as the adage goes.

The next two days passed without incident. Paul remained on-track to bring his life back into balance. He deactivated all fake profiles across the board, including the freelance sites. He actively worked to rebuild his real profile by severely slashing his bids to the point where he'd practically lose money on them. A few clients bit and he spent Wednesday writing for cooking blogs and a smattering of SEO articles. The money was ludicrously low, but it was a start.

He dropped the sex toys into a large box scrounged from the basement and drove them to a dumpster outside an apartment complex on Woodbury Street. He destroyed the printed postage labels in his office shredder. He kept the reading glasses because he needed them to read now.

The number with the foreign code called twice again, both on Wednesday night. Paul ignored the calls. Telemarketers were the last thing he needed to deal with now.

He spoke to Michelle each day, and he'd managed to convince her everything on the home front had been quiet even if the police had no leads. The kids seemed to be having a wonderful time in Springfield and everything seemed to be balancing out nicely. Paul felt a relief so deep it was nearly palpable.

Then, on Thursday morning, New Year's Eve Day, Michelle called with panic barbing her voice. "I got a call late last night from someone who said she needed to speak with you about an urgent matter."

"Okay, calm down. Did they say what that matter might be?" he asked, feeling his own panic rise. Had someone found out about what he'd been up to? The LWPD? If so, why hadn't they come to him directly?

"No, but she sounded distinctly European. German, maybe. Or Austrian. She said she needed to speak with you at once."

The international caller. Whoever it was had contacted his wife as well in order to try to raise him. Son of a bitch. If this had anything to do with Lucine Korth, which he somehow knew it would, he hated that they'd drawn Michelle into it. Now he'd have to think of some explanation. Christ, *why* had he gotten mixed up with her?

But he hadn't, not really. He'd merely gotten mixed up with a name, a face. Nothing more. He'd never laid eyes on the real Lucine Korth, just some digitized, pixelated version of her. Was she captivatingly, enchantingly beautiful? Without a doubt. But he'd not so much as heard her speak a single syllable. How had this gotten so far out of control?

"Okay, can you give me the number?" he asked, though he already knew he had it in his call history. He didn't want to sound worried to Michelle. He would take care of this and be done with it for good.

She rattled off the string of numerals. "Once you figure out what this is about, call me. Okay, Paul? This is scaring me."

"Nothing to be scared about. Probably a client wanting clarification on a project or something. I've had quite a few lately."

"Just keep me posted."

He promised he would, and she seemed content to let it drop.

"Have you figured out what you're doing tonight yet?" she asked.

"Hell, I'll probably just get some more work done and pop a bottle of Brut Extra Dry at midnight."

"That sounds boring. What are Sean and Jerome up to?"

"Get this. They're taking the NYE Magical Midnight Cruise on the lake. Can you believe it? It's actually called the fucking NYE Magical Midnight Cruise."

"Yeah, you'll have more fun proofreading."

"Tell me about it," he said. "Listen, I know your folks are throwing that party tonight, so just try to have a fun time. I'll check in with you later, okay?"

"Okay. Love you."

"Love you, too. Happy New Year."

They hung up. Paul hesitated before pulling the foreign number up from his history. The phone purred in his ear. After a dozen rings, someone answered. A man, not a woman. His accent certainly sounded Germanic, though he spoke English. And he spoke to Paul by name.

"Hello, Mr. Jeske," he said. "How good of you to finally feel compelled to return our call."

"I don't answer calls from numbers I don't know."

"You Americans are a paranoid lot, no?"

"My wife said someone wished to speak with me. You've got me. Speak."

"Alas, the person who wishes to converse is currently unavailable. I shall have her return your call at the earliest possible convenience."

Paul gritted his teeth. "That might not work, chief," he said. "I'm a very busy man and tonight's a holiday."

"Nonetheless, I'm certain you'll find time. The conversation is of utmost urgency." A pregnant pause. "To you and your family."

Paul's mouth dried so quickly he could barely get out a response. "What did you say? Who the hell are you? What is this about?"

"Be available to answer the telephone, Mr. Jeske, when it happens to ring. Good day and happy New Year to you and yours."

The call dropped. He tried redialing the number, but it went unanswered. Paul paced his office, gripping the phone so tight his knuckles went white. He slung it onto his desk and dropped into his chair. God, he just wished this could all be over with. If this was the something wonderful preordained by the fortune cookie, he'd never eat Chinese again.

Chapter Twenty-Five

Paul kept busy. He vacuumed and dusted the entire house. He stacked dishes in the dishwasher. He cleaned out the fridge. The fucking busted shutter finally got nailed back into place. It felt good, like a king taking back his castle from enemy invaders. With the housework complete, he finally settled in his office chair and opened the file ROSETHORN.doc. He thought he'd be too keyed up to write but found the opposite true. Whoever this caller turned out to be, she would be dealt with accordingly. It didn't matter—what mattered was getting his life back together and he'd gone a long way to making that happen on the final day of the year. Perfect timing for a fresh start.

Paul wrote for a solid three hours without pause. At first he thought about changing the name of the witch terrorizing Rosethorn from Ethel Parks to Lucine Korth, but realized how stupid that would be—it would prove a connection if the matter ever came under investigation.

Young, beautiful Ethel was in the middle of enchanting Sheriff Norton into unlocking her jail cell after she'd landed herself there for stealing herbs out of Dawn Stallworth's garden when the phone shrilled on his desk. Paul jumped; he'd already forgotten all about the expected call.

Night had spread across the office window. Flurries fluttered against the glass like icy albino moths. Paul took a breath and answered.

"Mr. Jeske," a smoky female voice glazed in a thick accent said. "At last, we get to speak and none too soon at that."

"You didn't leave a voicemail. I don't call numbers I don't recognize unless someone leaves a message."

"So I gathered. However, my voice may not be recorded nor may any portion of our conversation. Is that quite clear?"

"Look, what is this about? I'm sick of all the mystery."

"I asked if that was quite clear?"

"Yes, it is. Now speak or I'm hanging up."

"That would be ill-advised, Mr. Jeske."

"I'm losing my patience. Tell me who I'm speaking with, or I'll call the authorities for harassment."

The woman laughed. "Is police entanglement really something you feel you can afford at this juncture?"

"Last chance, lady. Tell me what you're selling, or I'm gone."

"Mr. Jeske, I'm not selling anything. I'm giving."

"Giving what?"

"I'm giving you a second chance, Mr. Jeske. And since I'm the only way that will happen, I suggest you take it."

"Tell me your name."

"My name is of no significance, but if it will help you may refer to me Ms. Bloch."

"And whom do you represent, Ms. Bloch?"

"I head a very old organization called the Congregation of Sacred Splendor. We are based in Vienna. The reason we are contacting you is because you were witnessed in attendance at a branch of Haven Revival Church. Is this correct?"

"The sign out front says it's an open and affirming church."

"So you confirm our sources are correct?"

"Yes, I attended a service there once."

"Why?"

"I was curious. In this country, there's such a thing as religious freedom, Ms. Bloch."

"Please answer the question, Mr. Jeske. Why did you abruptly decide to attend your local branch of Haven Revival?"

"I already told you. I was curious."

"No one persuaded you?"

"Hell no. I saw their website and thought it might be a good fit for our family."

"Yes, your family. Let's talk about them. You've been thinking about switching houses of worship? You've discussed it?"

"I think I've answered all the questions I'm going to answer, Ms. Bloch. Happy New Year."

"Mr. Jeske, please understand we have only your best interests at heart. And the best interests of Michelle, Perry, and Jean."

Paul's finger, which had been moving to end the call, stopped. "What did you say?"

"We aren't sure you're aware of exactly with whom you're meddling, Mr. Jeske."

"How did you know the names of my children?"

"We take situations such as yours very seriously," the woman identifying herself as Ms. Bloch said. "Our organization feels strongly about warning potential new members against joining."

"Why? What's the matter with Haven Revival?"

Ms. Bloch answered with a question of her own. "What impressions did you take away from your visit this Sunday last?"

"I thought the whole thing was pretty weird, to be honest."

"Do you intend to return?"

"Not a chance."

"Good. Our sources indicate greater than fifty-two percent of new attendees become indoctrinated upon first visit. You avoided the status quo, Mr. Jeske."

"What makes the place so bad?" Paul asked, genuinely curious. "And how did you know I was there?"

"Haven Revival has its roots in Eastern Europe. It—or some iteration of it—has existed since the days Christ walked the planet and most assuredly earlier. Along the way, the church's ideologies evolved. Eventually they became twisted."

"From my perspective, that holds true of most religious ideologies."

"This goes beyond simple meandering interpretations of scripture, Mr. Jeske. Haven Revival's mother church has branched into morally and legally questionable practices, according to the myriad ongoing investigations we've opened."

"Since when did speaking in tongues become illegal?"

Ms. Bloch offered a humorless chuckle. "That's only the part the general congregation gets to see. It's the practices going on behind the curtain that move into darker territory."

"Well, you've sold me. I won't be returning to Haven Chapel, I can assure you."

"That's uplifting, truly." She paused. "But I must insist you reveal the identity of the person who turned you in Haven's direction."

"I told you. The website."

"Mr. Jeske, don't not play me for a fool. It was a woman, wasn't it?"

"I don't think I'm comfortable with this discussion any longer."

"Give me her name." Ms. Bloch's tone held no room for debate. Paul either had to give a name or hang up.

"If I tell you, I want your guarantee you'll never contact me or my family again in any capacity."

Her voice softened. A little. "It will be as though this call never took place."

"First tell me why you're so itchy to know who pointed me toward the church?"

"Haven Revival uses quiet recruitment methods. I won't go into their means, but it's usually women involved in the process. These women are quite dangerous, Mr. Jeske, and my organization needs to keep track of them via strict contact tracing."

"What will happen to her?"

"That's of no concern to you."

He started to argue, then reconsidered. "Fine. But if you so much as misdial my number, I'll have you in court so fast your eyes will roll out of your head."

"Acknowledged."

"Her name is Viola Datsun."

"Thank you. Where does she live?"

Paul paused, licking his lower lip. "How would I know?"

"I asked you not to play me the fool, Mr. Jeske."

How could she possibly know I slept with her? he wondered. Something occurred to him, though. What's the worst that would happen? Viola might disappear? Ms. Bloch's people might come snatch her out of her crappy apartment and drag her across the ocean to Europe? That would actually solve a problem—he wouldn't have to worry about running into a one-night stand while out on the town with his family.

"Mr. Jeske?" Ms. Bloch prompted. He gave her the address without another thought. "Very good. One final thing before we end the call."

"Yes?"

"How do you feel?"

159

"Come again?"

"Are you healthy?"

"As a horse. Why?"

"You may have dodged a bullet, as you Americans are fond of saying. Good evening, Mr. Jeske. May the coming year bring you something wonderful."

Something wonderful. Like the fortune cookie.

"What did you say?" he demanded.

The call dropped. He tried redialing, but the connection would not go through—as if the number itself had abruptly been terminated.

No amount of digging online could turn up a single shred of information regarding any organization called the Congregation of Sacred Splendor. Nor anything deeper about Haven Revival that didn't appear on their website. If this all came down to some kind of denominational dispute between churches, Paul was glad to be done with it.

Chapter Twenty-Six

He took a walk to clear his head, kicking through two inches of new snow covering the sidewalks. The temperature had bottomed out around the freezing mark. Paul hunched deeper into his coat against the chill.

Before he realized it, he'd made it downtown. He had decided to let the Ben Gehant project slide away along with Lucine Korth as a means of getting back to normal, but now curiosity took over. Gehant's new apartment following his separation was above Chico's Mexican Cuisine just up the block. Paul moved toward it to see what he could see. Maybe he'd stop in for a few pre-New Year tacos. Chico's made the best in town, with the perfect amount of fresh cilantro and shredded smoky Gouda.

The iron staircase bolted to the restaurant's brick exterior was frosted over. Paul gripped the cold banister and looked up at the peeling door with the number 3 stenciled on. The adjacent window was dark. He wondered what Mr. Gehant might be up to tonight.

Probably downloading freaky fetish porn, Paul thought grimly. The smoldering rage he'd tried to smother returned when he remembered how the man had scared Jeannie and subsequently threatened Paul.

But he didn't *scare Jeannie,* another part of his mind countered. Jeannie had confirmed as much. Still, the son of a bitch *had* threatened him.

Let it go, the rational side of his brain pleaded.

Paul drew his hand away from the railing and stepped into the restaurant.

♀

"Well, look who it is," someone said when Paul stepped up to the bar. "Mr. Family Man."

Paul turned, his wallet halfway out of his pocket. The bartender was helping a woman at the far end, but it looked as though Ben Gehant hadn't suffered from lack of service. A shot of tequila and a Tecate stood on a coaster before him. His eyes were bloodshot, and his misshapen nose looked red and bloated like a vine-ripe tomato. He appeared to have aged ten years since they'd last met.

"Mr. Gehant," Paul said, extending a hand. "Good to see you again."

"I kind of doubt that," Gehant said, ignoring the hand.

"Look, I think we got off on the wrong foot—"

"You're damned right we did. I should have called the cops that day." He half-turned in his stool and called to the scant patrons. "Hey, did you know this guy leaves his kids alone in a running car?"

No one looked around, probably because the words came out as mostly indecipherable mush.

"I don't think that's necessary, do you, Mr. Gehant?" Paul said, copping the adjacent stool.

"I don't give a fuck what you think, buddy."

Paul lowered his voice. "Look, I know you're hurting. Because of the divorce."

Gehant looked sharply over, overcompensated, almost dropped off his stool, jaw working like a cow at its cud. He struggled to focus on Paul's face, the eyes rolling and crossing. He'd about hit his limit, that much was clear. This could be a perfect opportunity.

Paul leaned in. "Why'd she toss you? Couldn't wiggle the pickle anymore? Or were you beating on little Benny Junior? Maybe I should be the one calling Family Services."

Gehant uttered a single choked syllable and climbed to his feet, ready to swing, but was clearly in no condition to fight. Instead of throwing a punch, he threw up on his shoes.

"Whoopsie daisy," Paul said.

"You sumbitch," Gehant exhaled, his breath a fetid mix of vomit and agave.

"Let me help you home," Paul said, slinging Gehant's arm over his shoulders and drawing the ski mask over his face. A barback, probably a college kid, came to swab up the mess. "I'll be back to pay his tab," Paul told him.

"Don't worry about it," the college kid said. "Mr. Gehant always pays in full Sunday nights."

"A regular, is he?"

"You bet."

"Listen, we're old friends. I'm going to see him home. I'd be grateful if you had half a dozen tacos ready for pickup when I return."

"Crispy or soft?"

"Soft shell all the way."

"You got it. Name?"

"Tom. Tom Rood," Paul said, the lie feeling natural and automatic on his lips. He'd gotten pretty good at this scheming shit. Paul hauled Gehant out the door and, with some difficulty, managed to get him up the stairs to his apartment. He patted around the man's pockets until he found a set of keys and unlocked the door.

The place was a studio with a hide-a-bed sofa pulled out and an ancient TV atop a rolling microwave stand.

"Man, you're really living the high life, Benjamin," Paul proclaimed, dumping the guy face down on the mattress and toeing the door closed behind him. "This is precisely the kind of fall from grace I wished on you, my friend, did you know that? Karma is definitely a sawdust-on-the-floor whore, ain't she?"

Gehant uttered something between a grunt and a snore. Another cursory search of the man's pockets turned up a scuffed leather billfold stuffed with cash. Payday for Paulie.

Paul poked around the studio while Gehant snored his way into hangover hell. He riffled through his host's mail, tearing up some utility bills and a renewal notice for a newspaper subscription, dropped the pieces into the toilet, and flushed. Gehant's Visa, Amex, and Discover cards met with a pair of scissors scrounged from a kitchen drawer. Ditto his driver's license, the shards dumped into the nearest heating vent.

He found the man's cell phone, called up the contact list, and sent an obscenity-laced threatening text to the impending ex-Mrs. Gehant before dropping the device and driving the heel of his boot into the screen three times and then a fourth for good measure. He found a laptop beneath the bed, opened the Documents folder, and permanently deleted all the contents. Disappointingly, the computer seemed devoid of illegal porn—he would have loved nothing more than to call Detective Sanders with an anonymous tip from the payphone in Chico's lounge.

The only other item of interest—and of personal interest to Paul, no less—was a familiar picture tacked to a corkboard in the kitchenette. It was a computer print-out of Lucine Korth. The one of her in cutoff shorts and checkered shirt. Paul's favorite. Apparently she was Lake Winona's best-kept secret. The idea she may have been the cause of Gehant's marital woes never occurred to Paul.

"Benjamin, I have to say I admire your taste in women," Paul said. He leaned in close to the sleeping man's ear and said, "Don't even fucking think about it, asshole. She's mine."

Then he did his best to wipe down everything he'd touched with his sleeve before dropping everything he'd broken into the trash bag and taking it with him out the door, satisfied he'd exacted all the revenge he needed. He dropped the bag in the dumpster behind the restaurant and went inside to collect his dinner.

"Think he'll live?" the barback asked with a grin when Paul reappeared.

"He'll wish he was dead tomorrow, that's for sure," Paul replied from behind his mask. He paid for the tacos with a stolen fifty-dollar bill and told the college kid to keep the change.

"Wow, thanks, man," the kid said.

"Don't mention it," Paul said.

He ate two of the tacos on the walk home, relishing the way they steamed in the winter air and filled his belly with spicy fire. So much for going good; being bad felt so much better. He only had the remainder of the weekend to do it, and he refused to waste it.

Fuck it. Fuck everything.

Chapter Twenty-Seven

He washed down the tacos with a beer. Then another. He dressed in his best club attire (based on what he'd seen the kids wearing upon his first visit to Cabana Girls), gelled his newly-dyed hair to the max, and squirted on a generous dash of cologne. He dabbed more of Shell's skin cream around his eyes, swished a mouthful of Listerine, and dug out some of the douchey thumb rings he'd worn during his college days. Yep, he could pass for someone five years younger. At least, he hoped, in chancy nightclub light. It wasn't as though he was all that older than the target clientele, anyway, right? It had been less than a decade since he was one of them.

He drove to Cabana Girls without a care in the world, windows down, radio up. This was his time, goddammit, this was *Paulie* time. There would be plenty of time to play family man for the rest of his life. Or not. Who knew anymore? Hell, he might even give Viola another spin—she'd taken a lot out of him, but she'd been a hell of a lay.

Except Viola wasn't there. Paul made it past the bouncer with no trouble this time—the frat boy disguise duped him, at least—but when he merged with the throng and made his rounds, could not spot Viola nowhere. Maybe she had the night off. But what pseudo-titty-club server would want New Year's Eve off? With as much cash transacting in here, Paul would consider donning a wig and a bra.

He approached a questionable-looking blonde server and said, "Excuse me, is Viola working tonight?"

She shook her head, spraying frosted locks in all directions. "Sorry, hon. She didn't show tonight. Can I get you a drink?"

Paul ordered a whiskey sour and paid with Ben Gehant's cash. He may have fooled the bouncer, but the club kids seemed to smell his age. They flowed around him and away like river water around a rotten log. He tried smiling at a pretty brunette, but she only sneered and turned away. He finished his drink and pushed away from his table, deciding he'd find a bar more suited to his tastes.

"It's a two-drink minimum," the server said as he headed for the door.

"Are you shitting me? I already paid a fifteen-dollar cover just to step foot in this hole."

"I don't make the rules."

"So break them."

"Sorry. Can't."

Paul opened his wallet and thrust a ten at her. "You're not going to get very far in life if you're always following someone else's orders."

"Thanks, Dad," she said, taking the bill. She returned five minutes later with another drink. Paul contemplated tossing it in her face but tried a different tack instead. "What say we go back to your place after your shift."

The server curled her lip, an unconscious gesture of revulsion. As though she'd rather fuck a rattlesnake than consider taking Paul Jeske to bed. "I have a boyfriend," she said, recovering quickly.

"Fuck your boyfriend."

"I plan to," she said, turning away. "After my shift."

Paul watched her bitterly over his glass and when he finished his drink, whipped it to the floor. People danced away from the spray of glass. Someone called him an expletive he'd never heard before.

He sauntered out of the place, vowing never to return. At least he had decided where his next stop would be, and he drove the distance to Viola's apartment in fuming silence.

Paul didn't know what to expect when he got there, only that what he found wasn't it even if it should have been.

Her door stood ajar, darkness swimming inside like the ocean floor. Paul reached in and flipped the foyer switch.

"Ms. Datsun?" he called, but they'd had sex. Using her first name had been earned. "Viola?"

He entered. The place had been wrecked: furniture overturned, television toppled onto the carpet, bathroom door smashed in. A window in the living room had been shattered, shards of glass littering the sill and sofa.

"Holy shit," Paul muttered, skirting an end table with a busted leg. It looked like every cop show he'd ever seen where a burglar had ransacked someone's home. He stopped in the kitchenette. A splotch of something he took to be blood the size of a medium pizza adorned the back wall, clumps of hair sprouting from it. Black hair with blonde highlights.

Paul covered his mouth to hold in a scream. He found his phone and dialed 911 before hitting END. He couldn't call emergency services. Not from his phone. He couldn't have his name or face tied up in this.

He backed out of the apartment and hurried around the corner to a drugstore with a payphone bolted to the brickwork and called the cops from there.

Detective Sanders arrived ten minutes later with a partner—a tall, pretty woman—and three uniformed officers in tow. They toured the premises. The unis milled around outside the door, smoking and swearing, as if awaiting permission to enter.

Paul watched them from the shadowed steps of an apartment complex across the street, ski mask in place. The cement froze through his jeans, numbing his ass. He had given his name as Ben Gehant when the operator had asked for it. Let Sanders chew on that for a while and let Gehant choke on it.

They hung around inside the apartment another ten minutes before Sanders brought something outside, clutched in forceps. Paul couldn't tell what it was from that distance, but both plainclothes and uniformed cops seemed interested; they all leaned over to examine it. Then Sanders produced a plastic bag and dropped the article inside. Hopefully they'd found evidence of whoever had abducted—or worse, murdered—Viola. Paul wished her no harm.

Then what did you intend to do when you got to her place? that nagging voice in his mind asked.

He found he had no honest answer to the query.

The cops sealed Viola's apartment door with crime scene tape and then prepared to depart.

Paul's cell phone, gripped in his fist like a talisman, rang then. He'd jacked the ringer all the way up at the club in case Michelle called and the sudden shrill startled him into dropping it. It clattered down the concrete steps to the sidewalk, still braying, its display screen bright as noonday sun. Across the street, the cops looked up.

"Excuse me, sir, may we have a word with you?" Sanders called, heading over.

Paul jumped down the stairs, retrieved his phone, and rushed up again. If he ran down the street, the cadre of cops would head him off and have him cuffed before he made it to Wilson Street. He prayed this complex didn't keep their entrances security-locked.

It didn't. In this part of town, it wasn't much of a surprise. Paul rushed down a corridor lit with a buzzing, blinking track of fluorescent bulbs and smelling heavily of radishes. The door wheezed shut behind him on its pneumatic arm. Soon enough, Sanders & Co. would tear it open again in hot pursuit of what they'd likely consider their prime suspect. If they caught him, game over—it wouldn't matter that he'd never laid a hand on Viola except when laying her.

Paul found a steel door marked STAIRS and slid inside, taking them upward two at a time. Someone bellowed behind him, but whether it had come from a cop or a resident he couldn't tell.

He dodged around the second-floor landing and up to the third. Then the fourth. The building topped out on the fifth and when he reached it, he pushed into the corridor. Sweat slithered down his sides. He tried to appear as if he belonged, adopting a casual gait. Doors painted industrial gray stretched out before him. The threadbare carpet had worn through in places. Someone's television blared a beer ad.

Paul tried to steady his breathing. He needed to think. Most likely, the cops had all exits covered by now, with backup on the way.

He hurried to the door beneath the glowing EXIT sign at the other end of the hall and shoved it open. Voices drifted up from below.

"Second floor, clear," a cop called.

Only three floors remained between Paul and a turn in a county jail cell. And divorce court, don't forget about that. He jogged back the way he'd come.

A door on his left opened onto a small laundry complete with a pair of coin-op washer-dryer combos and a dispenser selling single-serve packets of Tide. One of the dryers was nearing the end of its cycle. A plastic basket with the number 522 stenciled on it stood nearby. He hauled open the washer door and dropped hot, damp clothes into the basket. Then he found apartment 522 and knocked.

"Who the hell is it?" a man called. Old and tired, by the sound. Good.

"Pardon me, sir, but someone threw your laundry all over the place. I picked it up for you."

Footsteps sounded from the staircases on either end of the corridor. He had ten seconds, fifteen at best.

"Again?" the old man hollered and dragged the door open. He looked even older than he sounded, but he grabbed the basket with surprising strength. "I bet it's that Ramsey kid. Goddamn teenage pranksters."

Paul shoved the man inside and eased the door closed behind him, throwing the bolt and sliding the chain.

"What the hell's this about?" the apartment-dweller asked. His eyes held not an ounce of fear in their brown depths. Probably an Army vet who'd seen his share of terror. He wore stained boxer shorts and a white strappy T. His hair stood in white spikes like stalactites, and he towed an oxygen tank behind him like a steel dog. A rerun of *Cheers* played on a 17-inch TV situated on a scuffed chest of drawers.

"Listen, I don't want to be a bother, but I need a place to hang out for a few minutes."

"Like hell you are," the man said.

"Sir, I'm really trying to be polite about this."

"No one barges in on me, you punk-ass motherfucker. Get on out of here 'fore I call the cops."

"The cops are already here," Paul said.

The old man squinted. "A troublemaker, are you?"

"No, sir. A case of mistaken identity."

"That's what they all say." He stared hard at Paul's face. "This wouldn't have anything to do with what went on across the way, does it?"

"I don't know anything about that. The cops think I do, though."

The man cracked a smile, displaying shockingly white teeth for a man of his age. "You know more than you're letting on, I'd wager."

"Come again?"

"It was Viola's place that got busted into, ain't it? They didn't get away with much, I guarantee it."

"You know Viola?"

"Know her?" he cackled, a horrid, baked sound. "I'm one of her regulars. Or I was, anyway."

Paul gaped, not understanding. "You go to Cabana Girls?"

"You ain't as smart as you look, kid. But I see it in your eyes—you've climbed into Vi's bed a time or two. Don't deny it. I can tell. I can see it as plain as if you'd written it on your face."

"How the hell do you know that?" Paul breathed.

"Listen, kid, pull up a stool and relax. I ain't rat you out, don't worry about that. I want you to hear a story. It's one you're going to want to hear if you're one of Vi's."

Paul did as bid, finding an ottoman with cracked upholstery. Outside, perhaps halfway down the corridor, an officer called, "Fifth floor, clear!"

"How long do you think before they start knocking on doors?" he asked his host.

The old man waved it away. "Even if they do, you can go stand in the shower until they leave. I won't rat on you, don't worry. Not one of Vi's. Hell, we're practically brothers now. Tell me something, though, before I begin."

"If I can."

"Is she okay?"

Paul took a deep breath. "I don't know. I went to see her, and she was gone."

The old man nodded as if this was to be expected. He snapped off the TV before settling into an armchair. "She doesn't stick around anyplace long, but she usually comes back. Make yourself comfortable and hear me out."

Chapter Twenty-Eight

Michelle couldn't sleep. She checked the kids and went to the kitchen. This was the third consecutive night, and it was beginning to take its toll. She wished she could blame homesickness. Since they'd left Lake Winona, Michelle felt the rift between her and Paul growing. They say absence makes the heart grow fonder, but this seemed to be a case of out of sight, out of mind. She still loved him—that much she knew—but something had changed between them, perhaps unalterably. The idea unsettled her, made her queasy.

Michelle found a can of ginger ale and sipped it at the sink. The backyard she'd spent so many hours playing in during her youth lay shrouded in pre-dawn shadow. The crescent moon dangled on the horizon like a frozen omen.

The New Year's Eve party had gone terribly, at least for her. Fifty people, give or take, had crowded into the Craycraft abode. They'd had to crowd because while the house certainly had the capability of comfortably holding that number, her folks had cordoned off all but the living and dining room. Smokers were required to step onto the patio into the chill night air and deposit their butts in a sand-filled crock designated for such.

Everything had been going as expected until Tom Rood showed up.

It had been Emily's doing. Emily had always thought Michelle and Tom should have remained together. *The cutest couple on campus*, she'd often gush.

She'd said hello graciously to her long-ago boyfriend, then asked to speak with Emily upstairs.

"I thought upstairs was off-limits," Emily had said.

"I'm making an exception," Michelle replied, dragging her friend by the sleeve of her silk blouse.

"Will you also be making an exception for Tom tonight?" Emily taunted.

That had been the trigger that detonated the Shelly-bomb. She laid into Emily for ten minutes, admonishing her for inviting her ex to a party at a house where her children slept.

"I'm married, Em, goddammit. I moved on from Tom a long fucking time ago. Why can't you get that through your head?"

Emily had only shrugged and smiled. "No one's telling you what to do with him. For all I care, you can ignore him the whole night and send him home with hurt feelings."

"You're a bitch, you know that?"

Emily had chimed laughter. "You're goddamn right I do. I didn't get this far in life playing pretty-pretty-princess."

Of course, Michelle hadn't ignored him. In fact, they'd enjoyed a nice chat out on the patio, the steam from their breaths rising and twining into the starry sky. At midnight, he hadn't even tried to kiss her but instead offered a Tom Rood bear hug, which she accepted. She would never admit it to Emily, but being back in his arms and breathing his scent did have a certain appeal. She missed him, at least on some perfunctory level steeped in nostalgia. Tom was an undeniable part of her life, her pathway to adulthood. He'd been the second of only three men with whom she'd shared her body.

Michelle would be a liar if she didn't admit to herself she'd thought of asking her parents to watch the kids overnight and going home with him. But it hadn't happened. They'd said goodnight in the doorway beneath the sprig of mistletoe and when they both looked up at it sheepishly, Tom had taken the reins and shaken her hand. That had been it, end of story. But her brief thought of infidelity led, of course, back to Paul.

Who had the woman caller been, the one who'd wanted to speak with her husband? The one with the accent that somehow reminded her of every bad Gestapo movie she'd ever seen? And why hadn't Paul called back to update her? This, she realized, was the root of her issue with him: his damnable secretiveness of late. His deliberate distance from her and the kids. Something odious was happening—whether an affair or something worse—and she feared it would be the end of the family they'd worked to cultivate. Strange how everything you believe stable in the world can skew so swiftly. It's something you can hardly believe is real, like the Earth's wobble.

As if on cue, her phone buzzed. Paul. Thank God. She answered, sounding curter than intended.

"Hi, babe. I was going to leave a voicemail."

"It's okay. I wasn't sleeping." She dropped the ball in his court, waited for him to pick it up.

"Listen, I'm sorry. It's been a hellishly long day."

I'll bet it has, lover boy, she thought, but said instead: "Is that right?"

"Anyway, I wanted to tell you what the strange call was all about—"

"And you waited until now to do so?"

"I fell asleep. As I said, it was a long day," he replied, his voice carefully neutral.

Too carefully, she thought. "So who was it?"

"A telemarketer from Vienna. I guess our name somehow got on some product list that made it overseas. Didn't you order some of that cold cream from that infomercial last month?"

The bastard is actually trying to blame this on me, Michelle thought. Fury rose in her throat like hot bile. "You're lying," she said simply. "You're flat-out lying, Paul, and I fucking know it."

A startled pause from the Lake Winona end of the line. When her husband spoke again, it hardly sounded like him. "Okay, listen up. If you want to entertain some half-assed delusion that a phone call was something more than just a call, that's on you. If you don't believe me, call the fucking number back. I will not be accused of something at this ungodly hour by an ungrateful, suspicious, paranoid *bitch*."

The call dropped as dead as the old year. Michelle, stunned, stared at the phone. They'd had their share of disagreements over the course of their marriage, including one screaming match that had resulted in police contact, but she'd never heard him use that cold, dead tone before. It was far worse than when he raised his voice. To her, it implied a severance, a turning away. And as the final bullet in the head, he'd called her a *bitch*. Part of the reason she'd married him was because of his reputation around campus as Mr. Nice Guy—all the ladies loved him. He held doors for people, stepped aside to let someone pass, said *Excuse me*, *Please*, and *Thank you* automatically as if those words had been etched in his genes. Paul could have had his pick of the student body. He'd chosen her. And she'd chosen him. In all their time together, she'd never once heard him use a disparaging word against a woman, least of all her.

More hurt than she thought possible, Michelle placed the phone on the table. She didn't cry. A year ago—hell, a month ago—she would have. But not this day. Not now.

She found a quiet corner of the house and dialed a number from memory. It rang twice before being answered.

"Hi, Tom. It's Shelly. I know it's late and you just left. But are you busy right now?"

Chapter Twenty-Nine

The old man's name was Major Stanley Olson, U.S. Army, retired, though he claimed he wasn't very old at all.

"Go on, guess my age," he challenged. The oxygen tank beside him snuffed.

Paul rubbed his jaw. "I don't see what this has to do with Viola."

"It has everything to do with her. Go on, guess."

"I don't know. Sixty?" Paul guessed, though he'd pulled his punch. Stanley looked seventy if he looked a day.

"Fifty-two years old come May."

Paul opened his mouth, then closed it again, unsure what to say.

Olson laughed. "I know what you're thinking. I haven't aged well. Don't worry, I won't hold it against you." He sobered and leaned forward in his chair. "But if you don't want to share my fate, you'll want to hear about Vi."

"I'm all ears."

"Good. This may take some time. And you may want a drink for it."

"I think I've had enough to drink tonight."

"I'm guessing you'll change your mind before we're through."

"Major Olson, what's this all about?"

"I'm retired. Just plain Stan will do."

"Okay, Stan."

"Tell me your name."

Paul hesitated, trying to decide whether to lie. "Ben Gehant," he said at last.

"Bullshit. I know Ben."

Paul took a breath. "Fine. My name's Paul Jeske. You're friends with Ben?"

"Hell, no. Ben Gehant is the biggest prick I've ever had the displeasure of meeting."

"I concur."

Olson grinned, displaying those pearly teeth—the only part of him that didn't seem positively ancient. "You and I are going to get along fine, Paul. Now listen up. It's story time. You feel free to interrupt whenever you like, especially if you change your mind on that drink. Wait one while I fix my own."

Paul waited, sitting tall and straight on the ottoman, an ear cocked at the door. The corridor behind lay silent.

Olson returned to his chair, eased down, and sipped scotch. "All right. I'm ready. Hope you are, too."

Paul wasn't sure about that but nodded anyway. Olson started speaking.

"I first met Vi Datsun while stationed in Iraq," he said. "She called herself Shia then, but it was her."

Paul laughed. "Come on. She must have been an infant. If she was even born at all."

Olson leaned forward over his generous belly, unsmiling. "She looked exactly as she did yesterday."

"Bullshit."

Olson climbed to his feet, hobbled to an ancient, scarred credenza against one wall, and shuffled around inside it for a time, muttering. "A-ha. Here it is," he said, and dropped a photo album onto Paul's lap. Its cover wore cracks and a coat of dust. "Open it to the first page."

Paul did as instructed and found himself looking at yellowed photographs taped in neat double rows. "What am I supposed to see?"

"The picture, top right."

Paul squinted at it. A woman lay on her belly in bed, covered in only a sheet. The curve of her back led up to a head of bouncy curls and beneath them he could just make out a face peering at the camera over one shoulder, her mouth a puckered moue. It certainly could be Viola Datsun or a close relative. The date embossed in the lower corner of the photo read Feb 96.

"You're saying this is the same woman who lives across the street from you now?"

"Swear on my mother's grave."

Stanley Olson at least believed what he said. Paul decided to hear him out. What else did he have to do? He wasn't about to go waltzing down the corridor until he knew the cops had cleared out. He said, "How is that possible?"

Olson eased back in his chair. "I'll get to that, but I intend to do it my way. Pay attention. To look at someone as beautiful as Viola Datsun and then attempt to look away is impossible. An exercise in futility. In fact, *beautiful* doesn't come close to describing her—she transcends beauty. Ethereal might be a better word.

"My company was stationed in Abdali, along the Iraqi border, and we had a lot of downtime. This is after Desert Storm and before the war, remember. I doubt you've ever seen combat—you don't have the look of it—but you may have gotten yourself an unscratchable itch from time to time. That's what us boys had as we awaited our orders: unscratchable itches. Well, unscratchable by the likes of us, at any rate. We found relief in the premiere Abdali brothel, and that's where I met Viola Datsun.

"She worked most every night. She was the only girl who spoke English and that was important to me. Most of the other boys, hell, they're glad they can't understand what their lay is saying. Some of 'em get off on hearing her moan in that alien tongue. Not me, though. I want to understand what my woman says. And I want her to understand me.

"The first time, I thought my brain might explode right through my skull cap. Didn't make me wear a condom or pull out, and I think I came for thirty seconds straight. You've been with her, you know what I mean. I'd had my share of women, being career military and moving around and such, but nothing compared to Viola. And good Christ, she got off on it, too. Or if she didn't, she ought to have earned herself an Academy Award for the performance. She moaned and writhed like a goddam cat in heat, I tell you what. The way she moved her hips, good God. Unreal. But, hell, what am I telling you for? You know."

Paul nodded but did not interrupt. The story had enchanted him as much as it perplexed him.

"Prostitution was illegal over there—still is; those men hold a tight rein on their women—but our CO had some connections. He knew some fellas who headed the sex trade. It was big business back then, but nothing like it is now. Anyway, we could get in once or twice a week and, my God, those nights were heaven. The nights I couldn't see her—those were the worst. Those were hell. I couldn't get her out of my head. My CO recommended I try one of the other girls. He told me Abeer was his personal favorite, said he'd buy me half an hour, let me try her out. But no. I just couldn't. The thought of anyone other than Viola turned me off. Revolted me, really. She had become a drug I couldn't live without and when I couldn't have her, I went into withdrawal."

"How do you mean?" Paul ventured when the old man stalled, lost in thought.

"I mean just as I said. My hands shook. I sweated through my uniform, and it wasn't because of the damnable heat. Sometimes I puked and other times I couldn't breathe." He closed his eyes and inhaled deeply as if recalling some memory through scent alone. "The last time I saw her in a bed was the fifth of March in the year 1997."

"What happened?" Paul asked. Olson appeared near tears.

"We were redeploying, breaking camp. Our CO told us if we needed anything from town, we had two hours to get there and get back. Of course, I ran straight for Viola—or Shia, as she was called at the time. I barely waited for the jeep to stop before I leapt out and bolted for the brothel.

"She was there, lounging in her usual silk robe the color of sapphire. Her hair hung in gorgeous chestnut ringlets and her face glowed when she saw me arrive. She was one of the few girls who seemed to enjoy being there, like she was made for the job. Nothing seemed to dishearten her. One of the grunts bragged once about how he'd beat on her a little bit and she'd just laughed. I kicked the shit out of that guy, by the way, and told him never to touch her again. He didn't—he died a month later. Heart attack.

"Anyway, as I stood looking at her that last day I felt tears in my eyes. I couldn't stomach the thought of never seeing her again and a crazy idea hit me—we could run away together. We couldn't stay in the Middle East or return to America, of course, but we could find somewhere. Maybe Canada. Maybe South America. Somewhere we could live out our lives together in bliss."

"But that didn't happen."

"Not exactly," Olson said. "We made love on that last day, and it was as shockingly incredible as ever. After, as we lay spent through the remaining minutes of my purchased time, I finally found the guts to outline my plan.

"God bless her, she listened to the entire pitch before shutting it down. She said her place was there, with the other girls. My heart broke. I tried to reason with her, then plead with her. Finally, in tears, I begged her. But nothing I said—no promise I made—changed her mind.

"Eventually, one of the pimps came and banged on the door, cursing at me in Kurdish and I had to leave under threat of violence. Even then, I almost couldn't do it. The only way I could tear myself away was by telling myself I would sneak out of camp in the night and return for her. Which I did."

"You did?" Paul said, on the edge of his seat.

Olson nodded. "I went back armed to the teeth, prepared to take out the whole fucking operation, Rambo-style. Except the place was empty."

"Empty?"

"Entirely cleared out. As though no one had ever been there."

"I don't understand. Where did they go?"

Olson shrugged. "I don't know, and I never found out. But I did find out where Shia—Viola—went."

"She wound up here in suburban Lake Winona, Illinois. And so did you."

"Indeed, we did. But it was a long and twisted road getting here to the present moment."

"Do tell," Paul said. He wanted to know how this ended and perhaps determine what happened to Viola. Besides, he wasn't ready to stick his head out the door yet.

"I'll spare you the gory details but suffice to say through some careful inquiries and some intercepted intelligence I discovered she'd taken up with a new group of girls in Paris. So, of course, Paris is where I went.

"By the time I got there, I was a complete wreck. I'd sunk into a depression so grim I couldn't see any hope for the future. I'd dropped forty pounds. My hair had thinned and gone ghost-white. The only thing that kept me going was the idea I'd see Shia soon and could again plead my case.

"I finally found the new brothel on Rue de Rivoli, but couldn't get in. You couldn't buy your way in. Admittance by invitation only. Apparently those in charge had realized the quality of their product and had decided to maximize profits with clientele of the highest order.

"I tried repeatedly to gain access and finally a man—not an Arab, but an Englishman—appeared at the door of the dingy flat I'd taken six blocks over to try to dissuade further attempts. He spoke politely, but there was something in the undercurrent of his tone that spoke of pain and death should I refuse compliance.

"I tried to explain my plight, how I needed to be near Shia. I begged him to look into my hollow, haunted eyes and understand my position. I told him I would pay anything he asked. He told me he sympathized, but that there was simply nothing to be done about it. Their rules were not his to break.

"Finally, on my knees, I got him to agree to take a message to Shia and hastily scrawled some words of love and my address on a slip of paper. The man folded it into his pocket but said he would try but could make no promises regarding its delivery."

Olson paused to drink. Paul couldn't stand it. "What happened? Did he deliver it?"

"He did," Olson confirmed. "And what happened next about did me in." He took another drink and Paul could tell he needed it to proceed. "She showed up in my flat that night, in person."

Chapter Thirty

Darlene and Ned Craycraft woke when their grandchildren ran, screeching, into their bedroom and threw themselves onto the bed.

"What in the name of heaven?" Darlene said as Perry and Jeannie shrieked and gibbered, clawing their way between their grandparents.

Ned snapped on the lamp. "You two about stopped my ticker. What are you going on about?"

It took the children several long moments to calm, but when they did Perry spoke first. "W-we saw a woman outside."

"A woman? Heck, boy, it was probably your mama," Ned said. Jeannie had wrapped herself around him like a boa constrictor while Perry huddled near his grandmother.

"It wasn't Mommy," Jeannie said. "It was her. The lady with the dark eyes."

Perry nodded. "Mommy wasn't in her room either. We checked."

"What's this nonsense about a woman with dark eyes?" Ned asked. "You two playing a joke?"

"Ned, you can see they're not joking," Darlene replied. "They really think they saw someone in the yard."

Perry's head switched direction and he shook it vigorously. "We really did see someone, Grammy. But she wasn't in the yard. She was outside our window."

"I want to go home," Jeannie moaned.

"Honey, your window's twenty-five feet off the ground. There couldn't have been anyone looking in it."

"But there was, Grammy. Honest."

"I'll go have a look," Ned grumbled, throwing the covers aside. He opened the closet.

"What are you doing?" Darlene asked.

"Taking my piece."

"Good God, are you insane? Don't take that out while the children are here."

"If there's a burglar, I'm going to protect my family."

"There's no burglar, Ned, really," Darlene countered, but her husband ignored her. He fought a Beretta out of a shoebox on the top shelf and left the room.

"I wish the paranoid old goat would get rid of that thing," Darlene said, mostly to herself. To her grandchildren, she said, "Now, tell me about this lady."

"It was the same one I saw in the car," Jeannie said.

"She had dark eyes," Perry added.

"How could you see her eyes? Did you turn on the light?"

"No, Grammy. The darkness ... it *crawled out* of her sockets," Perry said.

Ned returned ten minutes later. By then, the children had calmed and were passively listening to one of their grandmother's tales from the "olden days."

"Didn't see anything," he reported, shelving the firearm.

"Is Shelly back yet?"

"Car's still gone."

"Good lord, it's only a couple hours into the New Year. Where could she be?"

"Probably went out again with those friends of hers, not ready to let the old year go. I don't like them. Not when they were kids and not now. Bad news, those girls."

"Oh, stop it. You sound so curmudgeonly when you talk like that. Next you'll be sitting outside on our porch all day with your little pistol and hollering at kids to get off our lawn."

Ned muttered something and started getting back in bed, but Darlene shooed him out again. "No, you don't. You're coming with us to the kitchen. We decided we could all use a midnight snack to settle our nerves."

"It's the middle of the night, woman," her husband moaned.

"Hence, 'midnight snack.' We're certainly not going without you to protect us." She leaned toward the children and said, "It makes him feel manly if you say it like that."

"I can still hear, you know. Come on, let's get this over with. The sooner it's done, the sooner I can get back to dreaming of Farrah Fawcett."

"Who's that, Pop-Pop?" Perry asked.

"Never you mind, love," Darlene answered in his stead. "Pop-Pop's visiting La La Land again."

"Where's La La Land?" Jeannie asked, goggling.

"Someplace better than here," Ned said, cinching his bathrobe.

Darlene clucked her tongue. "In his dreams, dears."

They went downstairs.

Michelle came in midway through their snack of bagels and hot chocolate. She'd glimpsed the light on in the driveway and thought someone had mistakenly left it on. She should have known better, of course—her father had ever been a stickler for such wasteful habits and had ingrained in his family the necessity of thrift.

"What's the occasion?" she asked, stepping through the back door.

"Oh, good you're home, dear," Darlene said. "Cocoa?"

"No, thank you. Why are the kids up?"

Perry and Jeannie had calmed considerably and were happily gnawing through their snacks, their faces a mess of crumbs and cream cheese.

"They had a nightmare," her father said blearily.

"It wasn't a nightmare, Mommy," Jeannie said. "It was the lady with dark eyes."

Christ, not again, Michelle thought. And both this time. "Come on, you two. Let's get you tucked back in."

"We want to sleep with you," Perry hollered.

"Fine, but let's go. I'm beat."

"Did you have a good time with *those girls*?" Ned growled, shoving the milk carton into the fridge.

"Yes. Thanks, Daddy."

Ned muttered something else, then stomped upstairs. Darlene gave her daughter a knowing look, which Michelle tried to ignore as she marched the children up behind their grandfather.

"Listen, Mommy needs to step into the shower for a minute," she told the kids after she'd gotten them settled in her bed. The protests began in earnest, but she assured them they'd be right across the hall. She smoothed their hair, sang a lullaby, and made sure they had their favorite stuffed toys with them—

unnecessary in Jeannie's case since she hadn't let Gussy out of her sight the entire week. Finally, exhausted, they let her go.

In the bathroom, Michelle faced the mirror but found she couldn't look at her reflection. "It was the last time," she whispered.

She undressed after she'd spun on the tap and stepped into the needling spray. Steam rose as she scrubbed Tom's smell from her skin. How could she have done it?

It was easy.

No, you *were easy.*

Paul's changed. Something's different about him.

So that justifies you sleeping with your ex? That will help things at home.

Paul's having an affair. I know he is.

Where's your proof, princess?

I know him. He's never acted the way he has been over the past month. Not in the decade I've known him.

So you conclude he's sleeping with someone else.

What else could it be?

But on that point, her warring mind fell silent. She rinsed her hair and was reaching for the towel when she heard the bathroom door snick shut.

"Perry? Jeannie? I'll be right out, okay? Get back in bed," she called as she wheeled the water off. No answer. She peered around the edge of the curtain, but the bathroom was empty. Someone had been there, though. On the steamed mirror someone had drawn Venus's distaff, the universal symbol representing the female gender:

Chapter Thirty-One

Stanley Olson paused his story long enough to freshen his drink. The clock ticked onward toward the New Year. At first, Paul had not wanted to spend it here in this codger's stuffy apartment, but as time drifted on and he'd become embroiled in the old man's tale, he decided there may not be a better place to do so. At the same time Michelle and Tom Rood were chatting amicably but dispassionately on the patio during her parents' party, someone banged on the apartment door.

"For Chrissakes, it's forty minutes till the end of the year!" Stan bellowed. "Who the hell is it?"

"Lake Winona Police Department, sir," a man called through the door.

"Whatever it is, I didn't do it," Olson hollered, hauling himself to his feet and shuffling toward the door. He jabbed a finger at the bathroom. Paul got the message and stepped in, easing the door closed behind him. He stood with an ear pressed against the prefab wood.

"Sir, we're sorry to trouble you, but we think there may be a fugitive at large in your building," the officer said.

"What d'ya want me to do about it? You're the cop."

"Have you seen anyone strange on your floor this evening?"

"I see someone strange on my floor *every* evening. Look, if you're going to arrest someone, make it that damned Jason

192

Ramsey from five-nineteen. He's a delinquent if I ever seen one."

"Sir, we're not making any arrests at this point. Will you give us a call if you see someone out of the ordinary?"

"Sure, why not. Got a description?"

"Male, about six feet tall."

"That's it?"

"That's all we have so far."

"Since that describes about a billion people, good luck in your search."

The officer thanked him, and Olson slammed the door, sliding the bolt into place and chaining it for good measure. Paul stepped out of the bathroom.

"Thanks. You saved my ass."

"Let's get this done. I want to ring in the New Year without having this hanging over my head."

They resumed their positions in the tiny living room and after Olson had poured them drinks, he picked up where he'd left off.

"I was sleeping—or the nearest thing I could manage during those dark days, sort of a drifting discontented drowse—when I became aware I was no longer alone.

"I rolled to face the window and saw her silhouetted against the Parisian skyline like a sculpture of Isis. She held perfectly still and at first I thought my mind had finally snapped like a length of rotted twine. Surely I must be imagining her there in my tiny loft. But then she spoke my name.

"'Stanley, come to me,' she said. It was all I could do not to babble and bawl. I fell to my knees and crawled. I grasped her ankles, terrified she might fly away. God, I could smell her— the intoxicating exotic scent that had long since etched into my brain. No one in the world smells like Viola does, you know."

Paul nodded. The old man was right. And while he'd found Viola Datsun exceptionally attractive, she did not hold nearly the sway over him as she did over his host. Paul's object of desire lived a mile away, in the middle of town. A mere handful of blocks from his own abode.

"'Stanley, I'll be leaving Europe soon,' she told me. 'You must not follow.' I begged her to tell me where her next destination might be, but she deferred. 'I realize the effect I have on most men, Stanley,' she said, 'and for that you must stay clear of me. I'm a danger to you, this above all you must understand.' I'd begun weeping by then, knowing all too well she meant each word. She was cutting me out of her life and discarding me like a diseased organ.

"'I'll be nothing without you, Shia, a shell,' I bawled like a baby. 'I need you.'

"'If you stay near me too long, you'll die,' she said simply. I told her I didn't care. Death would be preferable because at least I'd be in heaven while her earthly absence, to me, spelled hell. She took my hands and raised me from the floor, so we stood eye to eye. It was too much to bear, but I couldn't look away. She caressed my cheek with her long, strong fingers and said: 'Trust me, child. Such a death as you would suffer is preferable to nothing.'

"Then she guided me to the bed, tied my wrists to the headboard, and fucked me one last time. And you know something? She was right. Continuing relations would lead to certain death. I could feel my essence, or spirit, or whatever you want to call it—I could feel it leaving me as she straddled my hips. It felt as though someone had unanchored my consciousness from my body and was drawing it slowly free. I felt how it would be to die."

They sat quiet a moment, sipping. If Paul had heard this story a week ago, he might have laughed aloud. But he knew

Olson spoke true because he had felt the same sensation. At the time he wouldn't have been able to describe it the same way, but now that he'd heard it spoken there simply was no other way to put it. His initial assessment was that the sex with a stranger had brought on some kind of euphoric reaction. Or perhaps it had been the alcohol—he hadn't imbibed so much since his college days (and he'd come to suspect Viola had drugged it).

But no. Olson's description had been accurate. It had felt as though something had been taken from him. A ridiculous notion, of course—sex was sex, nothing more. Some women merely knew how to do it better. Hell, sex was Viola's *trade*. She'd done it professionally for … how long, exactly? That part of the story still didn't add up.

"One thing doesn't fit, Stan. You said you first met her more than two decades ago. That would put her near fifty years old by now. I know they've made advances in plastic surgery and skin care, but there's no woman alive whose body ages like that."

"Use your noodle, kid. And I don't mean the linguine between your legs."

"Are you suggesting Viola is … immortal?" He thought that would crack the old man up, but Olson only glared through his glasses.

"Ain't nothing lives forever," he said. "But some things may live longer than a normal human lifespan."

"How can that be?"

"Think about the morning after you spent the night with Vi."

"What about it?"

"Notice anything different about yourself?"

Paul blinked. "As a matter of fact, I did."

"You can't fool me. I can tell you dye your hair. I can see the crow's feet scratching at your eyes. If I didn't know better, I'd peg you at about forty-one, forty-two. But you ain't, are you?"

Paul shook his head. "I'll be thirty this spring."

"Thought so. See, that's why I look like I do. Because I've been with Vi a couple dozen times. She takes something out of men and puts it into her. It *rejuvenates* her."

"You think she … she steals our souls or something?" Paul asked and uttered a sharp, barking laugh. It didn't sound as crazy as he'd imagined.

But Olson shook his head. "A soul leaves its body intact or not at all. There's something else she absorbs. Our life force, maybe you could call it. Our essence. Not much. Just a sip each time, like when you drink a soda through a straw. Only problem with essence is, there ain't no free refills."

"So what can we do?"

"Do? There's nothing you can do. It's something you *don't* do. You don't go anywhere near that woman."

"That's funny coming from a man who set up camp across the street from her."

Olson shook his head. "It's too late for me. I can't be with her anymore—one side effect of our liaisons is the pecker don't stand at attention no longer—but I can at least watch her."

"Does she know you're here?"

"Of course. She'll come out some days and blow a kiss up at me from the street. She doesn't stay here very long, though. Travels a lot."

"Where does she go?"

The old man shrugged. "Who can say? I haven't had the energy to keep proper tabs on her in years. But she always comes back, at least so far. If she ever leaves for good, I'll find her."

"Even though you can't be with her."

"You haven't heard a word I've said. I *must* be near her. If I'm away too long, I'll just … I don't know. Shrivel up and blow away, maybe."

"Aren't you worried about why the cops were over there tonight?"

"Vi can handle herself. Trust me, if someone broke in they left with less than what they came with."

"Not this time," Paul said. He recounted what he'd discovered upon entering the apartment mere hours ago.

Olson, incredibly, burst into tears. "She may be in trouble. I've got to find her," he said, climbing to his feet and swiping the latest iteration of iPhone to life. It seemed somehow anachronistic in his liver-spotted hands.

"I'm not sure that's going to be possible this time, Stan."

"Why not?" he blubbered, finger shaking as he tried to dial.

"Better sit down and take a drink," Paul said and helped his host back to his seat.

Chapter Thirty-Two

Michelle strode to her bedroom, meaning to ask which of her children thought it would be funny to scrawl on the mirror while she was in the shower, but both were asleep. She stood watching them, their small fingers interlaced with one another's, breathing easy, their faces at last peaceful. Gussy had fallen to the crocheted rug beside the bed. She scooped it and tucked it in the crook of her daughter's arm, then stepped down to her parents' bedroom.

"You're still awake," Darlene said, glancing up over her reading glasses from her Harlequin romance novel. Beside her, Ned snored like a snow blower in overdrive.

"Can I talk to you a minute, Mom?"

Darlene marked her place, stepped into her slippers, and followed her daughter out.

"Were you in the guest bathroom just now?"

"That's what you wanted to talk to me about?" Darlene asked.

"Come with me. I want to show you something." Michelle led the way and flipped on the light. The room had cleared of steam and the mirror looked innocuously blank. Michelle spun on the shower's hot water.

"What on earth are you up to?" her mother asked.

"Just watch."

They waited as steam overwhelmed the room. In a few moments, the symbol reappeared on the polished glass. Her mother looked at it and then at Michelle.

"What of it?"

"Did you do that while I was showering?"

"I'm no prude, but I certainly don't go stalking about while someone's in the midst of cleansing."

"Daddy and the kids are asleep. Who else could it have been?"

"Did you happen to think it may have been one of your girlfriends having a bit of fun at the New Year's party?"

Michelle gaped.

"Of course, you're aware that once a glass is good and steamed someone can draw what they want in it and the pattern will continue to appear in future steamings."

"Why would any of them do such a thing?" Michelle asked.

"You have strange friends, dear. Don't deny it."

She couldn't. Her friends were strange, sure. But she still didn't accept Emily or one of the others sneaking up here during the party to scrawl the symbol for womanhood on the bathroom mirror. She reminded her mother that upstairs had been off-limits.

"Since when did rules stop any of your friends from doing something they oughtn't?" Darlene paused half a beat before adding, "Or *you*, for that matter."

"What's that supposed to mean?"

"You weren't with your friends just now."

Michelle's shoulders slumped as if some celestial puppeteer had dropped the strings controlling her. She wished she could blame a higher power for her actions, but she had only herself to blame. No point in try hiding it from her mother, either; Darlene possessed an eerily preternatural sixth sense when it came to things like this.

"I saw Tom," Michelle said, mustering herself.

"Oh, Shelly," her mother said, wincing. "Are things really so bad with Paul?"

"They've never been worse," Michelle said, dropping pretense.

"Come downstairs. I'll fix coffee."

"Mom, it's the middle of the night—"

"We'll get enough sleep when we're dead. Come, now."

"I really don't want to talk about it."

"Talk is the only way you'll get through this. If you won't with your husband, you will with your mother. March."

Michelle sighed and complied.

She was spared her mother's lecture, though, when they found the back door standing open. Streamers of snow had swept across the tiles to drift against the refrigerator. Perfect footprints—bare feet, about a woman's size nine—had been melted into the snow.

"Oh my God," Darlene said.

"I told you someone's in the house," Michelle said, her voice edging on panic. "I'm going to get the kids, you get Daddy."

The women hurried upstairs again to their respective bedrooms. The children were gone. She drew in breath to scream but stopped short when she saw them huddled together in the corner near the bedside table, their faces ashen, their fingers knotted together as they had been in sleep.

"Perry? Jeannie? It's all right. It's okay," she said, kneeling to embrace them. They crowded against her, shivering. "What's the matter, sweeties? Did someone scare you? Was it the woman?"

Perry nodded, his head dipping like a bird at a feeder. "It was her, Mommy. The one with dark eyes."

"Where was she?"

"She was standing by the bed," Perry said. "Right over Jeannie."

"Where did she go?"

"She went out into the hall. I don't know where she went," Perry answered.

Someone pounded on the bedroom door and all three of them jumped.

"Shelly, open up. It's me," Ned hollered. Michelle stepped to the door, her children clinging to her like baby koalas. Her father stood in the hallway holding the Beretta. "Your mother's on the horn with the cops. I want you to stay with the kids and keep the door locked until we get this sorted out."

"I want Daddy," Perry said. "I want to go home."

Jeannie kept silent, her eyes wide and staring.

"For now, you stay put, buckaroo," Ned told his grandson. "Pop-Pop's got this."

"Be careful, Dad," Michelle said.

"Don't worry about me. You just hang tight until I give the all-clear." He pulled the door closed and tromped off.

"Everything's going to be okay," Michelle said, herding them back to bed. She climbed in between them, and they pulled the covers up to their chins. As gently as she knew how, she asked them to describe what they'd seen.

Jeannie remained mute, but Perry piped up. "Just like we said, Mommy. It was a lady standing by the bed. Watching us. I woke up and there she was."

"She didn't say or do anything?"

Perry shook his head. "Just winked and walked out of the room."

Michelle studied the carpet, looking for wet footprints, but the floor seemed clear.

"She didn't walk out of the room," Jeannie said.

"What do you mean, honey?" Michelle asked, cradling her daughter to her chest.

"She *floated*."

"Floated?"

"Like a balloon. Or a ghost."

"People can't float, Jeannie," Perry said.

"You didn't see her. I did. Her feet didn't touch the ground."

"Jeannie, was it the same person who scared you that day in the car? It was, wasn't it?"

Jeannie nodded. "I think so. I couldn't see the face the last time, but the eyes were the same."

"The dark eyes?"

"Yes, those."

"Describe them to me."

"I can't. They were just dark."

Michelle turned to her son.

"It's like she says, Mom. The lady's eyes were dark. Like smoke. Or nighttime. No white parts. And the darkness, Mommy, it *crawled*."

It all sounded so fantastic Michelle didn't know what to believe. Her kids weren't liars—they'd always been honest as Abe Lincoln. She supposed that would be short-lived, once they reached their teenage years, but for now they shot straight. Neither had an ounce of guile in them. Only then, with her mind whirring a million miles per hour, did she recall the nightmare she'd had of Paul in bed with the strange woman.

Her eyes had appeared to leak black smoke. But dreams were only dreams, not real—

Red lights strobed through the blinds. Michelle tried to excise herself from her children, but they refused to relinquish their grips. They compromised by scooching to the bedroom door and opening it a crack so she could listen.

She couldn't make out much other than the officers taking the information her parents fed them. One asked to speak with the children, but Darlene refused by saying they'd been through enough for one night. Good for her. The last thing Michelle wanted was to have them interrogated.

The cops made a sweep of the house, peeking into the guest room long enough to peel off a pair of stickers in the shape of badges for the children. They accepted them without comment and Michelle had to prompt them on their manners.

"I'm sorry," she said. "It's been a long night."

One of the cops crouched and said, "Hi. My name's Officer Linda. What's your name?"

"Mom says we're not supposed to talk to strangers," Perry answered automatically.

"Smart mom," Officer Linda said. "But I'm a police officer, so I'm safe."

"How do I know you're a police officer?" Perry asked. "You could be *her*."

"You mean the woman you saw in your room tonight?" Officer Linda asked. It looked as if the kids would be answering a few questions after all.

"You kind of look like her," Perry said. "Except your eyes are light instead of dark."

"The woman had brown eyes?"

"Not brown!" Jeannie shrieked, startling them all. "*Dark!* Why can't anyone understand that?" Then she broke down sobbing.

"I'm sorry, but I'm going to have to ask you to leave," Darlene said from the hallway. "This has all been upsetting for everyone."

"Well, if there was someone here she's gone now," the other cop, a clean-shaven kid fresh out of the academy said, sounding important while probing the corners of the bedroom with his flashlight.

"We have your statement. Let us know of any other disturbances," Officer Linda said. Her tone suggested the whole incident may have been the manufacturing of a child's dream.

When the officers had gone and Ned had grumbled his way back to bed, Darlene asked if Michelle wanted to join her for the coffee they'd missed out on.

"Not tonight. I want to get the kids to bed and they're not going without me."

"Perfectly understandable. We double-checked the doors and windows. Everything locked up tight. And your father's sleeping with that godforsaken gun beside the bed."

They said goodnight. Michelle got the kids to fall asleep with surprising ease—she figured she'd be up half the night with them, but they dropped off at once. Michelle found no such luxury and dreamed of witches riding broomsticks across the face of the moon.

Chapter Thirty-Three

At the same time his wife was dialing her ex's phone number, Paul wrapped up relaying the conversation he'd had with Ms. Bloch and divulged what he'd seen at Viola's apartment. The clock had tipped into the New Year without either man knowing it and the snow had stopped.

"Congregation of Sacred Splendor. Never heard of them," Olson said after he'd listened to his guest's story.

"I wouldn't expect you to have. Couldn't find a word about them online."

Olson nodded. His oxygen tank sniffed. "I heard of Haven Revival, though. Vi never mentioned she went to any church, much less that den of nutjobs."

"From what Ms. Bloch indicated, they're a lot nuttier than they appear on the surface."

"How so?"

"She didn't get into specifics, but mentioned they might be into practicing ungodly rituals behind the scenes."

"Well, if Vi worshipped that sounds like the place for her. Woman's got black magic in her bones. But I don't have to tell you that."

"Look, you don't have to worry about Viola and me, okay? I'm not going to try to take her away."

"Oh, I know. Vi belongs to no man." He took another pull of scotch. "So you think these Sacred Splendor people have something to do with her disappearance?" Olson asked.

"I don't know. It didn't look good. Ms. Bloch practically extorted me into giving up her a name. Seems like too big of a coincidence that only hours later Viola goes missing."

"This was the work of more than one person. There isn't a single man on the planet who could overpower Viola on his own."

"So what do you want to do?" Paul asked wearily. The first dawn of the New Year would soon rouge the horizon.

"I'm going to this Haven Revival church first thing in the morning and see what I can find out."

"I doubt anyone will be there on a Friday," Paul pointed out.

"Didn't say nothing about anyone being there," Olson said. "You in?"

They caught a few hours' sleep right there in the living room. Olson took to his easy chair and Paul stretched out on the sofa. It seemed sensible to give the cops extra time to finish investigating the building anyway. With little more than forty-eight hours until Michelle and the kids returned home, Paul wanted to put this whole goddamn thing behind him. He'd only agreed to help because the old timer had given him sanctuary. He woke when Olson jabbed his shoulder.

"Let's get moving."

Paul drove them to Haven Revival, Olson riding shotgun with the oxygen tank between his knees. The parking lot stood deserted, as he'd predicted … but someone occupied the building, he felt sure. Some instinct in the back of his mind nagged at him to be careful.

"Someone's watching us," Olson said.

"You feel it, too?"

"Yup. We got eyes on us for sure, from the instant we pulled in."

"There aren't any cars."

"Ain't cars I'm worried about," Olson replied, shaking his head. "This feels off."

"What do you want to do? Turn around?"

The old man considered, his watery eyes blinking hard behind his spectacles. "I think we better. Let's wait until dark."

Paul found he liked that idea even less but couldn't deny he felt something wrong here as well. It could be his paranoia fed off his passenger's, but no—the feeling of being watched, observed, *evaluated* remained. It became practically palpable the longer they sat.

"Okay. Let's get breakfast. We'll discuss what comes next."

They talked over heaping plates of omelets and bacon in the back corner booth of Dot's Place, which was open every day of the year without exception. After they fashioned a detailed outline for that night's activity, Olson cocked his U.S. Army Veteran cap back on his head and said, "You never told me how you got involved with Vi."

"It's a long story."

"We've got hours."

Paul hesitated, scratching a mushroom out of his eggs with the tines of his fork.

"If you're worried about me being jealous, don't. Vi's been with many men. Thousands, I suspect. Jealousy isn't something one can readily apply to her."

"It wasn't Viola I was after," Paul said at last. "She was a steppingstone to my goal."

"Your goal?"

Paul paused again, unsure whether he ought to proceed. Saying her name aloud in front of someone else would be akin to giving himself permission to try for her again. Part of him wanted to try for her, but the larger part understood having her would spell his undoing.

Finally, he said: "Lucine Korth."

Olson shook his head. "Never heard of her."

"She's the most beautiful woman I've ever seen."

"Ah. Like Viola is to me."

"Exactly. And they're friends, at least on Facebook."

"I haven't logged into Facebook in years."

"That's probably a good thing. It's nothing but trouble," Paul said as he drew his phone from his pocket. He called up his mobile account and showed Olson Lucine's picture.

"Aye, she's a looker," the old man said. "Nothing compared to my Vi, of course, but she's a looker for sure. You say they're friends?"

"According to this they are. Lucine's profile says she'll be in town tonight. She and Viola were planning to go out for drinks, probably at Cabana Girls." Something occurred to him for the first time. "Wait, do you think Lucine's one of them? Whatever Viola is?"

Olson shrugged. "Could be. Could be not. But the way she's got you hooked, I'd lay a bet on it."

Paul's phone rang. It was Michelle. He swiped to ignore. He'd talk to her later, after he'd forgiven her.

"You planning to meet up with this Korth woman?"

Paul drew in a deep breath. Was he? "I'm not sure. I want to, but everything inside me is screaming against it."

"You a married man?"

"I … yes. I'm married."

"Same here. Or I was, rather. After I met Shia—Viola—I hardly thought of my family. They seemed so … unnecessary by comparison."

"You have kids, too?"

"Three girls and two boys."

"You ever see them anymore?"

Olson drew a shuddery sigh. "Haven't in over twenty years. Yolanda—my wife—she moved them out west somewhere. I don't even know what state."

"You ought to try to find them. Maybe you can reconcile."

"It's far too late for that," Olson said. "It was too late the moment I climbed into that woman's bed. The rest of the world faded to a pinprick and that's what's going to happen to you if you pursue this Korth woman. You won't be able to think of nothing else."

"Do you really believe what you said about Viola drawing life force out of you?"

"It's the only explanation I can come up with," Olson said, leaning back from his meal. He seemed to have lost his appetite. "How else can you explain her sustained youth and my premature aging? Or yours?"

Paul still wasn't convinced Viola Datsun was the same woman Major Olson had bedded in the Middle East. But why shouldn't he be convinced of it? He'd slept with Viola, too, and had noticed significant changes happening to him the very next morning. He'd displayed open signs of aging, just as Olson said. But how was such a thing possible?

The old man seemed to read his mind. "I've researched the matter," he said. "I've found dozens of books and articles on sexual vampirism and—"

"Is that what you call this?" Paul asked, uttering a high, unnatural laugh.

"The term seems apt, no?"

"Vampirism. It sounds so superstitious. So archaic."

"Don't doubt what your senses tell you, Paul. Come back to my place, I'll show you what I found."

Paul dabbed his lips with his napkin. "Why not?" he said. "What else have we got to do?"

He raised a hand to call for the check, but Olson stilled him. "I got this."

"I couldn't possibly—"

"Trust me. I got this."

The waiter brought their check, but over the amount due someone had scrawled THANK YOU FOR YOUR SERVICE.

"That gentleman over there noticed a veteran and his son enjoying breakfast and picked up your tab," the waiter said.

"Please express our gratitude," Olson said. He adjusted the bill of his Army cap. When the waiter had gone to relay the message, he said to Paul: "Works every goddamn time."

Chapter Thirty-Four

Darlene found Ned in the downstairs bathtub early the next morning. When she woke after five to find him gone from bed, she went looking for him. Ned had always been an early riser, so his absence was not unusual; what *was* unusual was that he'd neglected to put on his robe or slippers as had been his habit going on forty years of marriage.

The kitchen stood empty, as did the front porch where he sometimes stood sipping coffee and watching the sunrise (even on brisk winter mornings such as this), the door still locked. She came up quietly on the bathroom door, which stood open an inch, and tapped. The light above the vanity glowed cool white.

"Ned, are you in there?" she called. When her query went unanswered, she pushed the door open, her heart already trip-hammering in her chest because she knew already something had happened.

Darlene noticed the mirror over the vanity first. The water running in the basin had gone cold, but the image still appeared on the steamed surface, identical to the one Michelle had claimed to see upstairs: the universal symbol for the female gender, Venus's mirrored cruciform distaff. She had time to wonder what type of burglar breaks into a house merely to draw on mirrors, and then the door swung wide, and she saw her husband.

Ned Craycraft lay naked in the spacious bathtub, knees drawn up to his chest. His pajamas had been neatly folded and placed on the toilet lid, his eyeglasses resting atop the pile. The gun—his stupid, useless gun—lay on the bathmat like a dead steel bat.

Her husband's face, quite clearly not living, held a mixture of fancy and fear and his already-fair complexion had been blanched even whiter. He seemed to have aged ten years. It was this last aspect Darlene clung to—this couldn't be her husband; it must be some sick hoax.

But Darlene had known Ned half a century and had been his wife only a smidge less, so she knew her husband when she saw him. The water in the sink ran on and on, a miniature waterfall to nowhere. Denial forced hysteria away. Darlene turned off the water and then looked up at the mirror. The symbol in the steam had faded and she caught a glimpse of her reflection, her blue eyes wide and shimmery, her mouth a hanging O of horror.

Only then did she find it in her to scream.

The same police officers who'd come to investigate the break-in—Officer Linda and her clean-cut partner—responded first to the emergency call. They looked nervous at the discovery in the tub as if they'd missed something on their last visit. A pair of no-nonsense detectives arrived and assessed the scene before calling in a forensics unit. The younger detective, a woman with soft features and hair as red and chaotic as wildfire, questioned Darlene and Michelle while her partner stood by, looking officious.

Michelle had sent the kids to Emily's house without telling them about Pop-Pop. She sat dazed on the living room sofa. The muscles of her thighs trembled no matter how hard she pressed her legs together. Her father was *dead*: it simply seemed too incredible to believe.

"You say you saw a woman in your parents' home last night?" the redhead asked for a second time and for a second time, Michelle shook her head.

"My children said they did. I never saw anyone."

"But you say you think someone entered the lavatory as you were showering."

"I heard the door open. I saw the thing on the mirror."

"The symbol identical to the one in the ground level lavatory?" the male detective asked.

Michelle thought if they kept saying *lavatory* she might start laughing and be unable to stop. "My father is lying dead in the bathroom, and you're worried about a steamed mirror."

"It's evident there's a connection," the female detective said. "If the offender drew both symbols, it's likely he left prints."

"It was a woman, not a man. Haven't you heard anything we've said?"

The redhead scribbled something on her pad. The medical examiner stepped in, and the detectives excused themselves to show him to the body. Darlene came in and the women collapsed onto the sofa, hugging and sobbing.

"I just don't understand what happened," Michelle said. "He was fine last night."

Darlene blew her nose on a tissue. "The way he was tromping around, you'd think he'd live another fifty years."

"What was it, Mom? A heart attack? I thought he took meds for that."

"That was no heart attack. A bad ticker doesn't make you look the way … the way he—" She broke off into a fresh torrent of tears.

"God, what am I going to tell the children?" Michelle asked slumping into the cushions.

"You don't say a word to them," Darlene said. "Not yet. There will be plenty of time to explain how Pop-Pop's with the angels after you've gotten them home."

"I'm not going home tomorrow," Michelle said. "I'll stay to help with the arrangements."

Darlene dabbed her eyes then looked at her daughter gratefully. "Thank you, love. Have you called Paul yet?"

"I tried but he didn't answer. Another thing I'll have to deal with when I get home."

Michelle buried her face in her hands. Too much had happened too fast. Who was she now? She gave it some thought and found she had no idea. The world had come unhinged in the span of weeks and dropped her like a trapdoor into this dungeonous half-life. She stood, wiping her hands on her pants.

"Where are you going?" Darlene asked.

"To call my husband again. To keep calling him until he picks up his fucking phone. He needs to know about Dad and I'm sure as hell not leaving it on his voicemail. He needs to know we won't be home for a while." She checked her mother's red-rimmed eyes. "Maybe ever."

"But the kids have school. Your job—"

"There are schools and jobs down here. And you're going to need help now that Dad's gone."

"You do what you feel you must," her mother said, pulling her into a deep embrace. Michelle let her. "I'm here for you, darling. Always and forever."

The female detective approached and asked to speak with Mrs. Craycraft in private.

"Did you find something?" Michelle asked, clutching her elbows.

"Maybe," the detective said, her eyes flicking between the women. "But it's of a sensitive nature and I need to ask bluntly."

"Anything you say in front of me, you can say in front of my daughter," Darlene said.

The detective sniffed. "Very well. I need to ask you if you and your husband were intimate at any point last night."

The question came so unexpected that Darlene uttered a choked giggle. "Are you joking?"

"What the hell?" Michelle cried.

"I assure you, Mrs. Craycraft, jokes are the last thing on my mind."

Darlene mustered herself. "If you must know, Ned and I have not been intimate in three years. He's suffered from erectile dysfunction since then." She snapped a glance at her daughter. "Sorry, dear."

Michelle waved this off. "What are you saying?" she demanded of the detective.

"From what we can determine, your father had sexual relations with a woman sometime with the past six hours."

Darlene put a hand over her mouth. "How can you possibly know that?"

"Ma'am, we found a large volume of what appears to be vaginal lubricant on your husband's genitals. Of course, we won't know for sure until the lab tests come back, but—"

"Are you … are you suggesting," Darlene said, her voice unsteady, "that you found Ned with a *hard-on*?"

Michelle felt as if she might be sick, but a laugh identical in tone to her mother's not-quite-sane giggle bubbled up out of her instead of vomit. She pressed her fingers to her lips to keep hysterics at bay.

The detective blushed crimson to her hair, matching it to the shade. "He was found in a state of arousal, yes."

"Well, I'll be damned," Darlene said, her voice distant and haunted. "Who knew the old rooster still had it in him?"

Chapter Thirty-Five

M ichelle called twice more before the men left Dot's Place. "Don't you think you ought to answer that?" Olson asked.

"She's not leaving voicemails, so it must not be that important. It can wait." The idea his wife might be calling because something had happened to one of the children or her parents never crossed his mind—so deep ran his resentment of her at that moment. The idea she had used a trip to her parents as a cover to see that ex-boyfriend gnawed at him. He might have forgiven, but he'd never forget.

They returned to Olson's apartment. Paul figured the heat would be off the building now that the cops hadn't found their suspect, but when they reached the lobby he got a nasty shock when a uniformed officer opened the door for them. By then it was too late to draw the ski mask over his face.

"Good morning, gentlemen," the officer said.

"Fine morning, ain't it?" Olson replied, patting his belly.

"Would you fellas mind answering a few questions?"

"Is this about the thing last night?" Olson asked. "I'd be happy to tell you the same thing I told them then."

"And what would that be?" the cop asked.

"I didn't see no strangers lurking around in the shadows."

"Sir, are you a resident here?"

"You see me here, don't you?"

"What about your friend?"

Olson laughed, deep and hearty. "With friends like this guy, who needs enemies? My favorite nephew just skinned thirty bones off me in gin rummy down at Dot's."

"Your nephew, huh? He got a name?" the officer asked, staring Paul down.

"Well, hell yeah he's got a name. Everyone's got a name, don't they? If you want to know, ask him."

"Sir?" the cop prompted.

"Paul. Paul Jeske." He could have lied but sensed it would get him in deeper than he already was. A slow trickle of sweat began at his hairline and traced its way down one sideburn.

"Mind if I see some ID, Mr. Jeske?"

"Are we under arrest?" Olson demanded. "If we are, you'd better start reading our rights."

"No, sir, you're not under arrest. I simply asked if I could see his ID."

"No, I don't think you can," Olson said. "We're up in five-twenty-two if you change your mind about Miranda."

The retired Army major stepped around the cop and to the elevator. Paul followed.

As the ammonia-smelling elevator bore them up five floors, Olson removed his cap and wiped his brow. "That was close."

"But I didn't have anything to do with Viola's disappearance."

"You called it in. To their mind, it's the same as leaving fingerprints in her blood. Fucking cops, I tell you what."

Olson snatched up a copy of the *Sun* lying on the mat outside his door and shed it of its rubber band without checking the front page. When they had locked themselves into the apartment, Paul asked, "What if they do change their minds and arrest us?"

"They got nothing to hold us on."

"I was in her apartment last night. And last Sunday. There must be a shitload of my DNA in there."

Olson eyed him. "You use a condom?"

Paul flushed. "No."

"I guess Vi took the better part of your DNA with her then." Paul started to sputter something, but Olson held up a hand. "Look, if you're worried they might find a pube in the potty, forget about it. Vi keeps a spotless abode."

Paul could not corroborate this claim as he had almost zero recollection of the layout of the place or its degree of cleanliness. The place had been completely destroyed last he'd seen it, so maybe that would help cover any lingering evidence. Then something occurred to him.

"Oh God, I left a sock behind," he said.

"Come again?"

"The morning after I spent the night, I couldn't find one of my socks. I left without it."

Olson didn't seem bothered. "So? There's nothing tying you to it."

"It could have my skin cells in it. My hair."

"Chances are Vi found it and either tossed it in the washer or tossed it in the trash. Garbage pickup is Wednesday around this neck of the woods, so either way you're safe."

Paul allowed himself to relax. He hated that he gave the cops his real name—it wouldn't take much digging to figure out he wasn't really Olson's nephew—and then they would be on to him. Maybe. Or maybe the cop bought the old man's story and wouldn't give either of them a second thought.

"What do you want to show me?"

"This, for one," Olson said. He stood skimming the front page of the *Sun* and then held it up for Paul to see. The headline read: Local Man Dies Amid Odd Circumstances, Police Baffled.

219

Paul read the article over his host's shoulder. It discussed the case of Andre Diaz and how his wife had found his skeletal remains draped over their privacy fence Sunday evening. His wife had given the lurid details to the press in an effort to aid in the apprehension of those responsible for her husband's death.

"This guy lived right by Lucine. I was there when the ambulance came to pick him up. A detective questioned me, the same guy investigating Viola's apartment last night."

"What were you doing there?"

The question took him by surprise. "Oh. I, um. Well, I—"

"You don't have to come up with some bullshit story, kid," Olson said. "You were there because you were checking up on Lady Lucy."

Paul shuffled his feet but said nothing.

"I know. I've been in that situation. You probably broke in and went through her stuff, didn't you?"

He couldn't deny it. "Yeah. I did. You gonna tell the cops?"

"And turn in the only friend I've made in decades?"

"It was like I couldn't help it," Paul said.

"I know, kid. I know all about it."

Paul cleared his throat. "Anyway, it says this guy was a skeleton. What could have done that?"

"Christ in a crucible, use your noodle."

"Holy shit. You don't think Viola had something to do with this, do you?"

"What else could suck the life right out of a man down to his bare bones?"

"This is crazy," Paul said. It sounded weak and ineffective, but turned out to be the only defense he could muster.

"Vi had her way with Mr. Diaz and maybe Diaz's people retaliated," Olson said.

"No. I told you about that Ms. Bloch and her Sacred whatever-the-fuck."

"Either way, someone got wind of Vi's ways and took her out," Olson said. His voice cracked on the last word—his grief over her absence still worked on him like methadone.

"You know, there was someone in Lucine's house that night," Paul said.

Olson narrowed his eyes behind his glasses. "Who?"

Paul shook his head. "I don't know. Someone was in her basement, rummaging around. I ran but then realized I'd left my phone behind and when I went back for it, someone was lying in her bed. It was dark and I couldn't see much, but I felt a headful of hair."

"Are you sure it wasn't your Lucine? After all, it was her place."

"I don't think so. The hair felt dead. I thought I was touching the head of a corpse."

"You been back there? Maybe she offed herself."

"We'll find out tonight at Cabana Girls."

"We're not going there, for God's sake," Olson said.

"I am. I need to see her in person."

"You don't even know that's where they agreed to meet."

"True, but I have a feeling she'll wind up there."

Olson sighed. "Okay, is this before or after we commit felony B and E at Haven Revival?"

"After. We're hitting the church as soon as the sun goes down. I'll drop you off if you won't come clubbing with me."

"Clubbing. Jesus, the stupid names you kids make up."

Paul grinned. "You know it, Grandpa. Hey, maybe Viola will be there. Maybe the thing at her apartment was some big misunderstanding." He didn't believe it but wanted to convince Olson to accompany him. He didn't want to step foot in Cabana Girls again without backup.

"We'll see how the church goes. Then I'll make up my mind."

"Deal. Now show me what else you've got."

Chapter Thirty-Six

"He's still not answering," Michelle said. "In fact, he turned his phone off."

"You don't suppose something's happened to him, do you?" Darlene asked.

"I'm not sure of anything anymore."

"When are you picking up the kids?"

"Emily's keeping them overnight. They're playing Go Fish and watching Disney movies."

"Do you think she's the wisest choice to babysit?"

"She won't have a man over with the children there."

"Are you sure?"

Michelle flung her arms in the air. "Like I said, I'm not sure of anything anymore."

"I'm going down to Salerno's to make the funeral arrangements. Will you come with?"

"I wouldn't let you go alone, Mom."

They didn't speak on the drive, their thoughts privately devouring each of them. Salerno's Funeral Home sat on a square lot a few blocks from the State Capitol. Lionel Salerno, the director, met them with a sympathy which seemed genuine and a sort of delicacy Michelle rarely saw in a man. His eyes seemed perpetually dewy and concerned. Mr. Salerno led them to his office on the far side of the building where he invited them to sit in wide plush chairs.

"I'm very sorry for your loss," Salerno said, taking a seat behind his desk opposite the women. "Losing someone too soon is never easy."

"We just want to make things as easy as possible," Michelle said when her mother found herself temporarily unable to speak.

"Of course," the director said. "That's what we all want."

"Can you make him look how he did?" Darlene at last asked.

"Our staff is skilled in making your loved one appear lifelike," Salerno said.

"You haven't seen our loved one yet," Darlene replied, followed by a sort of belching titter.

"Mom, you—" Michelle began but her mother broke down sobbing into her hands. Then she laughed, a high, maniacal sound.

Mr. Salerno, accustomed to hysterics, took this behavior in stride. He took Darlene's hand in his. "Ms. Craycraft, I understand your pain. You go on and grieve any way you please—there's no wrong way to do it."

Darlene looked around wildly at her daughter. "Oh my God, we're going to have to close the casket, aren't we? We can't let your father's friends see him that way—"

"I assure you, we'll do our very best, Mrs. Craycraft."

"Thank you," Michelle said for her mother, wiping her eyes. "I suppose we ought to discuss casket options."

The timing couldn't have been worse. The hearse bearing what remained of Ned Craycraft swung into the lot at the same moment the women stepped out the door.

"He's in there, isn't he?" Darlene asked her daughter. She appeared to have shrunk in the forty minutes they'd been inside the mortuary.

"Yes, Mom. He is. Let's get you home." She tried to guide Darlene to the car, but Darlene broke free and rushed to the funeral car.

"Goddamn you, Ned! Goddamn you to hell, you unfaithful son of a bitch!" she screamed. She drew back a foot and kicked the fender. The driver got out but made no move to stop her.

"Mother, that's enough," Michelle said. This time she took Darlene firmly by the shoulders and got her in the car.

"I'm sorry," Darlene wept. "I just can't believe what he did to me. To us. To *himself*."

"We don't know what he did or what was done to him, Mom. The police are investigating. They'll find out."

"They better. I can't go lie beside him in Green Hills cemetery for all eternity thinking he boffed some floozy burglar. I just can't."

"Daddy would never have done something like that," Michelle said. She still hadn't started the car and she still hadn't shared her theory about what happened. Her mother would likely take it bad.

"What do you think happened?" Darlene asked, as if reading her mind. "I know you've got an idea."

Michelle took a breath. "I … I think Daddy was raped."

Darlene's eyes unfocused and Michelle feared she'd devolve into another attack of hysterics, but her mother held it together. "Do you really think so?"

"It's the only thing that makes sense. Dad would never cheat on you, Mom. He was more devoted to you than a

Rottweiler. I've never seen anyone more in love with his wife." She took another deep breath. "That's part of the reason I married Paul. I'd never seen more devotion in a man, other than Dad."

"Who in creation would do such a thing?" her mother asked.

"There are sick people in this world," Michelle said. "We'll have to wait and see. But in the meantime, don't convict Daddy just yet. He loved you more than he loved himself."

Darlene closed her eyes and pressed her nails into the dashboard as if steeling herself. "You're right. Of course, you are. Let's go home. We haven't eaten in twelve hours and if we don't soon we'll wind up joining your father. I don't know about you, but I'm not ready to just yet."

"I'm not either," Michelle said and keyed the ignition. "I'll cook steak and potatoes. We can drink the leftover booze from the party and cry ourselves into hangovers."

Darlene managed a tight smile. "That doesn't actually sound half bad, love."

When they got home, Michelle tried Paul again to no avail. This time she left a message for him: "It's me. Something's happened. Call me as soon as you get this. It's a matter of life and death." She paused. "Scratch that. It's only a matter of death."

She figured he'd call back immediately, but halfway through dinner, when he still hadn't, she began to worry. Had something happened to him as well? Could he be lying on his office carpet, dead of some previously undetected illness like a brain embolism or a heart attack? Could he have endured an assault similar to the one that had taken her father?

"Mom, I think I better head home tonight," she said. "Something might have happened to Paul. It's not like him to not call back."

Darlene, who'd only picked at her meal but had finished three glasses of wine, looked blearily around.

"But you've been drinking, dear."

"I'm all right to drive. Will you be able to handle the kids when Emily drops them off tomorrow if I'm not back?"

"We'll manage."

Michelle took her mother's hand. "I won't leave you alone in this, Mom. I promise. I just need to figure out what is going on with my husband. I'll be back by tomorrow afternoon at the latest and I'll drag his deadbeat ass with me."

Normally her mother would admonish Michelle's language, but tonight she seemed too fogged out to bother. "Whatever you wish, honey."

"Will you be all right alone tonight?"

"The police said they'll be stationing a man outside until they can find out who did this to your father. I'll be fine."

Michelle stood and kissed the top of her mother's head. Her hair smelled of sweat and sorrow. "Tomorrow afternoon, tops."

"Get some sleep while you're there. I don't want you dropping off behind the wheel."

"I couldn't sleep now if you sedated me."

"Just be careful."

Michelle promised she would, then hurried to the car. She swung by Emily's place on the way out of town to kiss the kids good-bye and explain her plan to her friend. Emily sounded uneasy about Michelle's departure, but reluctantly agreed it was the right call. Perry and Jeannie wanted to go home with her, but she told them they still had lots to do at Grammy's house. Jeannie cried and hugged her mom's leg, refusing to let her mother walk out the door. Michelle gently pried the sobbing child loose and crouched before her.

"I'll be back before you know it, my sweet June Bug. And guess what? I'll bring Daddy back with me. How does that sound?"

Jeannie turned off the tears and smiled hugely. God, she would be beautiful when she grew up. Michelle kissed them each again, then made a quick getaway. Lake Winona was a four-hour drive and she wanted to get going. If she pushed it, she could be home by 10:00 p.m. She had a sinking suspicion— no more than a hunch, but a powerful one—that time had become a factor, a celestial scoreboard ticking down the seconds until some doomsday final buzzer. Every minute counted because something was going to happen. If it hadn't already.

Chapter Thirty-Seven

As his host dragged out a cardboard box from the back bedroom and dropped it on the coffee table between them, Paul flicked through the battered photo album.

"You have any other pictures of Viola?" he asked.

"Only ever snapped the one. She told me photos weren't allowed in her place of business, but she let me have one because I was one of her best customers." He pried the box flaps open. "Ah. Here we are."

The box exuded the odor of some exotic spice, pungent but not entirely unpleasant. Olson removed a wooden chest carved in ornate and intricate symbols. A small gold-plated keyhole adorned the front in the shape of the universal symbol for femininity, winking in the overhead light. The lid bore the image of three interlocked snakes eating their own tails. In the center of their coiled bodies lay a rendition of The Eye of Providence, similar to the one printed on the back of a dollar bill.

"What's this mean?" Paul asked, touching the lid.

"From what I've been able to tell, the eye represents an all-seeing entity. In America, this is nearly universally meant to be God's eye. Only this item isn't American. It's Middle Eastern in design, probably Egyptian. The serpents swallowing their tails represent cyclicality or re-creating of oneself. It's one of many symbols for vampirism I've come across."

"What's inside?" Paul asked. He no longer desired to touch it, as though it may transmit some deadly disease.

Instead of answering, Olson produced a gold key identical to the one Paul had found taped to the bottom of Lucine's silverware drawer from a chain around his throat and unlocked the chest. Paul guessed his stolen key must also open an identical trunk his lady had stashed somewhere, and he leaned forward, intrigued. When Olson opened the lid, a far more powerful smell than the dusty aroma of exotic spices wafted out: some type of ancient organic incense. Paul found it offensive and had to restrain clamping a hand over his nose.

"It don't smell pretty, but I don't imagine you will either when you're as old as it is," Olson said through a lopsided grin.

He reached delicately inside and pinched up something nearly too small to see. Paul dug the reading glasses out of his breast pocket and settled them on his nose. The thing in the old man's fingers appeared to be a small black worm, shriveled in on itself. For a moment, he thought it must be a tangible example of the serpent eating its own tail. The box appeared to be full of them.

"What the hell are they?" he asked.

"Foreskins," Olson said. "Mummified foreskins."

Paul leaned away and put a hand to his mouth. "Christ. Why?"

"During my many visits to Shia—Viola—I noticed this box resting atop her bureau. I never thought to ask about it until late in our relationship, if that's what you could call it. My focus was always on her. But one evening, after a particularly aggressive session, as I lay in afterglow heaven and she readied herself for the next john, I asked where she'd gotten it."

"And?"

"She told me a very powerful woman of her clan had gifted it to her. Shia was apparently some type of protégé, expected to take command after the current queen—her word—either died or abdicated."

"That still doesn't explain why it's full of … those."

"Ease off the gas, kid. I'm getting to it. I asked her what was in it, and she just grinned at me, this huge smile all full of those gorgeous white teeth of hers. 'Do you wish to see, Stanley?' she asked, her bare breasts painted gold in the candlelight. And suddenly I wasn't so sure I did. Something in her voice, in her stance, whispered of damnation." He paused, knuckling an eye beneath the frames of his glasses.

"And she showed you."

"She did more than show. She lifted the lid, dug her nails in, and lifted a handful for me to see. From where I lay on the bed, I couldn't tell what they were—they looked like flesh-colored wedding bands, shades and hues across the flesh-tone spectrum. They were still fresh then, you see."

"Fucking *hell*."

"And then she … God, I'll never forget it. She popped them in her mouth and chewed them up. Chewed them up like they were wads of Double Bubble."

"And this is the woman you left your family for? The woman who nearly killed you?"

He barked a brief, humorless laugh. "If anything, that act seduced me even further into her succulent web. I couldn't look away."

"I can see why," Paul said. His stomach rolled. He'd had his tongue in her mouth, had licked her teeth. The memory made him want to spit.

"Soon after, she was gone to Paris and I helpless but to follow."

"So how did you get the box? Did you steal it?"

He shook his head gravely. "I could never steal anything from my sweet Shia. No, during one of the many long months in which I lost track of her movements, in which I found myself most lost and contemplating ... well, contemplating certain unhealthy notions, the box arrived on my doorstep. No wrapping, no postage. It was simply there one morning. I could have wept for joy."

"Not exactly a present I'd ask Santa for," Paul said.

"Oh, it was far better than any Christmas gift. It was a remembrance of our time together. *She hadn't forgotten me*, you see. She *remembered*. She remembered *us*. And I think she sensed how lost I was without her. How utterly incomplete her absence made my existence. I think she sent me this box to *save* me."

"Couldn't she have sent, I don't know, an old bra?"

"You don't get it, Paul. She chose the only tangible object we'd ever discussed. The only piece of evidence proving we'd ever known one another. And it was an object she obviously cared very much for, as her leader had given it to her expressly as a kind of passing of the torch. She gave something sacred to her—and for that I'm eternally grateful. It sustains me. It gives me hope. What's wrong with something that gives a man hope?"

"She could have at least emptied it first, my God."

This time when Olson laughed, it sounded less forced. "No, not my Shia. Not a chance. These were her conquests, Paul. These made her proud and she wanted me to know it."

"Her *conquests*?"

"That leads me to the next item I want to show you," he replied, rummaging again in the box. He handed over a limp newspaper, yellowed with age. The copy appeared was printed in a foreign language. Something Slavic, he thought. A grainy image accompanied the lead story which appeared to depict an open mass grave. White-sheeted bodies stretched on for what seemed like miles with some official-looking men—police, probably—milling around.

"What does it say?" Paul asked.

"This is a from a Croatian newspaper. It details an enormous grave found in a remote part of the country in which two thousand eighty-seven bodies were discovered. All men. All circumcised. All castrated."

"Jesus."

"Oh, it gets better. It appears to have been an ongoing operation. The corpses at one end of the site were dated to be nearly three thousand years old while those at the opposite end proved to be only three *months* old."

"And you're saying Viola was somehow involved in this?" Paul asked. His extremities abruptly felt as though they'd spent significant time in a meat locker, and his pulse sounded in his ears.

"I'm saying more than that. I'm saying she did some of them herself. You think these foreskins simply appeared because the good lord willed them into being?"

Paul swallowed what felt like a lump of clay. "You're suggesting Viola Datsun, the church girl and nightclub server, helped castrate and kill countless men and then kept their foreskins to use as post-coital canapés?"

"Sounds crazy when you say it out loud, doesn't it?"

"It sounds crazy when I just think it."

"Well, it's the truth. Crazy or not, it's the truth."

"Why haven't I ever heard about this mass grave on the History Channel? Something like this, it's got to register somewhere other than some shitty local rag."

"Someone suppressed this information. And information about other, deeper graves found in other territories."

He removed a printout from a website detailing another tomb discovered in the Russian wilderness near Siberia. It had no picture accompanying it and the text itself appeared to a first-person eyewitness account rather than a credible news piece.

"Where did you find this?"

"I go to the library on occasion. Sometimes I dabble on the internet. I found this baby on a site devoted to uncovering things governments don't want uncovered."

"A conspiracy theory site. They're a dime a dozen these days, Stan."

"Not this one. This had a video clip at the bottom of the page. I saw the bodies."

"You saw what some prankster wanted you to see."

"Then why did the website get shut down?"

Paul blinked. "It got shut down?"

"I went back later after I bought one of those jump drives. I wanted to download the video and add it to my collection, but when I tried to pull up the website, it said the domain did not exist."

"Did you ever consider maybe the pranksters forgot to pay the bill and the site expired?"

"Maybe, except for one thing."

"What's that?"

"The next time I visited the library, a man approached and asked to have a word with me. At first I thought he must be an employee, maybe the circulation clerk wanting to let me know I had some late fees, but a closer look told me this was no librarian." Olson sauntered over to the kitchenette, found some fresh glasses, and poured a round of scotch. Paul tried to refuse, saying they still had driving to do, but Olson insisted. "Trust me, you'll want it."

"So what did this guy look like?" Paul asked, accepting the drink.

"Foreign. If you strapped me down and threatened to drill out my knees, I couldn't say from where exactly. His accent was muddled, his suit was Italian, and his skin tone looked Middle Eastern. Had eyes like smoldering coals, stoic, dead. He led me to an empty conference room and quietly closed the door." Olson took a slug of scotch.

"What did he want?"

"He was polite but firm. He told me to cease and desist in my search."

"How did he know it was you? You were on a public computer."

"Hell if I know, but he knew. He told me I was being watched and should I continue, the consequences would be dire. Not for me, but for my family."

That sounded ominously similar to Ms. Bloch's warning over the phone, but Paul refrained from saying so.

"Did you go to the police?" he asked, taking a sip of his own drink.

"These people are larger than the law. They're not simply above it, they exist outside it."

"But who was he? Where did he come from? Some foreign government hoping to cover up the graves?"

"He wasn't from no government. He was one of *theirs*."

"One of whose?"

"Theirs. The vampires."

"Christ, can we please stop calling them that?"

"You have a better name for them?"

Paul didn't. "So this guy, what—works for them?"

Olson cracked a lopsided grin. "In a sense. But not for money."

"For sex?"

"What else?"

"Did he look … "

"Old?" Olson finished for him. "Like me?"

"Yeah."

"Not in the least. Very fit, handsome."

"Then there goes your theory. If these vampires, as you call them, were paying in sex, he'd have had his life force sucked dry, too."

"Maybe not," Olson said.

"What do you mean?"

"Well, compensating your workers by taking from them is a fairly backward concept, wouldn't you agree?"

"I don't follow."

"These women get a man to attach to them—like Viola did with me—and then they get them to do their dirty work. In trade, the man gets the run of their bodies as often as possible, but the women don't leach from them. Or don't leach as much."

"Instead of taking a guzzle, they only take a sip. Like a tax," Paul said, fascinated. It still sounded crazy, only now less so.

"Exactly like a tax."

"So if they have bodyguards lurking around, how did Viola happen to get taken?" Paul asked.

"I don't know the ins and outs. I was never privy to that information. I just have a working theory and to my mind it works pretty damn well."

"I'm inclined to agree. Against my better judgment, I'm inclined."

"What other explanation is there? You've seen the evidence in the mirror."

"I'd still like to see more of it at Haven Chapel." Paul checked his watch and set his glass aside. "Come on, it's almost show time."

Chapter Thirty-Eight

Michelle had made it forty miles before realizing she'd left her phone behind in her haste to be home. A cancerous dread grew in her as she patted her purse pockets and checked the center console before giving in to the fact it remained on her mother's kitchen table—right where she'd left it. She imagined Darlene spotting it as her daughter backed out of the driveway and rushing to flag her down but missing out at the last second.

Now Michelle would be completely cut off from communication with her family until she arrived in Lake Winona. The idea sent a ripple of grief through her, followed by a wave of terror. Nothing happening today could possibly be construed as correct; everything felt wrong, as if the world had somehow slipped askew on its axis.

With rush hour tapering off on the tollway, at least there shouldn't be much traffic to battle (although who could be sure with the GPS app sitting uselessly on her phone resting 70,000 yards in her rearview mirror?). There hadn't been any noteworthy construction zones on the way down, fortunately. Michelle stepped on the accelerator and brought the car up to seventy-five. Four miles later she saw the endless line of taillights reddening the winter eve.

"Motherfucking pig-sucker!" she screamed. It must be an accident—there seemed no end to the line of stalled traffic a mile or so ahead. If she had had her GPS, it could have provided an alternate route. But no. She just had to run off all scatterbrained. Who could blame her, though? Her father had passed away in a terrible manner, if you believed the cops, and she'd left a distraught mother and two innocent children behind to go try to find out why the hell her husband wasn't answering his goddamned cell phone.

"Paul, you son of a bitch," Michelle whispered, tears trembling at the corners of her eyes. "You sorry, stupid son of a *bitch*."

An unmarked exit ramp appeared, and she took it. There would be a fueling station in town and maybe she could buy an old school paper map to plot an alternate route. It would get her there later, but any progress would be better than idling in traffic for the next two hours and once she found she had this country route to herself, she could cruise northward going a brisk seventy-five.

Thirty minutes later a battered, dirty sign appeared proclaiming she'd arrived in the village of Duck Valley, Ill., *Home of Creole Corn Stew!*—something Michelle never wished to sample let alone set eyes on. The town was the first she'd seen since leaving the Interstate. Secluded. Tucked way back in cornfields. A crossroads spread across the center with four businesses on the corresponding corners: a fueling station, a church, a post office, and a combination fire/police station. Far up the main avenue, residential roads spread out like tributaries from a river. Of the four trades, only the gas station showed signs of life and Michelle pulled in and parked.

The only other car was a beat-up old Ford Fiesta which might once have been red but had faded pansy pink over two decades of joyrides. Michelle pushed into the store, expecting the chime of a bell hung over the jamb but found herself disappointed on that count. The only sound came from a radio somewhere playing gospel music.

She found a rack of maps standing beside the Hostess snack stand, picked the one she wanted, and went to the counter. No one manned it. She called a hail in hopes of rousing some lazy attendant from his backroom porn haze. No one answered.

Somewhere toward the back of the store, a toilet gushed as loud as Niagara. Michelle spun toward it and a young woman in a smock and pink-framed eyeglasses stepped out carrying a copy of *People* magazine. She hummed something off-key, and when she saw Michelle standing at the counter actually jumped.

"Oh, holy *cow*," she said. "I didn't know you were in here."

"You might have if you had a door chime," Michelle said, more maliciously than she'd intended. The girl looked at her, expressionless. "I'm sorry. I didn't mean to startle you."

"It's okay," the girl said. "We don't usually get many customers from the highway."

"I'd like to buy this," Michelle said, flapping the map.

The girl edged around the counter. "You going north?"

"That's the idea."

"Why not just take fifty-five?"

"I just got off fifty-five. Traffic's backed up about ten miles."

"Oh, jeez. That's a bummer, for real."

"How much?"

The girl looked from the map to the register to Michelle as if unsure what to do. "You know what? It's only like a buck. Why don't you just take it?"

Michelle blinked. No one in a gas station had ever offered her something for free, not even high school boys trying to hit on her. "Are you sure?"

"Yeah, it's no problem. Sometimes I—" A high, screaming siren cut the clerk off. They looked out the window and saw a Village of Duck Valley police car whip around the police station and head for the highway.

"They're a little late," Michelle said. "The accident must have happened an hour ago with how far traffic was backed up."

"Our boys don't deal with the highway," the clerk said. "That's state police jurisdiction."

"Maybe it's worse than the state police can handle," Michelle said. "Anyway, thanks for the map."

She turned and pushed out the door and headed for the car, then thought of something and returned. The clerk stood in the same position behind the register.

"Do you have a pay phone?"

"Yeah. In back. Not sure if it works. You're the first person to ever ask about it since I've worked here."

Michelle thanked her and found it in an alcove between the restrooms. A phonebook from 2002 dangled from a steel cable. The cover read *Ashford – Ashford Heights – Derby Dale – Duck Valley – Hogan – Murdoch – Sommerville & surrounding areas.* Many of the pages appeared to have been torn out over the ensuing years since its publication. Michelle snatched up the receiver, fed in some change without looking at the denominations, and waited for a live line. She'd nearly forgotten how to use one of these relics and only knew how because she'd gone a semester in college without being able to afford a cell and had had to use the payphone at the end of the corridor on her dormitory floor to call Paul.

Or to call Tom, a tiny voice in her head reminded her. *We don't want to leave that chapter of your life out, do we?*

The line purred in her ear. She willed her husband to pick up so she could save herself the long drive and return to be with her mother and kids, but by the third ring she knew he wouldn't. At least he'd turned his phone back on. She stood studying a yellowed flyer for a country band called Wes Waters and the Six-Gun Shufflers who'd apparently been scheduled to perform at some bar in December of 2012. The clerk was right; no one must ever use this phone.

When his voicemail answered, she said: "Paul, I don't know where you are or what you're doing or why you won't respond to my calls. I can only think something terrible has happened to you and so I'm on my way home to find out." She took a deep breath, despair creeping in, and finished her piece. "I didn't want to say this over the phone, but Dad's dead. The police suspect foul play is involved. Paul, there was a woman in the house last night. Jeannie says it's the same one she saw before. The one who gave her night terrors. They think this woman might have killed Dad. I don't know what's going on, but I know somehow you're involved in this. Maybe the cause of it. We need to talk. I don't have my cell. Call me back at this number immediately." She gave the number listed on the payphone and clunked the receiver into its cradle. She couldn't wait long for him to call back, but if it meant avoiding another three hours on the road (or more, depending on traffic), she could spare five minutes.

Michelle dropped more change into the phone and called her mother's house. No one answered and her despair swelled.

Emily at least answered. Michelle explained the forgotten phone and how neither her husband nor mother were answering her calls.

"Don't worry, hon," Emily said. "The kiddos and I will take a drive over and make sure she's okay. I'll be happy to take a break from *Phineas and Ferb*."

"Thanks, Em. I'm sure she's just sleeping, but I'm worrying myself into old age here." She gave her friend the call back number, thanked her again, and then approached the front counter.

The clerk sat reading her magazine behind the register. No other customer had come in and the girl seemed to have forgotten Michelle altogether as a pinky probed one nostril and then the other.

"Excuse me," Michelle said. The girl snapped her head up and dropped her hand to her lap as though she'd been caught stealing.

"Do you mind getting me a cup of that coffee you have brewing back there?"

"That's for employees only, ma'am, but there's a coffee machine by the pop coolers."

Michelle found it and filled a large Styrofoam cup. She selected a pre-wrapped blueberry muffin, paid for the items, and took a seat in the waiting section primarily reserved for long-haul truckers taking a break from the road. Though she had little appetite, she ate the overly moist pastry, pored over the map, and waited for the phone to ring.

When it trilled ten minutes later, Michelle bolted to it. Emily happily reported Darlene had answered the door and had indeed been asleep when she missed her daughter's call. "In fact, we're moving the party over here," she said.

"I don't know if that's a good idea," Michelle said.

"Your mom misses the kiddos. I think she's lonely, Shelly."

Michelle sighed. "You're right."

"And there's a cop posted outside. A hot one. So, bonus."

"Don't get any funny ideas around my kids."

Emily laughed. "You know I'm joking. I'll stick around until she throws me out."

"Thanks again, Em," Michelle said, grateful. She felt better knowing someone not so close to the situation would be keeping an eye on her family.

They hung up and she decided she'd finish her coffee to give Paul time to call her back. A divide had opened in her: part of her knew she must continue homeward, but the other part felt a sickening dread at leaving her children and distraught mother behind.

Goddamn you, Paul, she thought for the hundredth time. *Goddamn you for putting us in this position*. She didn't think anything could be the same between them again. At this point, their marriage could still be salvaged, but something would always remain between them—a dark sliver of resentment that could easily widen into a chasm at the flip of a switch.

The door opened and a woman in a police uniform stepped through. She appeared about the same age as the clerk, and the two began chatting in chirpy tones. Michelle approached, pretending to scan a rack of candy bars in order to hear what all the excitement was about.

"… and Bobby called in that it was practically just a skeleton behind the wheel."

"No shit?" the clerk asked, awed disgust in her voice.

"No shit," the dispatcher confirmed. She sensed Michelle behind her and turned. "Hey, you planning on getting on the highway anytime soon?"

Michelle looked up. "I—no. I was checking this map for an alternate route. I saw the traffic jam and got off here."

"Good idea, ma'am," the dispatcher said. "I don't think they'll be clearing that stretch anytime soon."

"What was that about a skeleton?"

The dispatcher licked her lips as if deciding how much to say. Finally, she came up with, "Oh, hell. It's supposed to be confidential, but I already told Tanya here. What could it hurt?"

"You always tell me everything that gets called in, Maggie." She regarded Michelle with a gleam in her eye. "Especially the gooshy stuff."

"Twelve-car pileup near mile marker one-sixty. The first responders—the staties—say they found nothing but a dried-up mummy behind the wheel of one of the lead cars." She glanced between the clerk and her customer. "It had its fly unzipped and its pecker out."

Michelle couldn't help but think of her father. "Did they say what caused it?"

"What caused it was he died," the dispatcher said as if speaking to a particularly daft child.

"People don't just die and turn into a mummy."

"The M.E. usually takes twenty-four hours before he can figger out what happened to a body," the dispatcher said with an air of importance. "That is if you can drag him away from the fairway."

"Someone must have a preliminary conclusion," Michelle said. The others stared at her as if she'd spoken Sanskrit.

"I don't know anything about that, but Bobby—he's my boyfriend and a helluva cop—texted me this pic. They found it drawn on the windshield in lipstick."

Michelle edged forward, eyes fixed on the phone's screen, but she didn't have to look to know what it would be: Venus's distaff.

"Holy shit, it's an ankh," the clerk, Tanya, said. She dipped two fingers down the front of her blouse and brought up an emblem dangling from the end of a chain which strongly resembled the image on Maggie the dispatcher's cell and the ones found scrawled on the mirrors of her mother's home. They bore subtle differences but appeared similar enough to be kissing cousins. "It's an Egyptian hieroglyph that means 'life.'"

"There wasn't nothing alive in that car, girl," Maggie the police dispatcher said.

"I have to leave now," Michelle said, heading for the door. "I have to get home."

Before she could push through, though, the payphone rang.

Chapter Thirty-Nine

By 9:30 the snow had stopped, and Haven Revival appeared empty. No cars in the lot, no lights on in the chapel. Paul pulled around back so the car wouldn't be seen from the road. He sat hunched over the wheel, idling, making no move to switch off the ignition.

"Let's get this over with," Olson said.

"I'm trying to decide if we're being watched. I don't sense it like I did this morning. Do you?"

Olson held still. "My Spidey sense ain't tingling now."

They got out, Paul abruptly unsure whether he wanted to proceed. He wanted to untangle this enigma, but the idea of breaking into a fringe sect house of worship seemed precipitously unappealing.

Olson wheeled his oxygen tank behind him like a steel puppy. The tube leading from it to his nose occasionally gasped air into his lungs. They reached the back door and Paul set his ear against it. Aside from a constant low hum that could be nothing more than electricity running through cables, he heard nothing.

The door was locked, of course, but they'd come prepared. With a hammer scrounged from Olson's toolbox, Paul tapped the stained glass out of the sill before reaching inside to snap back the lock. He thought he'd feel a twinge of guilt at breaking into a church, but it never came. Neither did the sense of being watched. Maybe it had been only straight paranoia when they'd visited this morning, but he doubted it. Olson had said he'd felt it, too. But now the sensation remained at bay, and it settled his nerves.

"Hurry up," Stan whispered. "I'm freezing my ass off."

Paul pushed into the church and clicked on one of his impulse-buy flashlights. Olson switched on a second and they played their beams over the walls of some type of backroom storage area. Tupperware bins stood in stacks along the walls; Paul popped the lid on one and discovered a mess of broken crucifixes.

"Check it out," he said, hoisting one.

Olson adjusted his glasses. "What the hell?"

"There's a shitload of them. Some are melted."

"Doesn't seem very Christian, does it?"

"My thought exactly."

Down the hall they found a row of file cabinets, all locked. They explored two offices but found nothing of interest except a ring loaded with keys. From somewhere a clock chimed the quarter-hour.

The chapel opened before them when Olson stumbled on the stage left door. A pair of security lamps burned high up in the corners of the steepled ceiling, casting the rows of pews in shadow. Paul marked the place where he'd first spotted Viola. Had that been only last Sunday? It seemed ages had passed since then.

"Nothing," Olson said. His tank snorted.

"Wait. Look at this," Paul said, examining the back of the enormous crucifix hanging over the stage.

"I'll be damned," Olson muttered. From behind, the sacred symbol had been fixed to appear as the image of Venus's distaff, with the circular portion constructed from some kind of woven silk. He walked around the front it appeared as a halo around the savior's head. From the back, the effigy was all but invisible.

"I think we're onto something heavy here," Paul whispered. "Let's keep looking."

They found a heavy oak door and after a few minutes of fumbling through the keys, picked one that fit the iron lock set into the wood. When they'd dragged the door back—it took both of them—the odor that wafted up forced both to cover their faces.

"What is it?" Paul gasped.

"Smells like a mixture of incense, burnt cloth, and blood."

"This is a bad idea. Let's get the hell out of here."

"We're here. Might as well finish the job."

"You want to go down there?" Paul asked.

"Nope. Can't anyhow. It'd be hell dragging this contraption up and down those stairs." As if in acknowledgment, the machine sniffed. "You go."

"I'm not going alone."

"Sure, you are. You want to know what's down there as bad as I do."

"Not anymore."

"You said it yourself—this place is a ghost town. Go on. I'll stand guard. If someone comes, I'll holler."

He had a point. The place *did* feel empty. The sensation of being observed had not returned and surely someone would have come to investigate their presence by now, especially any hungry she-vampire who might be on site.

He tried a last-ditch effort to get out of this. "This whole thing was your idea, Stan."

"You're just as curious as I am, and you know it. You want to know what these people really are. Could be we turn up something newsworthy. Something that could change the world."

Paul thought that dramatic, but Olson was right. He did want to know what these people were all about. "Okay. But just a peek. Then we're heading to Cabana Girls. Deal?"

"Deal."

Paul took a shallow breath, mindful of the noxious odor rising from the cellar, and took the steps slowly. He became conscious of his pulse thudding in his temples and, incredibly, an erection throbbing in his jeans. He imagined Olson suddenly slamming the door and twisting the key, laughing maniacally. If that happened, his heart would probably seize, and he'd be dead before he hit the cellar floor.

But Olson stood where he'd promised, watching his back. The tank snuffed. Paul aimed the beam at the basement landing, but it did little to push back the shadows lurking there. When he reached the bottom, a cavernous space opened around him like a void. He flicked his light around in a sweeping arc. The rock foundation wept in places. The source of the odor remained unclear. An arched doorway led to a deeper chamber and Paul reluctantly stepped through it, heart thudding like a living animal against his ribcage.

The new space was even larger than the first and was not empty. An idol taller than the crucifix in the chapel dominated the room. This was a sort of crucifix, too, Paul saw, but one deeply sacrilegious: a naked white figure of Christ hung upside down from the arms of Venus's mirror, the legs splayed in a horrific parody of the splits. The arms dangled toward the floor as if something there may offer succor. The figure had been castrated. Red liquid—paint or blood, he couldn't tell—stained the figure's naked chest in streaks.

Paul could not recall a moment of deeper terror he'd experienced, not even after he realized someone had been in Lucine's house or when he felt the cold curls of the cadaver's hair in the bed. He was no longer a religious man but found this

248

affront to Christianity somehow an assault on everything he knew. He backed out of the chamber, unable to tear his eyes from the effigy. Whatever Haven Revival was, he wanted nothing more to do with it. What they had going on in their basement likely wasn't illegal, but Paul had an idea the church might be run out of town if the natives knew what he'd found. If anything, this would make national headlines. Maybe even international.

Get moving, Paulie, the rational part of his mind whispered. *You still have time to remove yourself from this situation. Get the hell out before something happens—*

But it was too late. Something happened.

The alabaster figure jerked. It lifted its face with what must have been an agony of motion and Paul realized with horror the face belonged to Ben Gehant.

Chapter Forty

When the phone rang again, Michelle rushed to it. "Paul? Is that you?"

"It's me. Michelle, I'm sorry I haven't called before now but you need to listen to me."

"What the hell have you been doing?" she said, her relief turning to fury. "Everything's in chaos and you disappear."

"I know. I know, baby, and I'm sorry. I'm sorry about your father but let me talk. Okay? It's important."

"I'm listening." She became aware that both the clerk and the dispatcher had stopped to eavesdrop. She turned her back to them.

"You need to stay at your mother's for now. Keep the kids there, help with funeral arrangements, whatever. Do not come home now, do you understand?"

"Why? Paul, what the *fuck* is going on?"

"I need you to trust me, Shelly. I promise everything is going to be all right."

"Is it about the person who broke into our house? It is, isn't it? It's the same woman who broke into my parents' house. The one who killed Dad."

"Maybe. Some very bad shit is going down here, and I need you to stay put. You'll be safe at your mother's."

"My father was just killed in that house. How can you say any of us are safe?"

"Because the person who killed your father is in Lake Winona now. Besides, she doesn't want anyone else in that house."

"How can you know that?"

"She only kills men."

"Paul, what are you going to do? You need to leave if you're in danger."

"I'm not in danger. She is."

"Did you call the police?"

His voice came through the line neutral, practically dead. "No. They'll only fuck things up."

Michelle shivered. "You're going after her yourself?"

"I have to."

"Why?"

Another pause, longer this time. "I have to atone for wrongdoings. And she needs to pay. For Ned and for scaring our children half to death."

"Who is she, Paul?" Michelle heard herself ask as if from a fathom underwater. "What's the name of the woman you fucked behind my back?"

No hesitation and no hint of guilt, just that same dead tone. "Viola Datsun. Go back to your mother's, Shelly. I'll be down in time for Ned's funeral."

Michelle opened her mouth to protest, but the line clicked dead. She stood for a moment in the unnatural silence of the store, staring at the receiver as if it might suddenly come to life.

"Ma'am? Is everything okay?" the clerk asked.

"No, it's not," she said before striding out of the store and to her car. She peeled out of the lot. She turned the car north instead of south. Toward Lake Winona. Toward her husband and home and whatever trouble lay ahead. Somehow she knew she'd have to handle it. She always did, it seemed.

Chapter Forty-One

Part of him knew Olson would be gone when he returned, but the old man still stood his post. For one horrific moment, he thought his companion had been reduced to a mummified skeleton but the former Army major tottered back from the head of the stairs to make room for Paul.

"We're getting the fuck out of here," Paul said.

"What did you find?"

"Tell you outside."

Paul hurried to the car, relieved beyond reason to see it still sat parked in the back lot. He fumbled the keys into the ignition and cranked it, fully suspecting some murderous maniac to burst from the shadows with a bander and blade, ready to castrate. No one came. Paul waited for Olson to climb in, tapping the wheel impatiently, then swerved out of the lot and onto the highway, tires skidding on the slick surface.

"Paul, slow down. What did you see?" Olson gasped.

"We need to call the police. There's a mutilated man in the basement. It's Ben Gehant."

"Holy Christ, are you kidding?"

"Do I look like I'm fucking kidding, Stan?" Paul barked. He dug out his cell and dumped it in his passenger's lap. "Dial nine-one-one."

But the old man made no move to pick up the phone. "Hold on a minute. Think this through."

"All I'm thinking through is testifying against these bastards in open court."

"There could be consequences if—"

"I don't give a damn about consequences. Someone castrated a man and left him to die down there. If you'd seen it, you'd be on my side."

"I am on your side, Paul, but you need to think this through all the way to the end. I'm not saying don't call the cops; I'm saying call it in anonymously. Like you did with Vi. No reason to implicate yourself."

What the old man said made sense. Of course it did. But Paul couldn't get the image of Ben Gehant suspended upside down, legs splayed at that horribly impossible angle, the place where his genitals had been nothing more than a gaping red wound …

"If that bitch did this … if Viola had something to do with what I saw down there, I don't care if you're in love or obsessed or whatever. I'm going to kill her myself. You don't … you don't do something like that to a man and let him live through it."

Olson wisely made no reply.

Paul could think of nothing else to do but go to Cabana Girls. Perhaps Viola had set up her own disappearance. Maybe she'd gotten wind someone might be coming for her and tried to set them off her trail. If she truly was what Olson thought she was, Paul figured she'd possess the means to pull something of that magnitude off. Or maybe the blood on her wall had been from the person or people who'd come for her. The police should be notified about the poor bastard hanging in the cellar with his unit removed. Did the club have a payphone? He couldn't recall.

Tonight, even the overflow lot teemed with vehicles. The music pulsed so loud it penetrated the car's windows, like what a child must hear when he places his head against his mother's chest. Paul found a metered street slot three blocks up and parallel parked between a Dodge SUV and some sporty coupe which had no business being driven on sleet-slick streets.

"It's going to be a hike," he told Olson.

"You go. I need to catch my breath and I'll call the cops about Gehant, okay?" Paul opened his door, but the old man clutched his wrist. "Listen, if you find out what happened to her, you come get me. I need to know."

Paul nodded once sharply, then stepped into the street. He thought about laying eyes on Lucine Korth for the first time. Her, not her image. She would be here; he could practically feel her drawing him on as if she possessed a gravitational pull.

He found his phone and called up Linda Lopez's profile on his Facebook app and checked Lucine's status. No change since her last post, but he knew she was here just the same. Perhaps sharing drinks with Viola. And if Viola happened to be here, well, Paul would look for an opening to kill her. Not because he cared a lick for Ben Gehant, but the assault offended his manhood. Who did these murderous bitches think they were?

Something else occurred to him. How did one kill a creature such as her? A stake through the heart? No, that was merely mythology. Although, he argued with himself, the notion of vampirism had seemed mythical to him only yesterday.

If it bleeds, it can die, he thought, the phrase from some stupid late-night action movie rising to mind.

The phone's voicemail icon showed new messages, and Paul reluctantly called them up. Both were from Michelle, but the second made him stop mid-stride. She reported her father had died and that she was on her way home. She asked him to call an unfamiliar number, which he did, in the alley beside the bar, partly to console her on her loss but mostly to insist she stay in Springfield. He couldn't have her showing up tonight. Not with what he had planned.

Chapter Forty-Two

By the time he got past the Cabana Girls bouncer, Paul thought he'd convinced his wife to return to Springfield. Surely she would not wish to leave their children and her distraught mother to come home. And by the time he'd set foot in the nightclub proper, he'd dismissed the idea altogether.

The place thumped with electronica music. The air reeked of booze and body spray. Someone shoulder-checked him, swore, and disappeared into the throng. There must have been five hundred people drinking, gyrating, or engaged in mouth-to-ear conversation, but he picked out Lucine Korth at once.

Paul had never had an instant physical reaction by simply seeing someone and the sensation caught him off-guard. He could actually feel his pupils dilate. A bizarre ringing separate from the incessant music began in his ears. He salivated so swiftly he had to spit on the floor between his feet. The flesh covering his ribs tingled into gooseflesh and the erection abruptly tightening his pants shocked him with its immediacy.

Lucine stood in the center of a crowd like the pistil of a flower. She wore a nightdress of red silk, her hair—now platinum blonde—woven into a complex series of ladder-like braids. In person, her features stood out more prominently than any two-dimensional image could ever hope to convey: lips like moistened rose petals, petite nose with perfectly symmetrical nostrils, eyes as mysterious and shimmering as twin tropical pools at night. She cupped a gossamer goblet filled with wine between her delicate yet somehow strong fingers. Paul knew exactly how they'd feel when they gripped him in the night.

And he *would* feel them or die trying. All at once, nothing else mattered. Not Michelle, not dead Ned, not Ben Gehant or Viola Datsun or Stanley Olson. He locked onto her like a heat-seeking missile and moved in.

A server skated up and asked for his order. "Not right now," he said without looking at her.

She tapped him on the shoulder and pointed at the two-drink minimum sign posted near the bar. "What'll it be, handsome?"

He growled out an order for a vodka gimlet, then returned his gaze to Lucine. Only now the crowd had swallowed her, perhaps borne her away to some private backroom soiree. Yes—there she went, ducking behind a heavy curtain of red velvet.

Paul clenched his fists, a feral grimace on his face. When the server returned, he asked her if Viola was working tonight.

"She called in sick," the server replied.

"She called in herself?"

The woman shook her head and when she did, it shook all her other assets as well. "Her boyfriend. I guess she was too sick to call herself."

"What's her boyfriend's name?"

The server put on a tart smile. "Which one?"

Paul jutted his chin at the curtain, flanked by two bouncers as wide as they were tall. "How do I get in there?"

"You can't. It's a private party."

"For whom?"

"That's private."

"Come on. Tell me how to get past those goons." He brought out his billfold and showed her one of Gehant's fifty-dollar bills. He felt a little low for spending a dead man's money (for even if he wasn't dead now he would be soon), but not enough to pass up an audience with Lucine. Also, Gehant wouldn't be needing it anymore.

"It'll take more than that to get in," she said. He showed another fifty. She took both bills and folded them into her cleavage. "Wait here."

Paul loitered near the bar, eyeing anyone who ducked inside the curtain. Each person—around a dozen well-dressed men, most foreign-looking, had shown the bouncers some kind of invitation printed on card stock. He sipped his drink without tasting it, wondering what could be going on in there.

The ice in his glass had melted when the server finally returned. She slipped something in his back pocket and winked. "Have fun, handsome."

Paul stalked off. He thought she might insist on his second drink, but she only watched him move away. The bouncers stared at him stoically as he approached, arms crossed over the drums of their chests.

"What do you want?" one asked, the same guy who'd chased him off the first time he'd dropped by.

Paul presented the purchased invitation. The guy looked it over. "Man, get outta here with this fake-ass bullshit," he said.

The partner glared at Paul. "Marissa give that to you? She's always fucking with the new guys."

"That bitch ripped me off?" he replied.

"I've got a mind to take you out back, teach you some manners when it comes to our lady friends," bouncer number one said.

"I doubt your manager would appreciate you beating up the clientele. You might find yourself on the breadline come morning."

"It'd be worth it," the guy said.

"Let him through, Jay," the partner said. "Might be he wants to leave on his own once he sees what's behind curtain number one."

The guard name Jay gave his partner a sidelong glance and shook the thick bulb of his head. "He's got to earn his invitation, like everyone else." He leaned in close, his breath a putrid mix of grain alcohol and peppermint gum. "I see your face around here again, I'll put you in a coma."

Paul's heart skipped at that—what could possibly be happening back there that a man would threaten bodily harm? Something illegal, no doubt. He backed away, thinking he'd simply go back to the car, drop Stan off, and go home ... but the allure of Lucine forbade such nonsense. He needed to gaze upon her glory again, if even for a moment.

I'll just have a peek and then get the hell out of Dodge, he told himself. *I'll go home, take a shower, get some sleep, and in the morning I'll drive down to Springfield for the funeral.*

There had to be a back door somewhere.

Another bouncer stood guard outside, of course, but Paul knew how to handle him. He watched the guy kicked back on his stool and scrolling on his phone—this job would be boring as hell since the only traffic to come back here would be some wayward club kid too drunk to find his car.

Paul watched from the shadows as the guy giggled at something he saw on his device—a crazy cat video or perhaps bestiality porn. Paul felt along the ground for something he could use as a weapon and finally turned up a length of rusted pipe. Then he crept forward, cat-quiet.

The bouncer never saw him. One moment he sat perched and browsing and the next he was down and drowsing. Paul didn't think he had hit him hard enough to kill him, but he didn't care. Pure primal instinct drove him. He wondered if it would feel the same to club someone with the cudgel he kept for home defense.

He found the bouncer's keys beneath the guy's mass and used them to unlock the back door. He faced a short, dark vestibule leading to an interior door standing dead ahead. Some kind of bastardized baroque music seeped beneath it, the notes emanating from what sounded like the bowels of an enormous pipe organ.

This door, too, stood locked against him, but Paul picked out the correct key and fixed the problem. Over his shoulder, the bouncer still lay on his belly, guttural breaths issuing from his maw.

Paul inched the door inward. It opened into an alcove flanked by restrooms. A polished oaken bar began at the outside of the recess and ran halfway around the room, though no one tended it now. No one was drinking.

The chamber lay bathed in blood-red light. A spotlight shone into the center of the room, where two dozen naked men stood in line, stretching back into the shadows. On a raised dais, directly beneath the light, lay Lucine Korth. She, too, was naked, her legs splayed before her as she accepted each man into her body, one by one.

Paul had watched his fair share of porn in college (and in his home life, truth be told, though its grip on him had eased over the years) and he recalled one clip in particular of some rising star fucking five hundred men. She'd been situated exactly like this, face impassive as each man pumped into her one after another in thirty-second spurts.

He could pick out only two differences in this scenario. First, Lucine's face was less than impassive. It was stoic, completely devoid of emotion. The second difference was that as each man spent himself inside her, they began to shudder in a series of seizure-like spasms, before dropping away on his knees. Each man who'd completed his part in this ritualistic scenario sat huddled against one wall, knees to their chests, heads down, like men taking siestas on a hot street in Juarez.

It took only the third man to reach this slumbered state before Paul understood they had crawled away to die. Each had paid an undoubtedly vast sum in order for this to be his final act in this realm. Had they been hypnotized? Drugged? No, Paul understood. They each did this of their own free will. Lucine had dug into each of them deep, as she had with him. How many times had Paul thought that if he could just be with Lucine once, a single time, it would be enough for him and he could die? A hundred times? A thousand? Michelle's face rose in his mind and he nearly vomited right there.

He took a stumbling step backward but Lucine's head turned toward him as if on a piston. He watched her eyes mark him, store his features.

Her voice, clear as day in his head, said: *My lover, my slave. You've found me at last. And I've found you.*

Only then did she smile, and darkness slid from her eyes.

Chapter Forty-Three

Paul ran, leaping over the fallen bouncer. He didn't want to see anymore. Olson had been right—Korth was a vampire. Or a succubus. Or something unnatural. Maybe there wasn't a word for what she was. All he knew is he'd seen enough. He only wanted to get to his family.

Part of him knew he'd find Olson dead once he returned to the car, but the old guy merely looked up in anticipation as Paul slid behind the wheel.

"You get a look at her?" Olson asked.

Paul opened his mouth to answer, but only a wheezing squeak came out. He tried again, this time able to explain what he'd seen. And what had seen him. "Her eyes. Stan, good God, her *eyes* … "

"She's the queen," Olson said, mystified. "She's the one who passed the carven box to my Viola."

"What the hell are you talking about?"

"The darkness you saw coming from her eyes—Paul, that means she rules the colony. You have no idea how powerful she is."

"I'm leaving town. Now. Tonight." But the words sounded hollow in his ears.

Olson grabbed Paul's wrist before he could get the key to the ignition. "You'll want to be careful, my friend. Once she's seen you, she can find you anytime she wants. Christ, I would never have figured their queen would come *here*."

"I have to go," Paul said. "Thanks for everything, Stan. Really. You've been a great help."

He dropped Olson at his apartment building without offering to see him inside. As Paul pulled away, he glimpsed the old man standing on the curb, gazing longingly at the apartment complex across the street. As if willing his favorite lady to return. But Paul didn't think Viola would be coming back. Ms. Bloch had seen to that.

When Paul got home, he found Ms. Bloch's number and dialed it. He meant to spill everything he'd seen in Cabana Girls' backroom. Maybe she still had some of her people still lurking around who could send Lucine wherever they'd sent Viola.

Ms. Bloch's assistant answered on the first ring and said, "Good evening, Mr. Jeske."

"I need to speak to your supervisor."

"Ms. Bloch is currently unavailable, sir."

"This is urgent. It's about the queen."

A long pause. "Please hold."

As the line clicked through miles of relays, Paul imagined a dim, smoky backroom in some Viennese villa with chaise furniture and a view of the city with a full moon hanging in the sky. He clearly saw the phone on that end of the line ringing — a black thing with a rotary dial from a bygone era. The hand picking it up would be porcelain-white and crosshatched with blue veins, a cigarillo in an ivory holder clasped between the first two fingers while the remaining three lifted the receiver.

"Hello, Mr. Jeske."

"Ms. Bloch—"

"I'd like to thank you for your assistance in helping our agents apprehend a very dangerous woman in your area."

"Ms. Bloch, listen—"

"So we're clear, this number will no longer be active after this call is terminated. Take no offense—it's merely a security measure to ensure our organization is not compromised or influenced by external entities."

"Ms. Bloch, there's another one."

"I beg your pardon?"

"There's another … whatever the hell they are. I saw her tonight. She's far more powerful than Viola. I think she's the queen. Or *a* queen. Or whatever the head of their group is called."

A considering pause. When Ms. Bloch spoke again, her voice had gone flat and toneless. "What makes you say so?"

Paul described what he'd witnessed. When he finished, he said, "Please tell me you still have agents in the area, Ms. Bloch. She's dangerous. She looked right at me and *knew everything about me*."

"Give me the address, Mr. Jeske."

"She was at a club called Cabana Girls up on Lakeland Drive, but when she's here in town she stays at two hundred Pace Lane."

"I'll have operatives investigate. Thank you for reporting, Mr. Jeske." Another pause from the European end of the line. "You're correct to assume she is dangerous. You'd do well to take precautions."

"Wait, Ms. Bloch, I need to know how to stop her."

Ms. Bloch said, "You can't stop her. No man can. Stay away from her, Mr. Jeske."

The call terminated and Paul stood staring at a dead phone. Behind him, the front door creaked open.

Chapter Forty-Four

Michelle hit the city limits at midnight going better than seventy miles per hour. Their house stood a few miles up the road, but here the highway turned residential, and traffic forced her foot off the gas.

"Fucking *move* already," she muttered at a minivan ahead of her. She wondered how the kids were faring. And her mother. Good God, her poor mother.

Traffic did not move faster following her directive. In fact, it slowed to a crawl before stopping altogether. Michelle pounded the steering wheel in frustration and cursed anything holy she could think of. Then, up ahead, she saw exactly what had everything stalled.

A cadre of LWPD cruisers and a pair of ambulances sat, full strobe, in the parking lot of that weirdo church on the south side of town. What was it called again? Something Revival she thought.

"Michelle? I thought I told you to stay with your mother," he called, already understanding it wasn't his wife who'd entered the house.

As he stood rooted to the floor, a woman drifted into the kitchen: literally Paul saw—her feet did not touch the floor. She was naked, lithe, beautiful. Pearly semen dripped down her thighs. The same discordant music he'd heard at the club chimed from somewhere seemingly far distant. His breath caught in his throat, and he struggled to speak her name.

"Don't bother, my love. You must come and find me," Lucine Korth said, darkness spilling from her eyes. It floated toward Paul, wrapping him in a black cocoon-like cloak, and stole him from consciousness.

He awoke on the kitchen tiles, head throbbing. He peered wildly around, searching for the she-demon who'd come to take his balls and his life, but the kitchen was empty. Had it been a hallucination? A vision of some kind? God forbid, a premonition?

Paul climbed to his feet and checked the clock. Less than five minutes had passed since he'd hung up with Bloch. Good, he hadn't lost much time. He needed to pack, he needed to get in the car, he needed to drive to ...

Except he needed none of those things, he discovered. He needed Lucine Korth. The desire to lie with her overpowered him, killing all rational thought. An erection that felt as long and hard as his billy club pulsed painfully against his thigh. Paul groaned in abrupt animal desire and prayed the vision of Lucine had been real, that she perhaps awaited him in the bed he and his wife had shared for going on a decade.

But the house was empty. Paul growled in the manner brought on exclusively by sexual frustration and thought maybe he could masturbate to her Facebook picture. But no, God no—he needed *her*, not her fucking image. It didn't matter if she mutilated or murdered him. He had to have her.

I'll be different than the others, considerate, he thought. *I won't simply use her like all those bastards. I'll show her passion and compassion. I'll make her love me.*

Another more distant voice in his mind spoke up: *Get a grip, you stupid son of a bitch. She'll kill you. Your family needs you. Your children need you.*

Silencing that voice took no more effort than swatting a gnat. Paul grabbed the keys and went to the car, in desperate need of relief, a man possessed by that most powerful and natural drug known as testosterone.

Michelle missed her husband by minutes. She could still smell his cologne in the air—cologne and something else. Something musky and organic.

"Paul?" she called, already knowing the house stood empty. She'd seen the vacant space in the garage, the fresh tire tracks in the driveway snow. Still, she searched room by room. Michelle paused in the bathroom, assessing the scattered toiletries on the vanity. Cologne. Hair gel. Her wrinkle cream, sitting there with the lid off and generous dollop missing off the top.

She called his cell and again it went straight to voicemail. Michelle bellowed in frustration. Where would he be? Where would he go? The worst part about it was *he'd just been here.*

Michelle sunk down in his office chair, trying to hold her tears at bay, and waited for her husband to call. Then she spotted an envelope addressed to a Lucine Korth resting on his desk, pinned beneath her husband's stupid surplus store truncheon.

You're a fool, his mind whispered.

Shut up.

You're going to your death … your death or worse.

I'm not.

You have a family who depends on you.

That last almost made him pause again. Almost.

I'll make her love me, he insisted to himself and drove the rest of the way to Pace Lane in resolute silence. The conflict that had opened in him like a chasm at last had been resolved. He knew what he had to do and was powerless to stop it even if he wished to.

The house appeared as dead as ever, the brown grass overlong where it poked through the snow. The gate shrieked as he pushed it open, the steel latch freezing beneath his hand. He hadn't bothered to put on gloves or even a coat for that matter. He'd be warm soon enough.

The front door stood open, and he could smell her: a feral musk of complex pheromones. He could smell the other men who'd spent themselves inside her. The mixture drove him mad with jealous lust, and he climbed the stairs gingerly, one hand gripping the front of his jeans as if to contain an escaping animal.

Paul wasted no time—he headed straight to her bedroom. He drew her scent through his mouth as though wanting to devour her. Any rational part of his brain which had argued against this had irreversibly shut down. Not even the recollection of the head of hair attached to that dead scalp he'd felt in the dark upon his last visit here could sway him. If anything, it propelled him onward with greater urgency.

He could smell her more strongly now, an unparalleled aphrodisiac. By the time he reached her door, Paul practically tore it off its hinges. The things he'd do to her body, the absolute annihilation he'd perpetrate on her, would be written of in history books and epic poems for eons.

Paul prepared to commit even more felonies than he'd already committed, felonies on top of felonies, except when he dragged his pants down and leaped onto the bed, he found it empty.

"No," he moaned. "No, no."

She was here. She had to be. He could *feel* her. And she wanted him here. He could feel that too, somehow. She'd looked at him and known his name.

Paul dug at the deep pile of blankets like a man trying to unearth a corpse but found only the mattress beneath them. Lucine had left him. She had teased him and flown off to one of her other lovers. One of the men who sent her all those boxed up sex toys she kept lying around. Paul began to weep, quietly at first, and then building into big blubbering sobs. It wasn't fair. He'd seen her and she'd seen him. She'd driven him insane with lust. He would lose his mind now, he thought.

You've already lost it, an echo whispered in some deep crevice of his brain. Had Paul seen himself then, a grown man with his Levi's around his ankles, howling into a pillow on a bed that wasn't his, a painful erection poking the air like a fleshy flagpole, he would have understood wholly the true depth of obsession. At that moment, Paul Jeske had gone away completely and left behind a broken shell.

But then, when all seemed lost, the lovely lilting verse rose from below, as if sung by an angel: the song he and Michelle had chosen for the wedding, God he couldn't recall its title now, only that the Beatles had sung it originally and now Lucine serenaded him with it, coaxing him, baiting him, calling him home.

Hope so refreshing it was nearly orgasmic flooded through his body. She hadn't abandoned him after all. The wind moaned around the eaves as if in warning. Paul didn't hear. He heard only the voice of the woman who would learn to love him back. The woman who would take him into her bed and into her body, would bear his children, would call him *husband*. Yes: Lucine was *here*.

Paul staggered toward the stairs, forgetting the shackles of his jeans, and fell face-first to the carpet. He imagined Lucine departing before he could get to her, and he bellowed out for her to wait. He scrabbled along the floor, jerking at his waistband, the nap of the rug rubbing his swollen member raw. Paul didn't care; he knew where to find the cure, the lovely, musky salve, and he lurched toward it.

Only Lucine did not appear in evidence on the ground floor either. He held his breath, listening.

"You're teasing me again, aren't you?" he called. "That's okay, Lucine, that's just fine. I'll play your game. I'll find you."

Paul stepped into the kitchen and noticed the door which had been barred against him before now stood open, emitting a warm, pink glow from the cellar.

"So that's where you're hiding," he said, no longer feeling anything but wild animal lust. "Here I come, my love. Here I come."

He took the stairs two by two and missed his footing in his haste, tumbling to the cellar floor and knocking his wind loose. Paul lay gasping, still throbbing with blood and desire, wanting only to find his true love and bury himself in her. The rosy glow emanated around him, strobing in time with his pulse. He scanned around for its source, unable to locate it but wanting to be in it, for it undoubtedly came from Lucine. He couldn't see her, couldn't see anything but the peaceful, pulsing glow. Another taunt then. Another trick.

And then she was there: his Lucine.

Chapter Forty-Five

Lucine's face, beyond ethereal, drifted into view. She smiled, revealing teeth white and straight as sun-bleached tombstones. Her naked shoulders resembled a pair of dunes, the hollow of her throat a peaceful valley nestled between them. Paul fought to say her name, to say anything. Then her hand, blessedly cool, found his manhood and he thought he might die before he ever got a chance to consummate their love.

"I've found you," she said, her voice like warm exotic oil in his ears. "At last, I've found you. One who has willfully forsaken his family in service of selfish pursuits."

She lifted him as she might a child, her small frame belying a strength she could not possibly possess and carried him deeper into the cellar. Toward the pink emanating light. Toward the place she would take him into her, her hand somehow still caressing the place he needed it most with slow and practiced strokes.

The light, he saw now, spilled from a sphere the size of an aspirin tablet. It hung suspended between rafters, softly revolving like a miniature planet. He'd never seen anything like it, not even in his sweetest dreams, and knew it must be some type of ancient magic.

Something else emanated from the back portion of the basement, an odor he'd not noticed before. It smelled of moldering material and ancient sweat. Organic and meaty, it overwhelmed Paul and he gagged. Corpses of men had been stacked like firewood along the walls. Their eyes and genitals had been removed.

"Stop," he pleaded. "Please, stop, please, I'll do anything, I'll—"

Lucine's hand, the one that had so expertly kept him rigid, appeared on his feverish brow. "Hush now, dear heart, we're almost through. It's almost over now. Come with me, be my lasting lover, and together we shall be forever one."

With the same easy strength, she cast Paul onto the earthen floor, sat astride him, and guided him inside. In that moment, he knew perfect hell. The pleasure of the flesh meant the damnation of the soul.

Lucine grinned, her teeth sharp points in the gentle pink light, and bucked her hips against him. Visions of chaos filled Paul's mind and he prayed to something—anything—to save him.

Then the thing astride him squealed in pain. Its sagging weight rolled away and the icy air on Paul's member made him groan in relief. Had his senses been intact, he would have heard the thick chunking sound of an unyielding object striking flesh. He opened his eyes and peered around in the pinkness.

"Back off, you cunt," a voice as familiar as his mother's growled. Paul wept with relief. Michelle, as otherworldly as an angel in that moment, stood over him, her face as hard and ageless as granite. She gripped the police-issue truncheon in one fist, its polished mahogany length reflecting rosy light.

"The interloper," Lucine growled. "The good wife, Eve."

"Run, Paul," Michelle said, never taking her gaze from Lucine.

"Michelle," he croaked. "Shelly, I—"

"Run, Paul, for fuck's sake," she hissed. "Run if you still give a damn about your family."

"Do you think you can stop us, sow?" Lucine said, though her voice no longer sounded like spun honey. Now it carried with it a terrible edge, a hoarse omen of impending doom. "We mean to have your man. He has been chosen. Once the ritual has begun, it cannot be stopped."

"I don't give a rat-fuck about your ritual," Michelle said. Her voice dragged its own terrible power, something Paul found so shocking he hesitated to obey his wife's command. "You killed my father, you tried to kill my husband, and you scared my children half to death. If you think I *can't* stop you, you're sadly mistaken, whore."

Lucine grinned, a malicious, diabolic leer. She slid a tongue between her lips that in the shadows created by the strange pink sphere seemed forked. "Whore. On that you are correct. Of the line of Lilith, the original whore. Now we are many; now we are legion. The orphaned whores of Lilith shall overrun your filthy patriarchal, puritanical world. And we'll use your husband as stock to aid in our increase."

Michelle's face contorted in fury. If Paul didn't know better, she might have been one of them.

"Shelly," Paul tried again.

His wife kicked him in the thigh with the toe of her sneaker. "Paul, get the fuck out of here, you stupid *bitch*."

Paul ran. He bolted blindly up the rough-hewn risers and out the front door, naked, and collapsed onto the lawn of 200 Pace Lane. Silent snow drifted out of the sky, melting against the heat of his skin. Behind him, someone screamed from the bowels of the house and a second voice answered it. The moon, pallid as the face of a corpse, seemed to dim before winking out completely, and Paul sunk into a darkness so deep it defied understanding.

He deserved nothing less, he supposed, and went to greet it.

Epilogue

Five years later

When the phone rang, Michelle knew who would be on the other end before she even checked the caller ID. She set her glass of merlot on the coffee table and tapped TALK, then listened to the caller's careful instructions, stated she understood, and ended the call.

"Who was that, dear?" Darlene asked, stepping into the family room.

Michelle glanced at her mother. "Work," she said.

Darlene clucked her tongue. "The freelance gig? Oh, don't say you have to go out tonight. Last time you didn't get home until, what, eight or nine in the morning."

Michelle retrieved her wineglass, drained it, and stood. "I have to go out tonight. I'll be home as soon as possible. Will you watch the kids?"

"Of course, dear. Have they finished their homework?"

"Perry has a couple more algebra problems and Jeannie's reading. I'll sign their worksheets before I go."

Darlene glanced over her shoulder toward the two bedrooms down the hall. She hadn't minded moving in with her daughter and grandchildren after what had happened with Paul. In fact, even despite the close quarters, she relished having her remaining family close during her golden years.

Perry had grown into a tall, strong, younger version of his father. He had inherited all of Paul's best features along with all of Michelle's. He would be quite a hit with the ladies (or the gents—the Jeske-Craycraft household was open and affirming), to be sure. And his athleticism seemed to be off the charts, something he'd gotten somewhere else as neither parent had ever shown an aptitude toward sports.

Jeannine, now 10, had become a sweet tween who loved reading and watching cooking shows. She got straight A's in school and had taken a liking to running track. Her old friend Gussy had not yet been retired, even if she didn't need him to sleep in her arms every night anymore. One time Darlene had even found the poor thing forgotten on a kitchen chair long after its owner had gone to bed. Ah, the way children grow could break your heart sometimes. It just goes by so damned fast.

In a lowered tone, she asked, "Is Jeannie still having nightmares?"

"Night terrors, Mom," Michelle corrected, stepping into her sneakers. Her phone buzzed with a new text, and she checked the message for the required coordinates she'd need to carry out tonight's task. Chicago Heights. Not too far. Good. She wanted to get this over with so she could kiss her kids goodbye before school in the morning.

"Nightmares, night terrors, it's all the same to me," Darlene said, pouring her own generous glass of wine.

"They're the same to you because you've never experienced them. To Jeannie, they're very real and very scary. She hasn't had one in going on a year now, but if she does, just be there for her and tell her everything is going to be all right."

Darlene paused with her glass halfway to her lips. "*Is* it going to be all right, Michelle? Their father—"

"Please don't talk about their father," Michelle said as gently as possible. She knew Darlene worried about her and the kids, but right now Paul was the last thing she wanted to think about. She changed the subject. "Could you also make sure Perry's baseball jersey is clean? He tossed it in the hamper, but I haven't gotten to it yet."

Perry would be starting high school in the fall and had become a bit flighty in recent days. Michelle supposed it could be because the poor boy was in the full throes of puberty. Hormone spikes had led to surliness, sloppiness, and even a spate of sleepwalking, something he'd never done as a child. Michelle had found him twice out of bed at ungodly hours, once in the kitchen rummaging through the fridge and another in the hallway, pacing and mumbling something under his breath. He'd been fast asleep on both occasions and on both occasions she'd managed to lead him back to bed without waking him. It could be dangerous to wake a sleepwalker, she'd read somewhere.

Darlene sipped her wine. "Of course, dear. He's willfully ignorant when it comes to the washing machine, something I bet will continue well into manhood, until he finds a strong wife who makes him do it." She hesitated, considering her next words. "You know, you can always talk to me. I'm here for you."

Michelle gave her a gracious smile. In the past, her mother might have made a joke about being there for her at least until the grim reaper came calling for her, but her mother's sense of humor seemed to have died with her husband. "I know, Mom. I appreciate it. And thank you."

After giving her mother a peck on the cheek, Michelle went to the garage and got behind the wheel of her brand-new Cadillac Escalade. After tonight, if all went as planned, she would be able to pay this baby off. For now, though, she thought of it as her Batmobile and herself as Batwoman. It made the task at hand seem more manageable, but she knew not to take what she had to do lightly.

She keyed the ignition and then bent and felt beneath the driver's seat. For one horrible moment her fingers failed to find her weapon of choice and she wondered for about the millionth time what would happen if Jeannie—or worse, Perry—found it.

Like father, like son, her mind whispered, unbidden, and she quieted it in a hurry. Thinking like that would be unproductive. And Perry would never be like his father. Michelle would see to that.

She entered the address she'd received into her GPS and started off. With little traffic at that hour, she made it to her destination in an hour. Good time.

The place appeared to be a rundown tenement. She parked along the curb and waited. Ten minutes later, a black van pulled up behind her and sat idling. This would be her assigned partner, sent directly by Ms. Bloch's authority. Michelle was still considered a trainee, even though she'd been on nearly a dozen assignments. It took time to learn everything, every fine nuance of the craft, Ms. Bloch had explained.

The woman who got out of the van had a bluff, stern face with eyes dark as coal, evident even in the Escalade's mirrors. Michelle had not worked with her before and already hoped she wouldn't again. The woman approached her car and rapped on the glass. Michelle rolled it down.

"You are ready, yes?" she asked in a thick Eastern European accent. "You have your weapon?"

"Yes to both," Michelle said and hefted the surplus store truncheon.

"Good. Come along. We strike now and be done quick."

Michelle got out and followed the woman to unit 4, where they had been tipped to go. The woman did not bother to identify herself or bother to knock on the door. She drew back and kicked the door in. It slammed against the wall, shattering the cheap drywall within.

"Move quick, before she fully wakes," the woman said and Michelle did as instructed, rushing to the studio apartment's single bed and bringing the club down on the shape beneath the sheets again and again in rapid succession. By now her muscles had grown used to it, even if her mind had not. Nor had her mind grown used to the sound the creatures made as they died, and when it finally had, the women together rolled it into the bedsheets and hauled it to the back of the van. The needn't worry about police response. Not in this neighborhood.

"You have done well," the stern trainer told her. "Efficient. No wasted movements. Tonight, you advance to full recruit."

Michelle thought she would feel pride when the promotion came, but she felt nothing at all. Pure numbness.

"You take it from here, right? I want to get home."

"Correct. The funds will be deposited in your account within forty-eight hours. Be ready when next we call."

"I will," Michelle said and got into the Escalade. She waited for the van to pull away and then drove back toward home.

Before she got there, though, she had a stop to make. An hour later she pulled onto Pace Lane.

Michelle picked up the mail that had piled up on the porch and took it inside. She collected the utility bills, placed them in her purse, and made her way to the door in the kitchen. She unlocked it with a key from her ring and stepped down the rough-hewn steps.

"Good evening, Lucine," Michelle said to the thing chained to the wall. It raised its head to stare at her through a mop of matted hair with eyes so deep-set they could barely be seen. But what could be seen of them revealed a gleam of famine so profound it was palpable.

Lucine herself had been reduced to a bag of bones, barely recognizable as human. Or humanoid, rather — Michelle did not consider those of Lucine's ilk people. They were monsters.

Lucine's once-lustrous hair had dried to a colorless straw-like thatch. Her bronze skin had paled to an unhealthy paper white. Her voluptuous thighs had slackened and atrophied, and her breasts had shrunk to withered apples. The thing tried to say something, but her throat emitted only a dry scrape.

"Oh, don't try to talk," Michelle said. "You'll want to conserve what little energy you have left. I'm still curious to see how long you'll last without the company of men. How long do you suppose? Another year? Two? Ten?" She cracked a malevolent grin. "Forever? Will someone find you like this, broken, starved for sex, a mere mummy, long after I'm gone? A girl can wish, can't she?"

Lucine tried to make another sound, a low hissing like a snake slithering through scrub. Michelle took a step toward her, raising the baton, and relished the sight of her prisoner recoiling in fear. She had not reported Lucine's presence to Ms. Bloch. No, Michelle planned to keep Lucine for herself. For the foreseeable future, at any rate. Perhaps when she got bored of playing with the thing that had sunk its claws into her husband, she would report it.

And if Lucine turned out to be the queen of the coven, well … Michelle imagined the reward would make her quite a wealthy woman.

"I just stopped by to say hello," Michelle said, her smile still hanging in place. "We'll catch up again soon."

She retreated up the stairs and had reached the top when her phone rang. Darlene. Michelle swiped TALK. "Mom? What's up? Is everything—"

Darlene's voice issued frantically through the earpiece. "Michelle, are you on your way home? Perry's gone."

Michelle's heart stalled. "Gone? What do you mean? Are you sure he's not in the bathroom or—"

"He's gone!" Darlene shrieked. "I've checked everywhere."

"Did you call the police?" Michelle shrieked back. She prayed it was only another sleepwalking incident and they'd find him in the closet of Paul's old study or maybe the garage, rummaging around the workbench while mumbling and snoring.

"They're on their way now."

"I'll be home in two minutes." Michelle rushed out the door and down the walk to her vehicle without bothering to lock the cellar door or even shut the front door to the house at 200 Pace Lane. She would come back later and close up. Perry was her number one priority now and she jumped behind the wheel and sped off toward home.

As Michelle turned onto William Street, Perry rounded the opposite corner onto Pace Lane. The new teen had already sleepwalked a dozen blocks. In his bed, he'd heard a voice singing his name to strange and wondrous music and had been powerless not to pursue it. He stopped before an old ugly house with its door standing open and cocked his head. The song came from within, a sweet and sour melody it seemed to him,

281

one that beckoned him on. Yes, it originated here, from inside the sad gray house. From the basement, to be exact.

Perry started up the walk, taking the steps of the old porch slowly, one at a time. He'd grown large enough that he could've taken them easily enough by twos, but tonight he was moving carefully. He wanted to hear more of the lovely macabre music that lulled him on. He knew that whoever made such a luscious melody would also be luscious. In fact, he could even see her face rising in his mind like morning mist. His heart raced, and in his sleep he grinned.

When he stepped over the threshold of 200 Pace Lane, he closed the door gently behind him, flipped the lock, and stepped over to the cellar door standing wide. He hesitated. Through his closed eyelids, he could see a gentle pink light down below, at the bottom of the stairs. A light to guide his way.

Perry, the voice whispered, though it seemed to come from inside his head. From the same place he could hear the music. *Perry, come to me. I need you, Perry. We can make such wondrous music together. Come and find me.* The face that whispered those words rose again behind his eyes. Never before had he beheld such wicked beauty. The music's tempo increased in time with his pulse, rising quickly to crescendo, and from somewhere he saw the beautiful pink light like the first flush of dawn on the vernal equinox. He longed to be in that pulsing light, to bask in it and to bask in the lovely mysterious music with which it kept a hard and throbbing tempo.

Perry took the first steps slowly, blood flushing adrenaline and testosterone, those deadliest of fluids, through his body, and by the time he reached the bottom, he began to run.

About the Author

Aaron Gudmunson lives and writes in the Chicagoland area. His short fiction and essays have been published in numerous magazines and anthologies. He is the author of the novels *Snow Globe*, *Emma Tremendous*, *The Slingerman*, *Farmland*, and the collection *From the Dusklands*. Visit him online at www.gudmunsonic.com.

Curious about other Crossroad Press books? Stop by our
website: http://crossroadpress.com
We offer quality writing
in digital, audio, and print formats.

Subscribe to our newsletter on the website homepage and
receive a free eBook.

www.ingramcontent.com/pod-product-compliance
Lightning Source LLC
Chambersburg PA
CBHW020258200626
46816CB00001BA/358